A Shadow Stained in BLOOD

ICHABOD EBENEZER

ISBN: 1-7329796-0-X
ISBN-13: 978-1-7329796-0-4

Cover Art by Violeta Nedkova
https://violetanedkova.com/

Editing by Happy Self Publishing
www.happyselfpublishing.com

For my loving wife, who put up with a lot during my pursuit of a dream, and for the Twitter writing community that showed such love and encouragement to carry me through to completion.

And to ChaslyUK whose idea spawned this one.

Chapter One

It was a messy rain, the sort
that seemed to come straight at you no
matter which way you turned.
Transplants to Seattle swear it
doesn't exist anywhere else, but this
was early March in Puget Sound.

I stood under a streetlamp near
the sparse job postings board with my
collar turned up and hat pressed
tightly to my head. The gal I was
watching stood across the street,
curls held down by a scarf, and a
black umbrella clutched in both hands.

She was a nervous little blonde

number, pacing back and forth in tight
strides, and damned cute in her own
little way. She gave the impression
that she was trying not to draw
attention to herself, with the dark
glasses and understated makeup, but
the fancy line at the seam of her
stockings and the designer coat stood
out anyway. I had a photo in my
breast pocket that told a different
story. Megan Bowerman, trophy wife
and happy socialite. Bold lipstick
and angelic dimples, classic curls and
a lively glint in her pale eyes.

I was hired by her husband,
Rudolph, to catch her in the act of
cheating, and to bring in pictures to
prove it. The strap of my folding
camera was hanging around my neck,
shielded by my long coat, and I was
just waiting for her beau to show.
She had gotten a ticket to the theater
half an hour ago but didn't seem
interested in the film yet.

I didn't have to wait long as it
turned out, as a man approached from a
block away, and Megan stopped her
pacing when she saw him. I turned my
attention to the job posting board and

watched them from the corner of my
eye. He stopped an arm's length away
from her and looked in all directions.
Interesting that he was the one being
careful about who was watching them.
His eyes lingered on me, and I stepped
closer to the job board to examine a
particularly interesting index card.
'Longshoreman wanted,' it said. 'Must
speak Chinese,' it went on to say.
Then finally, and without a hint of
irony, 'No Chinese need apply.'

The man grabbed Megan by the arm
and led her into the diner and out of
the rain. I waited several beats
before turning to watch them. He took
her coat and hung it for her, then her
umbrella. She kept the scarf and
glasses. They sat on a couple stools
halfway down the counter and spoke,
hunched over.

I reached into my pocket and let
the few coins there slip through my
fingers. Twenty-seven cents, or
thereabouts. A nickel would buy me a
cup of coffee. Another dime would get
me a plate of scramble with a side of
hash, but despite my insistent
stomach, I decided against it. If the

couple left the diner, I would have to follow them, and I couldn't afford to leave good food on the table.

I hurried across the street and entered the diner, taking a booth near the door. Setting my hat on the table, I pulled a folded newspaper from my long coat and put my camera down between the two. The waitress came by with a menu, which I immediately handed back to her. "Cup of coffee, doll," I said. The waitress wrote that down on her notebook, tore off the sheet, and laid my tab down on the table, then walked back behind the counter.

I unbuttoned my camera case, let the cover fall forward, and unfolded the newspaper, using that to shield what I was doing with the camera while pretending to read. Pressing the button to extend the bellows, I lined up my shot at the couple engaged in quiet conversation. I turned the page of my newspaper, pulling it out of the way just long enough to snap a photo. The two of them were drinking their dinner tonight as well. He took his coffee black while she preferred tea

with lemon. The waitress swung by
with the coffee pot to fill my cup, so
I dropped my paper on top of the
camera.

"Anything else?" she asked.

"Yeah," I said. "What time does
the picture get out next door?" I
didn't actually care, of course. I
just needed something plausible to
explain why I was waiting here.
Katharine Hepburn and Cary Grant were
arguing over a pet leopard next door,
twice a night plus matinees. Bringing
Up Baby was the biggest hit of 1938 so
far. I don't step out much, but if
you haven't seen it, I hear it's a
riot.

She looked up at the clock on the
wall. "That would be the ten o'clock
showing, so it should be out in twenty
minutes."

"Thanks, doll," I said and
stirred some cream into my coffee. As
tired as I was, I really needed the
Java. The last couple of nights, I
staked out the Bowerman place, but
Megan had never stepped out. I had
almost opted to give tonight a miss
and catch up on sleep instead, so of

course, this is when she met her man.

The waitress returned to her spot behind the counter. I returned my attention to the young couple. Their conversation was impossible to make out, but body language counts for a lot. She was frantic about something, speaking in a harsh whisper and gesturing aggressively with her hands, looking over her shoulder a bunch, and fidgeting with both her scarf and her glasses. His posture was relaxed. He took the time to blow on his coffee and nod while she complained. He laid a hand on her exposed knee several times and smiled knowingly as he spoke. I guessed she felt that her husband suspected them, and he was reassuring her that if they were careful, they'd be fine. I snapped several more photos as they spoke, advancing the film while the Seattle Post-Intelligencer covered my camera. Maybe I got one clear shot of her face while she was turned toward the door, but I got several of him. At least one with his hand on her knee. Disappointingly missing, though, were any shots of a more romantic nature.

A shot of them kissing would assure my payday, but even a good hug would do.

Fifteen minutes later, I was into my second cup, and the nature of the couple's liaison hadn't changed. She seemed a bit calmer, but not enough to touch her tea. She stood up and opened her purse. She threw some change onto the counter and headed for the door. I got one last shot of her and collapsed the lens-board of my camera as she threw on her coat. The man remained, sloshing his coffee around in the cup, so I had a choice to make. Follow him or follow her.

I was pretty sure I knew where she was going, so I opted to wait it out and see where he went. Megan shook off her umbrella and stepped back out into the rain. I buttoned up my camera, tucked it into the pocket of my long coat, and dropped seven cents on my tab. The waitress was two cents closer to retirement, and I was ready to go as soon as my mark made for the door.

He waited long enough that the two of them weren't seen leaving together, then he slugged back his coffee, grabbed his hat, and headed out the door. I made another note on my mental scratch pad: Megan paid the bill on this encounter. How thoroughly modern. Five beats later, I plunked my own hat on my head, folded the paper under one arm, and was out the door.

My mark was heading back the way he'd come from. I stood in the doorway and lit a cigarette until he was most of a block away. He headed up the hill at Spring Street, and I tailed him to First Avenue, where he used a key to enter a doorway next to a dress shop. After a minute or so, a light came on in the third-floor window. I walked up to the doorbell panel for the apartment and found the label next to 3A. 'B. Laslop,' it read.

Now I knew his name and where he lived. That was good enough for tonight. Time to find my own bed. I was overdue a few winks and willing the coffee to perk me up was doing little good.

I made my way on foot to my own apartment. My office would have been closer, and part of me ached to sleep behind my desk in the rolling chair, but I had some film to develop, so I trudged the few miles through the pouring rain.

I didn't mind it. It seemed these days that everyone currently living in Seattle came from somewhere else, but not me. I grew up in Ballard, and that's almost as far from the city center as I've ever been. When everyone else complains about the rain, to me, that's just Thursday. Folks from L.A. are amazed by the greenery and the luscious grasses, the clean air and clear view of the mountains, yet they complain about the rain that brings it all to us. It always makes me chuckle. They'll never understand. For a local, it doesn't just clear the air, it clears the mind.

I stumbled up to the door of my own flat and threw my coat and hat across the bed. I took the camera into the bathroom. Long ago, I had taped a dozen layers of butcher paper to the windows and replaced the bulb with one painted red. A clothesline hung over the bathtub, and next to the sink were tubs filled with developing fluid. Sure, it still functioned as a lavatory, but this was my darkroom.

I closed the door tight and rewound the film in my camera. I pulled out the roll and felt around the counter for everything I would need. Even though I didn't get a shot of them kissing, I could show up at my client's door tomorrow with these pictures and his name, and who knows? He might pay me enough to keep my landlord off my back for at least a week. I pulled the film out of the canister and let it coil, then I laid it in the developer bath and wound the agitator. In thirteen minutes, I would have to drop it in the fixer, so I found my way to the toilet and made sure the lid was down before sitting. I felt for the minute minder that was on a shelf under the blacked-out window and found the bit of tape that marked thirteen minutes. I set the timer and put it back on the shelf, then I crossed my arms on my lap and rested my head, waiting for the timer.

I must have needed my sleep worse than I thought because it was my stomach rather than the alarm that woke me. I jumped up and felt for the minute minder. It was pointing straight up. I ran across the room and quickly transferred the film to the fixer, knowing full well I was way too late, but opening a door or turning on the light to see the time would make sure it was ruined.

I agitated the film by hand, yawning and blinking away the last of the sleep. It was a long ten minutes until the fixer would do its job, and I could turn on the light. When I finally did, my fears were confirmed. The film was long over-exposed. I threw the film across the room and dashed aside the chemical trays.

Now, I don't want you thinking I've got a short temper. There were people I had to avoid because they would be there to collect from me, and splitting my twenty cents wouldn't get me very far. Those pictures were the difference between skulking in shadows and walking out the front door with my head held high.

Leaving the bathroom, I crossed the room to where my coat was lying on the bed. I pulled my pack of cigarettes from the pocket and shook out the last one. I decided to smoke it anyway. Setting it between my lips, I crumpled up the pack and threw it across the room. I pulled out the matchbook from the same pocket and found it empty. When would they make a matchbook with the same number of matches as packs had cigarettes?

I strode to the kitchen and lit my cigarette off the stove. I took two satisfying puffs before filling the kettle and setting it on the flame.

I cursed myself again for wasting the film and the chemicals. Those would cost me. Of course, the pictures that had been on the film weren't worth much.

My cupboard was bare except for a box of Lipton soup packets. I pulled one out and poured it into a mug while I waited for the water to boil. It may not have been much of a meal, but if I looked out my window, I could just see smoke rising from the shacks of Hooverville to the West and a little South.

A thousand men lived there, put out of work by what President Hoover called an economy. They had built shacks from whatever they could find and had spent the last six years surviving on canned beans and hunted rodents.

Suddenly, a packet of thin chicken soup, under a roof that didn't leak, felt a long way from a tin shack and smoke inhalation. I reached under the mattress and pulled out the money I was saving for rent. Two tens. I put one of them back and shoved the other into my pocket. I would need film, and now developer, sooner than I would need rent.

When the kettle whistled, I drank my soup, threw on my hat and coat, and headed to the office.

The sun was out, and any clouds from the night before had moved on to darken the Cascade Range. The streets had had time to mostly dry, and there was a scent to the air that was uniquely Seattle as well. A freshness that was part salty sea and part mountain brook with just a hint of your more modern scents, such as drying concrete and fresh linen.

I was renting a small space up a narrow set of stairs over a laundry. It got unbearably hot and humid in the summer, but aside from some steamy windows, it was a blessing in the winter because I couldn't afford a heating bill.

I walked through the door bearing my name. 'Drake Glover, Private Investigator,' it said on the frosted glass. Katie was already in, typing up the Dictaphone recordings I had left for her over the weekend. She stopped the playback when I came in.

Katie's husband was career military, stationed down at Fort Lewis. The two of them had raised a couple boys, both of whom had since married and moved out. She was no more than five foot one, but she was still pretty and didn't go in for the high heels and dye jobs that other women her age did.

Katie didn't need the job, but she liked to be busy. I couldn't pay her much, so that worked out just fine. She read her little romances and listened in on conversations about cheating spouses, and she lived a very full if vicarious life. I could only imagine the gossip she shared with the other Army wives.

Katie held the Dictaphone earpiece away from her ear. "Good morning, Mr. Glover," she said. "You have a client waiting." She looked meaningfully at the door to my private office.

My thoughts went back to the overdeveloped film lying in the bin of my flat, and I wished I had last night to do over again. "Mr. Bowerman?" I asked.

"No, a new client. A woman," Katie whispered.

I hung up my hat and coat then opened the door to my private office. A long-haired brunette in a red hat was sitting in my guest chair with her back to the door. She turned toward me when I opened the door. She had her small purse clutched in both hands and a handkerchief wound around the fingers of one hand. Her eyes were puffy and red, and her expression was one of a child caught shaving her sister's head, but she relaxed noticeably when she saw me.

I closed the door quietly and walked around my desk as I introduced myself. "Drake Glover, miss. There's no reason to be afraid. Whatever has happened, you're safe here."

"Oh, it's not me I'm worried about, Mr. Glover, it's my husband." She started dabbing at her eyes with the hanky.

"Alright," I said, standing behind my chair. "How about we take it slow. Why not start with your name?"

"Yes, of course. How forgetful of me. I'm Mrs. Evan Noble." She paused and gave a brief, sweet smile, then added, "Claire."

"That's better, Claire, how do you do?" I said, flashing her my friendliest smile. "Now, what can I do for you?"

She took a deep breath and began

her story. I sat down to listen. "My
husband and I moved here from Denver,
six months ago. It's been hard for
Evan to find a job, so we've been
living off our savings ever since."
She paused, and I nodded knowingly.
"Well, our savings didn't last as long
as we'd planned, and we were starting
to get desperate. I started to see
how it really is around here. People
are friendly when they know you have
money, but heaven forbid you stop
throwing parties quite so often, or
you show up in the same dress twice...
But Evan, he's always the optimist.
He went out, day after day, looking
for work. The longer it went, the
more work he was willing to do. He
waited for three days outside the
cannery just hoping for a job!" she
said with a look of disgust on her
face.

It looked like she expected a
reaction from me, so I said, "Imagine
that."

She was quiet for a while longer,
gathering her thoughts. She didn't
look at me, and her hands were
nervously playing with the clasp on

her purse, twisting it open, snapping it shut. When she finally spoke, her tone had completely changed. "Two weeks ago, he came home. It was late in the evening, but not so late that I was worried. He threw open the door, all smiles, and announced he finally had a job. I was so relieved, I rushed in to jump into his arms, but he handed me a package wrapped in butchers' twine. 'We're eating steak tonight!' he said."

Claire stopped toying with her purse and sat up straight. "'Well, tell me all about it!' I said, 'The girls will all be dying to know.' But he just said, 'I can't. It's secret.'"

She was quiet again, but rather than looking away this time, her eyes drilled into me. I rode out the silence, nodding gravely.

"What kind of job could Evan have that he can't tell me about?" she blurted out all at once. "At first, I kept my silence. Our friends are friends again, the money is coming in again - and it is a lot of money. But it's eating at me. My husband is not a secretive person by nature, Mr. Glover. What could he be doing that makes that kind of money, and he has to keep it secret? He doesn't have what it takes to be one of J. Edger's men, and the only other thing I can think of is crime. Mr. Glover, Evan is no criminal."

"Mrs. Noble," I said, leaning across the desk, "have you tried confronting your husband with your concerns?"

Now she looked down at her purse again. "Well, no. He asked for my trust. I don't want to betray that."

"So you turn to a shamus," I stated flatly.

"I have to know, you understand. When he leaves home in the morning, I worry that I'll never see him again. As much as I wonder where the money comes from, that's the worst part. Evan isn't cut out for that life," she pleaded.

"What is your husband cut out for? What did he do back in Denver?" I asked.

"He's a cook. Not some diner fry cook either. He's a chef, you know?

He ties up chickens and has those paper boots on the drumsticks and sauces on little bits of meat with truffle shavings and things."

My stomach growled audibly. "Fancy cooking. He's educated," I said to cover up the noise.

"Exactly," she agreed.

"Why did he think he could find work in Seattle?" I asked. "Maybe more to the point, why did you two leave Denver?"

Telling her story seemed to calm her down quite a bit. She hadn't needed to use her kerchief in some time. "Evan lost his job at Chez Marseilles. A rather snooty customer called him out to complain about his soup. When my husband explained that gazpacho was intended to be cold, the man blew up and insisted that Evan was fired on the spot for daring to serve it and for insulting him. As my husband was run out of the restaurant, he was told he would never work in Denver again. We left that day," she explained. "As for why we picked Seattle, I don't really know. I suggested L.A., but Evan said he'd have to start from the bottom again in L.A. or San Francisco." She shrugged. "He liked Seattle, so here we are."

I nodded again. "I see. So, you'd like me to follow him, see where he goes of a day and let you know if it's the mob. Is that about right?"

It was her turn to nod. "But if it is the mob, I want you to get him out of there."

"Mrs. Noble, it doesn't work like that. I can let you know what I see, and I can get you some pictures as proof. If he is being threatened, I can step in or call the police. But if all he's doing is cooking and being paid for it, that's his business."

Suddenly, she was all tears again. "But you must! I can't stand the thought of him with thugs and murderers all day! One slip up, and he won't be out the door, he'll be found in an alley!" She turned her face from me, and her shoulders shook with uncontrollable sobbing.

I stood up and came around to the other side of the desk. I put a hand on both her shoulders. "Mrs. Noble, please calm down. I'll take your case. Let's get those pictures first and decide what to do once we know, alright?"

Her fingers patted my hand. "Yes, of course. You're right," she said. She looked up at me and forced a little smile. "I must seem very silly for all this."

Nodding reassuringly, I returned to my seat behind the desk. I pulled out the top drawer, removed a pad of paper, and grabbed a pencil from the container on my desk. "Now, Mrs. Noble, I'm going to need to know a few things to get started on. First off, have they ever contacted your husband at home?"

"Yes, more than once. He sends me out of the room when they call."

"Have you ever picked up the extension when they do?" I asked, knowingly.

"No, never," she said. I raised my eyebrows to convey my suspicion. "Not because I didn't want to. You see, we only have the one extension in the kitchen, and you can see it from the phone in the living room."

I nodded my understanding. "All

the same, I'm going to need your number. I may be able to find out who's been calling."

"I understand. It's Klondike 5312. But you won't call, will you?" she asked.

I wrote the number down. "No, Mrs. Noble, I won't. Now, does your husband drive a car?"

"Yes. A 37 Cadillac Series 60. Beige," she said.

I nodded, writing all this down. "License plate?" I asked.

"A 85182," she said.

"And your address?" This one she had prepared. She opened her purse and handed me a folded piece of paper. I unfolded it and copied the address onto my own sheet, just to have it all in one place.

"And what times does he leave for work and return home?" I asked.

"He always picks out the freshest produce, so he leaves the house at 5:30 every morning." I must admit, I didn't like hearing that. "Getting home is harder to predict. He should be home by 8PM, but many nights, he crawls in the door at 2AM just to be up again in a couple hours."

"That doesn't sound like an easy life," I commented. I felt I should move this along. If I was going to take on a second case, I'd better start making some headway on the one I already had. I tore the top sheet off and folded it in half. "I've got what I need to know to get moving on this. Now, there's just the matter of payment."

"Yes... Of-of course. I've never done this before. How much will it cost?" she asked.

"Thirty a day, plus expenses, for which, I'll have receipts. If it's going to cost a lot, I'll get your okay first. Normally, I like to get two days' worth in advance."

"Sixty dollars, then." She snapped open her purse again and pulled out three Jacksons. She slid them across the desk to me. I let them sit there as if I didn't need them so desperately. "Please, Mr. Glover, save my husband."

With that, she stood up and left.

I waited until she was out the door, and I watched her through the window blinds as she climbed into a cab. Her story didn't quite add up, but I wasn't sure yet which part of it gave me trouble. A woman who moved in the circles that she did couldn't be nearly as innocent as she was acting. But her concern for her husband came across as real. On the other hand, if it was real, then it was impossible that her husband was as innocent as she believes. I picked up the money and stuck it in my wallet. Of course, it was always possible neither one was who they seemed. But then, why come to me?

I looked up at the wall clock and allowed a smile to cross my face as I reached for the phone and dialed zero. Betty would be manning the switchboard, and she was sweet on me.

"Operator," she said.

"Hello, Betty, it's Drake," I said. "I need a favor, and I'm hoping you can help me out."

"Sure, Drake, you know I'm always happy to help," she replied. Her smile came through in her voice.

"I've got a client that's been getting some harassing phone calls at Klondike 5312. She's getting scared. Is there any way you can tell me what new numbers have been calling her?"

"A girl, huh, Drake?" Betty asked petulantly.

"The happily married type. Her husband's been taking a lot of the calls, but he's helpless to do anything."

"Gee Drake, I'd love to help, but I don't have access to the call records. I could watch from now on. I'll put a note on the line so the girls on the other shifts watch it too."

"That'd be swell, Betty. But they can't know who you're doing this for or why."

"No problem, Drake. It will just be our little conspiracy."

"Thanks a lot, Betty. I owe you one," I said.

"Actually, I think you owe me two now. Payable in the form of dinner?" she replied, the smile coming through in her voice again.

"Sounds lovely, Doll. We'll

arrange something in a few days. I've
got to run. Goodbye, Betty, and
thanks again."

"Catch you later, Drake."

I hung up the phone and stepped
out of my office. Grabbing my hat and
coat, I got Katie's attention. She
paused the Dictaphone and pulled the
earpiece out.

"I probably won't be back in
the office today. I've got a new
case. I assume you were listening
in?" I peeled off a twenty and set it
down on her desk.

Katie slid the bill off the desk
and stuffed it into her bra. She
smirked at me and said, "Since when do
you charge thirty a day?"

"Ever since my clients started
complaining about having it too good.
Go ahead and take off once you've got
those typed up. Just leave them on my
desk."

Katie picked a key up off her
desk and tossed it to me. "Joe
Freeman left his car downstairs," she
said simply.

"The usual?" I asked.

"Affirmative," Katie said and

went back to the Dictaphone. When I got down to street level, sure enough, there was Joe's car, with his hat and coat in it. I got behind the driver's seat and made a U-turn. I needed to see a friend at the police department, and for that, I would need a bottle of scotch.

Chapter Two

This poker buddy of mine likes to
play the ponies, but he's got a
problem, and I'm not talking about a
gambling addiction. He works for his
old lady's father, and she doesn't
like him gambling. She knows he
places a bet now and again, and she
uses her dad to keep an eye on Joe.
If he gets caught, not only does he
lose her, he loses the job; something
no one can afford in this day and age.
Joe's a clever cat, though, even if he
isn't all that smart. We're about the

same height, so we have a little arrangement. I run a couple drops in his car wearing his clothes; maybe buy a paper in Pike Place where the newsie knows me as Joe, and meanwhile, he hops onto the bus down to Longacres for a couple hours.

Anybody who's watching on behalf of Joe's other half, only sees Joe's car doing his rounds. Anyone who asks, finds out that Joe ate his regular hot dog, picked up his usual newspaper, and made all his deliveries. And meanwhile, if he ever wins it big, he gets real grateful. Every now and then, I need access to a car, and as long as his wife doesn't know about it, I can borrow Joe's.

I parked the car in front of Delaney's, swapped out my hat and coat for Joe's, and ducked inside. I paused just inside the door to let my eyes adjust to the dark, smoky interior after the bright sun outside. Peggy slowly resolved out of the darkness behind the bar. She blew out a cloud of smoke and called out to me. "'Morning, Drake. Scotch on the rocks?"

Peggy was a heck of a gal. A redhead through and through, though the shade of red has been a bit unnatural for the last ten years or more. Her husband died halfway through the war, and this business was her only livelihood. Then, less than a year later, the good people of Seattle saw fit to abolish the sale of alcohol, and a few years after that, the Feds took up enforcement. Peggy always found a way to have some available for her loyal following, but she also managed to turn Delaney's into a successful greasy spoon. On October third of 1933, Washington state ratified the 21st amendment, and liquor was again the law of the land. That very night, there was a party in Delaney's, and the griddle was parked on the sidewalk the next day. The liquor mysteriously reappeared, and no one questioned it.

I walked up to the bar and leaned against it, ignoring the stools. "Not today, Peggy dear, I'm on a case."

She stubbed out her cigarette. "Anything interesting?"

I shrugged. "Worried wife, but

no concerns of infidelity. Her man's got a mysterious new job, and she worries that she's married to the mob."

She considered that. "Gotta beat the usual pictures 'in flagrante'." She poured herself a shot and downed it quickly.

I shrugged again. "Too soon to tell. Could turn out to be exactly that." There was no point in hemming and hawing. I needed a bottle, and I wanted to keep what little cash I had. It was time to ask for my favor. "Listen, Peggy, I've got to go talk to the cops. A bottle of scotch would sure beat a foot in the door when I've got favors to ask."

"Are you asking me for a favor, Drake Glover?" Peggy asked, hand on her hip.

"A bottle of your scotch, Peggy. Better make it the good stuff too, not what I drink. I'll pay you back," I said.

This made her snort laughter. She grabbed a bottle anyway. Dewar's White Label. She held it just out of reach. "You owe me, Drake Glover.

And I know where you live." She
handed me the bottle.

"I'll pay you back," I said again
as I left the bar.

"I'll just stay up nights waiting
then, shall I?" she called after me.

I dropped the bottle onto the
back seat of the car and headed down
to the precinct building on Third. I
turned left on Yesler and dropped the
car at City Hall Park.

I got out of the car and stuck
the bottle in my inside coat pocket,
that is to say, Joe's inside coat
pocket. I walked with my conspicuous
gift around the side and down to the
precinct. Shaughnessy was manning the
desk when I stepped through the doors.
He didn't say anything, but he set
down his pen and watched me intently
as I passed. I pretended not to
notice.

The officers in the bullpen were
a different story. Some of them knew
me from my days in the academy, and
they always had some choice words for
me. "Washout," someone called.

"Snoop," came from somewhere across the room, but I kept on walking. "Murderer."

That one brought me up short. Looking around for the cop that came with that accusation, everyone seemed to be doing something more important at that moment. I gave it a minute, but nobody made eye contact, and the only sounds I heard were the uncomfortable clearing of throats.

Never mind them. I had business here, so I continued on to the offices on the far side.

I gave Sergeant Benson a moment's warning by knocking on his door before opening it. He had his shades drawn and couldn't see me any more than I could see him. "What is it?" he demanded as I opened the door, and that was before he knew who it was.

"Damn it, Drake, you can't keep just showing up here," he said impatiently as I closed the door behind me. His eyes went to the bulge in my jacket, but his expression told me he thought I was packing. I suppressed a smile.

Mike was a little older than me,

but we went into the academy together.
He showed his age a bit more. His
hair wasn't yet where you would call
him balding, but those who've known
him for a while would tell you he
didn't used to have that widow's peak.
Ever since he got the desk job, he'd
gotten a bit rounder as well, and all
those lunches at his desk had taken a
toll on the front of his shirt.

"I understand it's inconvenient
for you, Mike, but I need a favor.
Don't worry, it's all above board."

Mike leaned back in his swivel
chair with a heavy sigh. "Okay,
Drake, what is it? And it better be
good."

"I've got a new client, and she's
worried about her husband. It's
likely he's into something shady, and
the only question is, does he know
about it?"

"You know the cops don't arrest
people for 'something shady,'
otherwise, we'd have you behind bars.
If you want someone to tail him, do it
yourself."

"Thanks for the pointers, Mike,
but don't worry, I've got that part

covered. What I need is his record.
I've got a plate and a name for you.
He's from Colorado. I want you to
look into him, see if he's got a
record, traffic or crime, I want to
know both."

Mike scratched his head and
puffed out some air. "Thing is,
Drake, I don't have any contacts in
Colorado."

"I'm asking you to make some.
Denver's a big city, police chief has
got to be listed, and he's more likely
to talk to a badge than a license.
But, I get it. You may need help from
someone who doesn't much like me.
Maybe this will help convince them."
I reached into my coat pocket.

"Now, Drake --" he started, but
once he saw the bottle, I knew we were
all right. I set it down on the
corner of his desk, watching his eyes
follow it the whole time. I didn't
take my hand off it, quite yet.

"Write this down," I said. He
fumbled around his desk for a pen, and
when he had it, he looked up at me and
not the bottle. "Evan Noble. A85182.
You got that?"

"Yeah, I got that," he said. He was back to being irritated with me.

"Good." I pushed the bottle to the center of his desk and let go. It quickly disappeared into one of his lower drawers. "I'll come back tomorrow, see what you've got."

"Now, you listen here, Drake. It's trouble for me every time you walk in here. You've got history here. I know some of it's true, and maybe some of it ain't, but you open it up for me all over again. I'll see you for poker on Sunday. You can hear about it then."

"No. This can't wait until Sunday, unless it's nothing. Then it doesn't matter when you tell me. Tell you what. You don't want me coming over day after tomorrow, you catch me at Delaney's before that. Or hell, arrest me for something. You know where I work."

"Don't get wise, Drake. But yeah, I'll find you. Probably won't have anything, but I'll find you just the same."

I nodded and went to the door. "Just the same," I repeated. "And thanks." I almost said, 'I owe you one,' but that wasn't right. I just owed Peggy one.

Having put my feelers out on this case, I turned back to my other one. I drove Joe's car down to Bartell's, bought another roll of film, a jug of processing chemicals, and some cigarettes, and headed over to the lover's house to wait.

In my experience, when a man finds out that his girl is definitively cheating on him, the first thing he wants to do is size the man up, make comparisons. Does he have a better job? Is he better looking? Does he come from wealth? Then there's all the spiteful stuff, things he can throw in her face. Is he lying to her about something? Pretending to be someone he isn't? Is she just one of many women that the other guy is leading on?

It pays to be able to provide some of this information to the client. I already knew Laslop lived in a mid-price apartment. A single, guessing by the spacing of the windows along Spring, possibly with an occluded view of the bay. Still, it was two or three large steps up from my own beloved rat-hole. But on the other hand, he let the lady pay for their date last night. If he's got money, he doesn't part with it easy. On the other, other hand, he may be just the sort of gigolo that relies upon women like Mrs. Bowerman to pay for his lodgings. I'd know more after watching him for a bit, maybe following him to work one morning, or visiting his apartment when he left.

That was all for another day, though. Today, I was busily winding a new roll of film into my camera and waiting for him to come home from work. I was curious whether he'd have someone with him. It wasn't unusual for the other man in these relationships to turn out to be married, especially with how carefully he made sure he wasn't followed. If Laslop was, I might end up with a second paycheck, selling pictures to her as well.

After that, I'd nose into his

evening routine. Did he cook his own dinner or would he head back out? If he went out, I'd follow along, just in case he had another date. If not, I'd find a view of his open window and get to know him. When did he call it a night? Was he a radio listener or a newspaper reader? Sloppy or neat? Whatever. The more details I knew, the more answers I would have for the questions Bowerman would inevitably ask.

I went through three cigarettes of my new pack waiting for him before I cut myself off. If I didn't pay attention, I'd need another pack tomorrow. Sometime after 5pm, the bus came up the hill, and several men got out. I had my camera ready, and I watched each as they exited. None of them were my guy, so I put the camera back down on my lap and settled in to wait for the next one, with one eye out for pedestrians.

Suddenly, there was a tapping at my passenger-side window. I'm not proud of the fact it made me jump. I looked over to see the barrel of a gun pointed at me through the glass. The man holding the gun pointed at the door lock with his free hand.

I leaned across and unlocked the door. Laslop opened it and got in next to me, holding the gun conspicuously leveled at me. "Why are you following me?" he asked.

I put my hands on the steering wheel to keep him from getting jumpy. I didn't put my hands up, as neither of us wanted people outside the car paying us any extra attention. "What makes you think I'm following you?" I asked, playing dumb.

"I saw you last night in the diner, now here you are casing my apartment. So I'll ask again, why is a detective tailing me?"

The surprise must have registered on my face. "Please. As if I can't spot a fellow dick?"

"You mean you're a detective too?" I asked.

"I can see whoever's paying you is getting their money's worth. You're quick."

Now, I was annoyed. "Look pal, I'm not after you, I'm tailing the dame."

"You're barking up the wrong tree then, friend. Only dame I've been around lately is my client. Strictly business."

"How about you put the smoker away? We're friends now," I said. "So, she hired you? What for?"

He stowed the pistol in a shoulder holster, and I relaxed a little. "She's worried that her husband is having an affair, and she wants me to watch him. She called me up last night wanting to meet, but it turned out she just wanted to see if I had anything yet. She's the impatient sort. Now your turn. Who hired you?"

"Her old man. He knows she's been sneaking out at night meeting with a man."

The man chuckled dryly. "So the two of them's got the two of us chasing each other. That's a hoot." He opened the door and stepped out.

Before closing the door, he bent down and looked me in the eye. "If I see you back here again, I'm likely to get nervous. And when I'm nervous, my finger tends to slip." He raised his hand, curling his index finger as if holding the trigger of a gun. "If you know what I mean." He held that pose for a moment, then he closed the door and crossed the street in front of me.

He hadn't been the first man to point a gun at me and certainly not the scariest. But there was one thing that all such men had in common. I didn't much like them. I'd be damned if this dick was going to know more about my client than I did. It was just a matter of professional integrity.

Time to pay Mr. Bowerman a visit. First though, I had to repay a favor and return the car.

I cruised around Seattle and dropped off a couple packages Joe had left in the back of his car. His route had me up as far as Ninth and Cherry, then back to Smith Tower, then a few stops down Fifth. Along the way, I bought a hotdog from a vendor on Marginal Way and got a paper at Pike Place.

I made plenty sure I was seen,

but not too well. Anyone who was
asked would say that Joe was there--
even Louis, the old guy at the
newsstand. He and I talked the big
three: Sports, weather, and job
prospects. When I was done with the
route, I stashed the hat and coat in
the trunk, returned the car to the
parking garage, and the keys to Joe's
little hiding spot under the hood.

I went out the side exit in my
own clothing. Then I took a streetcar
up to Capitol Hill to see Mr.
Bowerman. This time of day, the seats
were filled, leaving me to hang from a
strap. I tuned out the gabby
passengers and the sounds of traffic
and stewed in my own thoughts to
switch gears mentally.

I never used to do a lot of
thinking about my clientele. They
were just the people who brought me
money to do a job. It can be
dangerous deciding whether you like
them or not. You start getting picky
about what jobs you take in my line of
business, and pretty soon, you don't
eat any more. But that's what I had
to do right now.

I had a decision to make, and it came down to how much I liked my client, versus how much I liked my meal ticket. Rudolph Bowerman was a fat old bastard of a man, who got to a position high up the ladder and had a habit of treating everyone below him as if they were beneath him as well.

Now, I don't throw words like bastard around easily, and I know there's a percentage of people who shock easily. But Bowerman was the sort of fella who makes it his goal early in any conversation to put you off in some way or other. He didn't have friends; he used his influence and his money in lieu of charm, so it atrophied like an unused muscle. My own sainted mother, had she been forced to spend more than a few minutes in his presence, probably still wouldn't have used the word 'bastard,' but she'd have been thinking it loudly enough for anyone to hear.

Bowerman could say what he wanted because there was no one to stop him, and frankly, I think he was just daring people to stand up for themselves so he could pound them back down. Nothing made his day like a good firing, except maybe seeing that same person on the street a couple weeks later begging for change.

Technically, my job was done. I could simply tell him that his wife wasn't seeing anyone romantically. That was one way I could go. I could also tell him that she met up with a man last night, mostly innocent, but who knows? In that case, I would need more cash before I could find out more. Might take me a week or more to know whether it's an affair or not.

We'll call that one option B. My empty stomach was pulling me in that direction, whereas my heart was actually pulling for the wife. If I go with option A, with any luck, he lays off her, and whether he's up to something or not, well that's up to how good a snoop Laslop is.

There was a third option as well, and as much as I was against it, there was a nagging little voice in the back of my head called professional integrity that kept insisting I do right by my client. I tell him everything. Question was, what does a man like that do with such information?

I'm not sure I knew, but I also ran out of time to contemplate it, because my trolley stop was up.

His place was on the north end of Capitol Hill; a small triangle of land that jutted out just west of the Government Canal that linked Lake Washington to Lake Union.

When I was a kid, that canal didn't exist. Instead, it was just a small trickle of water winding its way through the marshy stretch of land between the two lakes. I remember taking a bamboo pole down there and coming back with the occasional fish. I remember they had to move the Madison docks because the shape of Lake Washington changed with the canal, but I can't remember much else, like how we used to drive from the north side of the river down to here. I only have the vague sense that everything is different.

The houses here were packed in close together, with no garage and no room to build but vertically. The sort of houses that are apparently quite popular in our sister city to the south, San Francisco. They were incredibly expensive, or at least, the land they sat on was. The only reason I could imagine people wanting to live in a house like that was the view. You turned to the right, and you had Lake Washington and the Cascade Range. You turned left, and there was Lake Union, and on a clear day, the Olympics out across the sound.

I rang the bell, and his servant, Chasly, opened the door. He had me wait just inside the door while he announced me to the master. The old British gentleman in the starched suit and impeccable gloves walked the eight feet or so to where Bowerman sat in his deep velvet chair. He was turned away, but clearly visible from where I stood, while Chasly informed him of my presence.

Bowerman leaned around the arm of the chair to regard me, as if he hadn't heard the door or didn't remember who I was, then nodded to Chasly.

"This way, sir." I followed him

around to where Bowerman sat facing
the bay windows, where he almost
certainly watched me walking up the
street.

"Glover. What have you got for
me? Did you catch the little minx in
the act?"

"Your lady's clean," I said. I
guess I wasn't going to string him
along. I was as surprised as you.

"Clean? What do you mean, clean?
Did you get any pictures?"

"I got some shots, sure. But
they were no good. There's nothing
there." Yeah, that's one way to put
it.

"Dash it all, I paid you for
pictures, Glover!" he said, slapping
his newspaper down on the floor.
"Now, what have you got for me?"

Suddenly, I didn't care if I got
paid or not. I wanted to get out of
there in the worst way before I got
his stench on me. "What have I got
for you, old man? I've got advice.
Your wife is a sweet kid and thirty
years your junior. You should be
doing what you can to keep her around
instead of driving her away. She's

not cheating on you; she's worried
you've got something on the side.
Now, maybe you do, and maybe you
don't. That's not my business, but
the reason she's been sneaking out is
to find out how you're spending your
spare time. My advice is to stay at
home once in a while and talk to each
other rather than hiring people to
find out what each other are up to.
Save yourself a few bucks. There's a
depression on if you hadn't noticed."

Bowerman came up out of his chair
in a flash. "Who the hell do you
think you are, you lousy two-bit
shamus?"

I don't have lice, but the rest
was fair.

Two men I hadn't seen earlier
came out of the back room and stood
threateningly in the doorway.

"I'm the two-bit shamus you hired
to do a job. Now I've done that job,
and I've given you the results. If
you want me to speak to you with
deference, that costs extra. My door
has my name over it, and that means I
don't report to anyone. And if someone
treats me like I belong to them, then

I get to say something about it. I
can tell you're the kind of man who
isn't used to that. You hire a man,
and that means he belongs to you.
It's about time someone told you
otherwise. Good day to you, Mr.
Bowerman. I think at this point, I'll
mail you the bill for services
rendered. I won't charge you for the
advice."

I put my hat on and brushed past
Chasly to let myself out. Bowerman
was shouting at me to come back, but I
had no intention of darkening his
doorstep again.

The trolley heading back across
Capitol Hill had already hit my stop,
and I ran to catch up with it.

I got change for the Jacksons at
Wells Fargo and stopped back at
Delaney's on my way home. There was a
slim chance that Mike would be there
with a rundown on that plate. He
wasn't, as it turned out, but Peggy
had a payphone in the bar, so I rang
up Joe to make sure I could use his
car in the wee hours.

He gave the okay as long as it was back in its spot by 8am, which was fine by me. I needed it to tail Mr. Noble, and if he left the house at 5:30, he could get halfway to Canada and still have me back by 8am.

After that, I took up my spot at the bar and had a couple glasses of my usual rotgut. I figured I'd give Mike a couple hours, and then I'd need to get in bed to be up at five. A two-bit shamus, like a soldier on the front, had to get used to sleeping when the opportunity came.

Delaney's usual crowd of misfits and orphans hadn't yet filtered in off the streets, and Peggy had some big band playing on the radio, which suited my mood. Deep rich male and high sweet female vocals. Nice and smooth with a wire brush for a beat.

The place got busier an hour and a half later, and I decided Mike wasn't going to show. There were five empties in front of me and a twenty-minute walk in the cool, Spring air ahead of me. I paid Peggy and asked her to tell Mike that he just missed me.

"Anything else I should tell him?"

"Thanks, doll, but no. This is more something he's got to tell me. If he's got some notes, maybe he can leave 'em with you. Otherwise, don't worry about it. Tell him I'll swing back by tomorrow."

The next morning, I got Joe's car again, and I waited down the street from the Noble house. Evan left promptly at 5:30. I laid back a couple blocks as traffic was practically non-existent. He headed West by North toward Ballard and the South-side docks. Looked like he was picking up some fish, fresh off the boat. Not too unusual for a restaurant man, I supposed. Dock workers loaded the fish onto a truck, ice packed along the walls, and when it left, Evan followed in his car.

I joined their little caravan as they went South along the Sound on Elliott then parted ways. The truck took a left up Mercer while Noble stayed on Elliot.

I stuck with Noble until he started looking for a parking spot near the Pike Place Market. I drove past him when he pulled over and continued on for another block before finding my own space. I watched him in my rear-view mirror as he jogged across to the market.

The streets were full of lumbering trucks this time of day, but I found a gap to park between them, and I followed Noble into the market at a leisurely distance. He met with a number of people and stuck his nose into several bags of mussels before selecting a few. They apparently knew him because they set the crate aside for him without payment while he moved on to other stands.

I followed him through the market, making stops at most of the stalls he vacated, watching what they did with his wares while pretending to be interested in what they were selling. For the most part, the smell of raw seafood turns me off. Don't get me wrong, I've never been so well fed that I could stand to be picky about what you put in front of me, but

there was a difference between what
they had on sale here and actual food.
That difference was a pot or a pan,
and a good long simmer in butter. All
the while I was conversing with the
various proprietors about the
freshness of their offerings or where
they were caught, I kept Noble firmly
in the corner of my eye, and I moved
on when he did.

All told, he picked up several
large salmon, a crate of live
Dungeness crab, the mussels I
mentioned already, a couple bags of
flour, an armload of daffodils, two
crates of fist-sized potatoes of
various colors, one with some rather
early asparagus, and another crate
filled with several types of onion.
Over the top of it lay a long string
of garlic.

Someone helped him back to his
car with it all, pushing a hand truck
down the incline, and loading it all
carefully into his back seat. He made
a U-turn and headed up Western. I had
to run to Joe's car to keep from
losing him. A U-turn from where I
parked was much more uncomfortable,

but I got there, and found Noble's car
as he was making a right on 4th Ave.

He wound his way up toward Queen
Anne Hill. A couple more turns
brought us to a section of town
painted with new money. The flashy
kind. Some of the places were still
under construction, but Noble turned
into the circular driveway of a modern
mansion with an elegantly manicured
lawn. I drove past it and noticed the
truck parked at a servant entrance.
There was a brass plaque on one of the
entrance columns that I was going to
have to come back later and inspect.

I drove on a bit and pulled over
in front of one of the unfinished
houses. After twenty minutes or so,
the truck took off, but Noble stayed
put. I watched over my shoulder for
another hour or so before deciding he
was there for the day. A stroll was
in order, so I got out of the car.
Along my way, I happened past the
brass plaque that announced the
mansion as the Brothers of Unity club,
est. 1919. There was no way this
mansion existed back in 1919, so
maybe, it was the Brothers of Unity as

a club that the establishment date referred to. I filed that information away to look up later. It felt as though I ought to know about something that was part of Seattle for that long, but it rang exactly zero bells.

I crossed the street two houses down, then circled the block and returned to Joe's car from the other direction. It was coming up on normal work hours, and I promised Joe he wouldn't be late for work. When I came back tonight, I would have a pair of binoculars and my camera.

Chapter Three

I dropped off Joe's car with
plenty of time to spare. He and his
wife lived in South Park, hoping to
raise a couple of kids. No luck so
far, but they had the house and yard
for it when the blessed event finally
came. But I had to get back to
downtown, and that's a heck of a walk.
I headed up Rainier Avenue until I
found a diner where I could wait it
out until bus service started up. The
sausage was questionable, but the eggs
were both crispy and runny, the way I

like them, and the hash helped fill my gut.

I stopped by my flat for a quick shower and change, then went to the office. Katie was there already, reading one of her bodice rippers. Without looking away from the page, she inclined an eyebrow toward the transcribed notes sitting on my desk.

"Thanks, Katie--you're a peach. Listen. I only got home last night about the time I had to head out this morning, so I'm going to shut the blinds and catch a few winks. Go ahead and wake me if a call comes in."

"You got it, Drake," she said without looking up from the novel. "Anything exciting?"

I shrugged. "Once I know who a few people are, things could get pretty interesting." I hung up my coat and hat and opened the door to my office, then a thought occurred to me. "Say, Katie, you haven't ever heard of the Brothers of Unity, have you?"

She frowned, resting the novel on her bosom. "Doesn't ring a bell. Should I ask around?"

"No, don't go to any trouble.

I'll get my answer by the end of the
day."

I stepped into my office, drew
the blinds, leaned back in my chair,
and put my feet up on my desk. Maybe
I wouldn't recommend this position to
anyone else, but I've always found it
comfortable. Outside my window, cars
were honking and people were shouting,
but inside a minute, I was fast
asleep.

I don't remember what I dreamed
about, but there was a lot of
shouting. It took a few moments after
I woke up to realize that the shouting
was still going on, and Katie was
doing most of it.

I jumped up and threw open the
door. There were two big men in there
with her, and she had her face up in
their space, right about chest height.

My father had been a boxer by
trade, and I recognized the look in
one of the men. The other one was
just plain big, so he might as well be
a boxer too. The suits they wore were
cheap but well-tailored to fit their

frames. They worked for someone who had money but didn't really want to spend it on them. The bigger guy's jacket bulged noticeably more on his left side than his right. I doubted he was bringing me whiskey though.

"I've got it from here, Katie. Why don't you take the rest of the day off?" I said, closing my office door behind me.   "What say you give the gal some space so she can grab her coat and hat, then you can have your say."

They stepped out of the way, and Katie pushed past the two of them to the coat rack. She pulled on her coat, staring daggers at them the whole time. "I could've taken them," she said as she stuffed her hat down on her head.

"I'm sure you could have," I replied with a smile. She returned to her desk for her paperback. I knew it wasn't for the bus ride, as she drove up from Fort Lewis--this little act of defiance was a show for the mooks. "But then, we couldn't have our chat."

Once she was down the stairs, I turned to my visitors.   "So, what

brings you two my way? Let me guess,
a missing cat?"

"Boss said you thought you was
funny," the bruiser said.

"Well, if you can't laugh," I
joked. Neither one looked like a
conversationalist, so I didn't have
much hope of keeping them going long,
but I pressed my luck anyway. "How is
old Bowerman?"

"None too happy wit youse," the
boxer said.

"Wants us to send you a message,"
said the other. "You should learn how
to talk to your betters. Thinks you
can do it just fine with fewer teeth."
The first guy cracked his knuckles at
that. We had reached the end of the
conversation.

Now, I don't look like much. I'm
a hair over five foot ten, and with my
lack of what you might call 'eating
habits,' I'm thinner than I'd like to
be. My hair is dark brown and likes
to stick up no matter what I put in
it, so I thank God that hats are in
fashion. My skin tone is darker than
average for this latitude. There's no
leading man in Hollywood that looks

enough like me that I'd make the comparison, but I'm not covered in scars or anything either. The point is, people have a habit of underestimating me when it comes to a fight.

My dad taught me a few things. The importance of keeping my guard up. The importance of footwork and of controlling the space around me. He taught me that no one ever sees a southpaw coming. Maybe it was his influence or maybe it was having a war hero for an older brother, but I grew up believing that you never back down just because the other guy is bigger or that there are more of them. I'm quick, and I have a glower like a Frankenstein mask.

There's one other lesson that I got from my dad that very few boxers seemed to ever receive. He was teaching me how to box, he wasn't teaching me how to fight. There was a very big difference.

In the years since his death, I learned how to fight.

They squared up to come at me from both sides, and the bigger one

tried to grab me. I batted his hand
aside and stepped outside his grasp,
facing the boxer.

He took a swing at me, and I
evaded him easily, taking another step
back. I was aware that he was pushing
me back toward the wall, but I was
also getting both of them in front of
me.

The brawler turned to face me,
and I moved fast to use his momentum.
I struck out and grabbed his tie while
sticking a leg behind his. I yanked
his tie to the side and got him off
balance. He started back-pedaling to
regain control, but I moved with him
so that he stayed at an awkward angle.
A mountain of a man like this could do
some real damage if I let him get his
hands on me for even an instant. So
every time it looked like he was going
to try, I let another inch of his tie
slip through my fingers. The man was
about as heavy as any I could manage,
but I had him on a leash now, and with
little effort, I kept his body between
mine and the boxer's. Reaching into
his holster, I pulled out the revolver
that was stashed there.

The two threw up their hands. I still didn't let the brawler get his legs under him. While I had them both under my control, I flicked the release and whipped the gun to the side, letting the cylinder fall open. I shook it until I heard all six rounds ping off the floor, then threw the gun out the open door Katie had left behind.

To my surprise, neither one of them seemed to wonder why I got rid of the gun. Not enough imagination between the two of them to strike a match off of. They just went back to the fight.

The boxer couldn't do much but try to get around the brawler, and I wasn't allowing it. Then he wised up, and with his own back against Katie's desk, supported his friend by the shoulders, so I quickly changed tactics. Letting go of his tie, I gave him a quick jab to the throat. He cupped his neck with both hands, and I put my knee in his groin with all my strength. I hate to do that to a guy, but I liked getting beaten to a pulp worse. And if I had let him get his hands on me even once, this fight would go a whole different way.

He curled up neatly, letting me in with my left for a haymaker, and he was out of the fight. The boxer rolled him out of the way and started circling. I brought up my guard. "When he wakes up, I'm going to give him enough of your teeth to make a necklace." Nice. I didn't have him pegged for the arts and crafts sort.

He threw a couple jabs, and I batted them down. I threw a couple back his way, but he didn't seem to care. I couldn't reach him without opening myself up to a grab. His reach outstripped mine, probably by six inches. We continued to circle until he had my back to the corner where my office wall met the side wall. He stopped circling and smiled a nasty, broken-nosed smile. This was right where he wanted me.

What he didn't know was that this was where I wanted to be too.

He jabbed a couple more times, trying to push me back, or maybe bring my guard down. I brought my left hand back, which he saw as his opening. He came in fast with an uppercut that never landed. My left hand came forward again, pulling with it the coat rack; a seven-foot length of oak four-by-four with a wrought iron core, weighing in at a hundred and eighty easy.

It crashed down on his skull and brought him to the floor. I wasn't entirely sure the fight was out of him yet, and he still had me trapped in a corner, so I started kicking at his ribs until he rolled the other way.

I walked around him, giving his arms a wide berth. His friend was coming around, so I grabbed him by the tie again and lifted. He put his arms out behind him, and I crab-walked him to the door and let go.

The boxer was trying to stand, so I got behind him and kicked him in the rear. I encouraged him to the door like that.

"Tell you what. Go back to your boss and tell him you roughed me up good. I won't be opening my left eye any time soon, much less getting involved in his affairs. There's no reason he won't believe you, and I won't disabuse him of this impression. I didn't hit you anywhere it will show this time, but if I see either of your mugs again, it's more of the same and maybe worse. Got it?"

The boxer, still on all fours, turned and gave me a look like I'd said something about his mother. The brawler, who was still in pain from breathing, just nodded at me.

"Good. Don't forget your smoker. And count yourselves lucky I didn't let Katie have her way with you."

I closed the door, propped my coat rack back up and re-entered my office. At the window, I pulled the edge of the blinds up a smidgen to watch the cars outside. My two guests didn't appear right away, but I hadn't expected them to, since if Bowerman was out there, they couldn't come out limping and sell our story. When they finally did, they got into a black Chrysler. The boxer did the driving.

Last time I saw Bowerman, it was my plan to be the end of things between us, but now it looked like that just wasn't to be. I suppose I only had myself to blame. If I hadn't been thinking about how much I disliked the man, I probably wouldn't have spoken to him like I did. It didn't matter whether I liked him or not. The man was a client. I agree to do a job, then I do it. Then the client pays me, and that's it.

But I had to go and mouth off. In the end, I did everything for him that I would have done anyway, and I told him what his wife was up to.

If he was going to send his mooks to rearrange my jaw just because I spoke to him roughly, what was he likely to do to the gal he's married to when she starts prying into something he's trying to keep secret?

It wasn't pretty, and any lawyer I'd ever met would say that I wasn't legally culpable, but that didn't stop me from feeling responsible.

Even knowing all that, I felt I needed to warn her.

My time was rather unoccupied until late that night. If I got everything ready now, I'd have time to find Megan Bowerman long before I had to get to the Brothers of Unity club.

I grabbed my camera and headed out, making sure to lock up behind me. A bus and a trolley later, I was back up Capitol Hill.

When I first started working for Bowerman, he gave me a detailed list of where Megan went, or at least, where she said she was going. On Wednesdays, she liked to take a walk around Volunteer Park and take in the view from the water tower. Seeing as how it was clear all the way out to the San Juans today, I thought there would be a good chance she'd be there.

When I got to the park, I could see several people looking off the edge of the tower. There was a woman, all on her own, dressed the way Megan liked to. I climbed the metal staircase and leaned against the railing next to her.

She spared me a sullen glance and returned to the scenery. "You wanna step off, fella. My husband doesn't like me talking to other men.

"Alright, Mrs. Bowerman," I said,

and she stiffened.

She turned, eyes wide, and as if she expected me to push her off, she gripped the rail tightly. "How do you know me?"

"It's okay, ma'am. I don't work for your husband. Not anymore, leastways. My name's Glover. Drake Glover. I'm a P.I. I've come to warn you."

I turned casually, lighting a cigarette and scanning the other onlookers. There was a decent chance that Bowerman didn't let his wife out unattended, and it wasn't too hard to find the man.

A big fella was eyeing me suspiciously. Made me wonder if Bowerman did all his shopping at King's boxing arena. It also made me wonder further if my father would have ended up working for him if he had lived a little longer.

I turned back around, keeping everything casual, and digging out a matchbook.

The tension hadn't gone out of her one bit. She pursed her ruby reds and waited, saying nothing.

She was even prettier by daylight. It must have taken her hours to get her hair and makeup that way, but in truth, she didn't need any of it. She would have been striking dressed in burlap. If she hadn't become Bowerman's trophy wife, she could have gone on to Hollywood or maybe become a New York model. Of course, they could never reproduce those green eyes on a magazine cover.

I struck a match and cupped my hands to cover my mouth while I talked. "Your husband hired me because he was worried about all the stepping out you like to do alone. He thought you might be seeing someone, you see. I followed you the other night and found out about Laslop. Don't worry," I said, holding up my hands at her sudden look of panic. "I know the two of you aren't romantic, and I told Rudolph so. I spoke to Laslop too. He let me know why you hired him. And that's where maybe I should have kept my mouth shut."

"You told Rudolph that I was having him followed?" she asked. She looked like she was about to faint, so

I grabbed her by the arm to support
her. Just on the edge of my vision, I
could see the big guy didn't like
that. I let go quickly and took a
step to my left. The goon glowered at
me but stayed put for now.

"Yes, ma'am, I did."

"You don't know what you've done.
I wanted him to be having an affair.
You don't know what Rudolph will do to
me, Mr. Glover."

"I'm afraid I have some idea.
Earlier today, he sent a couple of
these guys," I said, hitching a thumb
over my shoulder at the goon, "to give
me singing lessons the hard way. I
didn't give him Laslop's name, so he
won't be going after him."

"That just makes it worse! He'll
get it out of me! Oh, Mr. Glover,
you've got to help me."

"I'm afraid I can't, doll. I
have a client of my own I need to
help."

"I'll hire you!" she said. She
opened up her purse. "And then I'll
be your client too." That was too
much for the goon. He separated from
the others, heading toward us, but I

had a few moments with her.

I stepped back, giving her a warning glance. "Any other day, I'd take you up on that offer. But I have a prior engagement. There's another woman out there, this one loves her husband, and I need to make sure he doesn't get himself killed tonight."

Her eyes started filling with tears. "I don't know what to do!" she whispered with a sidelong glance at the goon.

I turned and straightened my tie, blowing out a cloud of smoke. I acted as if I had noticed the big guy for the first time and wandered off on my own to gaze in another direction. He lingered over her shoulder. I could feel his eyes on the back of my head. Eventually, he wandered off again.

Mrs. Bowerman was instantly back by my side. "Please, Mr. Glover. There must be something you can do."

"Just calm down. Take a deep breath and think. Call Laslop. He seems like a clever dick. You tell him what I told you. He'll get between you and your husband. Rudolph just needs a good talking to. Let him know

people are watching what he does. He
won't be able to get away with so
much. And if he lays a finger on you
after that, well, then you've got your
divorce."

     "Time to go, Mrs. B." The big
guy was back, and he put his hand
around her arm. I turned toward him,
and the big guy put one large finger
against my chest. "You shouldn't go
around talkin' to married women," he
told me.

     I put my hands up. "Just
enjoying the view, friend."

     He gave me a bit of a nudge with
that finger before turning and pulling
Mrs. Bowerman away toward the
staircase. She turned one last time
and gave me one of the most hopeless
looks I've ever seen.

     It was hard to leave her like
that. She was clinging to me like a
life raft, and I felt for her. I
could have taken care of the big guy
and bought her a little bit of
freedom, but it would have been
fleeting, and I had a job to do. If I

could, I would look in on her again
tomorrow, but for the moment, I left
the park and hailed a cab.

"Queen Anne and Mercer," I said,
and we drove in silence. He let me
off at the bottom of the hill, and I
walked the rest of the way. There was
a lot more traffic than I expected on
a road that was freshly paved and
flanked by the skeletons of houses
yet-to-be on both sides. They paid me
no mind as they passed, and as I
approached the Brothers of Unity club,
I realized they were hosting a party
of some sort.

I waited for a break in the cars,
then made a run for the construction
next door. Cars were lining up along
the horseshoe driveway, and folks
stepped out, dressed to the nines.
Men in tuxes and tails and women with
what could just about be described as
chandeliers hanging around their necks
were led in through the front doors.
I could just make out the faint
playing of live music each time the
bruiser at the door opened it.

I unscrewed the bulb from my
flash and stashed it in my left coat

pocket with the others. Several bulbs filled my pockets on hand for nighttime work. Fresh ones in the left, used ones in the right. But I wouldn't be using them tonight. If I did get close enough to take a few shots, I didn't want the burst of light to give me away. Nothing was going to happen for me while people were arriving, though. If Evan were still in there, he would be working late tonight.

I looked around at the framed-in house that was my base of operations for the night and decided to get familiar.

The floor I was standing on was a concrete slab, must have been two thousand square feet, and the frame of two stories was in place. Pipes and electrical wires wound through the structure, and wooden panels were going up along the north side of the first floor. Pallets of construction materials were distributed around the roughshod mud surrounding the concrete slab.

Just over the property line, a hedge grew to about chest high. There were several gaps where the individual bushes hadn't yet grown together, and that's where I'd make my crossing once the traffic had died down.

I moved toward the back of the construction, making sure to keep my head below hedge level just in case anybody got observant. From there, I could see around the back of the club. Security didn't seem to be their primary concern. Aside from the two big fellas on the front door, there didn't seem to be anyone guarding the place. Then again, with tall firs bordering the property on two sides, and no one else moved into the neighborhood yet, maybe they didn't have any reason for security.

It looked as if the last of the cars was pulling out of their driveway, and the goons out front were buttoning up. The two of them stayed outside but just stood quietly at the front door.

This was my best chance to see just what sort of club this was. I picked a gap in the hedge, hunched low and sprinted across to the back.

I made it into the backyard of
the club without being seen. The
manor was raised off the ground, and
the lowest windows were at head
height. So I flattened myself against
the wall and took a look inside.

I could make out two different
rooms from this angle. The closest
one had a buffet table. People were
standing around and talking while
waiters came past with silver trays
and refilled their champagne flutes.
I had no way of knowing which one
might be Evan, if any of them, but
from the view that I'd got of the back
of his head this morning, no one quite
fit the description.

Of course, it was always possible
that he was one of the party-goers
instead of one of the servants. I
quickly snapped off a few pictures,
hoping to cover most of the room.

Through an open doorway, I could
see there was a second room where
a pianist and bassist were playing.
From the sound of it, there were a
couple violinists not visible from

here. There were also guests milling
about in that room, and at least one
couple was dancing. Unfortunately,
most of the room was beyond my sight
from this angle.

I ducked down under the window
and tried my luck from the other end.
From there, I could see the front door
past the second room. More guests,
but still no sign of Mr. Noble. The
banister of a grand staircase was in
full view leading to the second floor.
I grabbed a couple shots again and
ducked down.

A couple men moved to stand right
next to the window. Neither one of
them looked down, though, thank my
luck. One of the men was a portly,
graying man who spoke with a cigar
pointing out between two fingers. He
held a small guillotine in the other
hand but hadn't yet chopped the end
off his cigar. The second man was
younger, and he was stuck holding both
the champagne glasses. "But with the
right packaging, we could use smaller
boxes and save twelve cents per unit!"
the older one said; the other smiled
politely. I noticed they both had a

small brass pin affixed to their
lapel. It looked like some sort of
animal, and maybe a couple letters
over the top of it, but I couldn't
make out any real detail from here.

A woman in a silvery dress and a
matching pillbox hat came dancing up
to them. "Have you tried the petit
fours?" The young man handed a
champagne glass to her, which she
downed while maintaining a Charleston.

"Waiter," the older gentleman
called to one of the passing servants.
While they were distracted, I chanced
a closer look and noticed the woman
had an identical pin on the strap of
her dress. I was going to want to see
that better.

I flattened against the wall and
sidled further along. Toward the far
end of the house, there was a door out
into the yard, and a ramp leading away
from me. The door had a window in it
with curtains drawn. I approached the
window and pressed my eye against the
gap in the curtains.

Beyond was the kitchen. Men in
white uniforms and aprons moved from
station to station, while other men in

servants' outfits dropped off empty
trays, picked up full ones, then left
the way they had come. Over the
sounds of running water and clanging
dishes, someone was barking orders.
"Coddled eggs! Coddled, not poached!
Hey! That one doesn't go out without
saffron threads!" It was a fair bet
that would be Evan, but he never came
into view. Even if he did, I wouldn't
be able to get a picture through the
curtain. I ducked back down behind
the high end of the ramp to come up
with my next move.

Turns out, I was just in time
too, because a moment later, I was
surprised by a man coming around the
far side of the house. He was dressed
in a flannel top and jeans with
suspenders and had a newsboy cap
perched on his head. Definitely not
one of the party-goers. He didn't
look my way, and instead turned back
the way he had come and started waving
forward and back with both hands. He
walked slowly backward, and the back
end of a truck followed him.
"Alright, that's good!" he yelled, and
the truck engine shut off. He rolled

up the door on the back of the truck.

I had nowhere to hide. If he turned this way, I would have to make a run for it.

Just then, the kitchen door opened, hiding me from view. Someone stuck his head out. "Hey, Mack, you guys ready?" he called. It was the same voice barking orders from a moment ago, probably belonged to Noble, but I had no chance at a photo.

"Yeah, just let us get the ramp down. How many you got going anyway, chief?" Mac asked.

"There will be twenty-four. Twenty-four going, twenty-four coming back. If any are missing, it's coming out of your hide."

"Yeah, yeah, I've got it."

There was the sound of steel on steel. I poked my head around the side of the door and saw Mack and another similarly dressed man pulling a ramp out of the back of the truck. Once he had finished, Noble called to someone inside, "Okay, let's go."

A line of waiters came out through the door, down the ramp, and up into the truck; eight of them in

all. Each one was pushing something
that looked like a room-service cart
from the movies. There were covered
trays in both the top and bottom of
each one.

The eight parked the carts in the
truck, then came running back into the
house. I ducked back behind the door
as Noble propped it open and joined
Mack and his double. The three of them
disappeared around the side of the
truck.

It was time to make a decision.
As full as it was, I wasn't likely to
get into the main house or the kitchen
tonight. And a party is a party,
anyway, even a rich one. There was
nothing odd or criminal going on in
there as far as I could see. But this
was something else.

An investigator develops a
certain sense for when things were
hinkey. Many times in the past, it
had saved my life, and I understand
from cops and priests that the
feeling's not uncommon. If something
doesn't smell right, it usually ain't.
Now, I don't know what it means, by
any stretch, but I've been to a party

or two in the past. There's dancing,
there's music, people play dress up.
But I have never seen a party where
the waiters take the food out the back
door just when it's getting started.

The eight waiters came out with a
second group of carts and loaded them
up on the truck. I poked my head back
out after the last one, looking for
Noble to return, but he and his
companions were nowhere in sight. I
ducked back again and waited. The
eight waiters came running back into
the house, and I made a break for the
truck.

At the bottom of the ramp, I
could see Mack, Noble, and the other
guy up near the cab of the truck
sharing a smoke. I quickly ran up the
ramp and pushed past the food that had
already been loaded. The truck itself
was freezing, but the carts radiated
heat. Aside from them, there was a
bunch of lumber stacked up along the
right wall, a pile of linens, and a
dozen or so sawhorses. There were two
long metal boxes built into either
side of the truck. I lifted the lid
on the closer one, and sure enough, it

was filled with blocks of ice.

The waiters were coming back, so I hunkered down behind the furthest cart while they brought the last batch in.

There was Mack's voice again. "You coming with us?"

Then Noble. "Nah, I've got a party to attend. Kowalczyk's going with you. He'd better hurry with the forms too, I don't want that food to get cold."

At that point, someone pulled the roll-down door shut, leaving me alone in the freezing darkness.

Chapter Four

Being in a freezer truck for half an hour, roughly jostled back and forth at every turn, isn't as comfortable as I make it sound. I started off trying to memorize the left and right turns and estimate how far it was between them, but I was getting so cold, it was hard to think straight.

The carts all had little votive candles in cups beneath the chafing trays keeping the food warm, so I pulled one out to use as a heat source, but it didn't do much beyond burn my hands while the rest of me froze. After a few unexpected turns, I ended up with hot wax all over my shirt, and I put the candle back.

I did my best to take my mind off the cold and had some success in that. Unfortunately, that just made the voice in my stomach louder. Every part of this van smelled like mom's cooking, only better. I wanted to just open the closest dish and fill my stomach with whatever was in there. The only thing that stopped me was my desire to get out of that truck without them ever knowing I was there.

Now that I knew they were up to something, I had to find out what that was. If they found out that someone was on to them, they might change things up, maybe hide some information that would lead to clarity for me. No, I wanted them to think whatever was going on was working to plan.

Eventually, the truck came to a stop, and I heard the emergency brake ratcheting into position. I got ready.

The roll-up door opened, and I

was well hidden behind the carts. The two men in casuals started pulling planks of two by four from the pile of lumber, and another man in a decent suit grabbed a couple of the sawhorses. As soon as his back was turned, I sprang from my hiding spot and slunk to the truck's entrance.

I'm not sure where I thought the truck would end up making its mouth-watering delivery, but it sure wasn't here. A muddy, rutty road ran between hastily crafted shacks constructed out of whatever was lying around. Trash cans held not trash but fire, and men were gathered around them for warmth. The truck had stopped in Hooverville.

The man in the suit was placing the two sawhorses ten feet or so apart, and the other two were ready to lay the wooden planks across the top of them. For the moment, all three had their backs to me, so I let myself down off the truck and ran to the shadow of the closest shack. This one was made from flattened gasoline cans.

They set up another six tables end to end, and men started gathering around. The one in the suit started

putting them to work. He pulled white
tablecloths out of the cab of the
truck and handed them out. The men
started laying them over the makeshift
tables.

There was a lot of conjecture
about what was going on, but the three
from the club didn't say anything.
One of the men of Hooverville spoke up
for the group. He was close to seven
feet tall and dressed almost
identically to Mack. "Hey, what's all
this about?" he asked, even as he
flattened the wrinkles of a
tablecloth.

"It's about voices, my good man,"
said the little guy in the formal
wear. He spoke with a heavy Eastern
European accent, and his version of
'voices' sounded like 'woices.' I
thought back to what the waiter had
said, that someone named Kowalczyk
would be going with them. By my
guess, the little guy was from Poland.

The answer he had given them
wasn't the most satisfying, but it was
all the men got. The little guy went
to the back of the truck and pulled
down the ramp. Then he went inside

and emerged with one of the carts.
The other two went in after him and
pulled out two more.

The three of them started placing
the chafing trays on the tables, and
the murmuring from the crowd became
more interested.

A second truck pulled in while
they were going back for more carts.
The driver got out and went around the
back. I heard the sound of another
roll-up door.

"Gentlemen, I believe there are
some folding chairs on board that
truck. If you could start setting them
up?" the little guy said to the
gathered crowd.

Over the next few minutes, the
men of Hooverville set chairs around
the table, and after that, paper
plates and silverware. I watched the
little guy and the van driver go back
with empty carts and return with full
ones until the table was brimming with
food. Strangely, all I could think
while watching them was how many sets
of silver did they think they would
get back at the end of the night?

"Gentlemen," the little guy said

again over the voices of the men, "If there's anyone still in their homes who hasn't gotten word of tonight's spectacle, would you be so good as to retrieve them? There's enough here for everyone, I promise. And if there's not enough seats, well, we can manage in shifts now, can't we?"

A few men went running off into the sea of ramshackle houses around them, yelling for everyone to come out. A few others pulled out chairs and sat at the table. "Not just yet, please," the little man said. "I have something to say to all of you, and I would prefer not to have to yell over the sounds of fork and knife. Yes, please stand up. There will be no food until you've heard me out."

"And who's going to stop me?" someone in the crowd shouted.

The little man gave a look of surprise. "Why, your fellow man, of course. There's no reason this couldn't be a regular event, but if you make a mess of it, I can promise it won't be."

There was silence from the crowd, but those who had still been seated stood up and pushed their chairs in. They remained standing with their hands on the back of their chair, though, and the rest of the crowd spread out to reserve their own spot at the table.

The runners returned, and along with them were a few stragglers. Among them were a few women, one of whom had kids clinging to her. Two of the men started pushing other men out of the way, making sure the women and children got spots. I noted that those two men kept their places as well.

"Alright, I won't take long," said the little guy. He waited a few moments for relative silence from the crowd.

"You've all heard it. Maybe you heard it from far away because Seattle was calling to you. You heard its voice. And what did it say? "Come to me. I have jobs for you. Come to me, and I will make you prosperous. Come to me, and your children will be safe. And fed.

"You've heard its voice, and you've heard the voice of the

businessmen! We need good men to
build ships! We need you to build
airplanes! We need you to fish our
waters! To build our roads, to make
your mark in the world, and it is here
where you can make your mark. But
their voices have changed, haven't
they?"

He looked around at the men.
"Now they say, it's not worth it any
more to run the mill! The price of
timber is too low, and so they close
it down, and it's because they didn't
make as many millions one year! And
the cannery is the same thing! Who
knows how long it will last? If the
price of bulk salmon goes down or the
price of tin goes up, or they have one
too many tragic accidents in the
factory, they'll shut it down! But it
won't be for safety! Because what
they see is money. They won't fix the
problems because they don't care about
their workers; they'll just shut it
down and put more of you out of a job!
"The politicians are no better!
I hear their voices all the time, but
what do they say? They say, they're
going to find you jobs. They say,

they know there's a problem, and
they're going to find a solution. I
say, they aren't looking very hard.
Because the jobs are here! They're
right here. They're in the cannery,
they're in our fleets, they're in the
mill, they're in the forests, they're
in our mines. They're building houses
and schools and community!"

It was a stump speech. I
couldn't believe it. This whole thing
was a whistle-stop.

"And what about your voice?" He
paused again, watching the sea of
nodding heads. "Don't you have a
voice? No! You might think you do,
but you don't. Have you ever tried
using it? Nobody listens. My friend,
Jesse Jackson, has tried to use his.
He's walked right up to City Hall, and
he's demanded they do something about
jobs in Seattle. And nobody heard
him. He went to the papers, and they
wrote it down, and still, nobody heard
him."

"Well, friends, we've got a way
of making them hear you. If they
don't care about your job, I say we
put them out of a job! In just a few

weeks, Mayor Dore is up for re-
election, but we can put him out of
town on a rail. Friends, Lonnie Seger
is running for mayor, and on day one,
he will start working on jobs. He
will open the mill back up. He will
get our mines and our forests back up
to full production. He will make them
fix the problems at the cannery, and
he will expand. Seattle will once
again be the place that people come to
because the jobs are here. More jobs
than people. No longer will you be
forced to do everything you can just
to hold onto a job you hate because
you can just get another job at the
next place over, and if they don't
treat you right, you can quit that job
too!

"And the best part is, Lonnie
Seger will listen to you. If you
don't think he's doing something
right, friends, his door is open. He
will give you your voice back."

"So, sit down. Eat. Remember
that Lonnie Seger brought you this
food, and imagine a world where Lonnie
Seger is running Seattle."

Mack and his friend went down the

line pulling the lids off the chafing
trays. Everyone rushed to take a seat
and start filling up their plates as
quickly as possible.

The little guy had to start
shouting to be heard over the din.
"Vote for Lonnie Seger! And if anyone
here isn't registered to vote, I
brought registration forms and pens!
If anyone can't read, just raise your
hand, and I will help you fill out
your forms!"

I realized that I had just been
standing there watching through the
whole thing, and I started snapping
picture after picture. I got the guys
lifting lids off trays, I got the
little guy waving forms around, and I
got plenty of shots of the men eating.

I watched the men of Hooverville
filling their plates with meat,
potatoes, green beans, and corn, as
well as the salmon I saw Noble buying
just this morning. I couldn't
remember when I had felt hungrier.
I've mostly learned to ignore that
feeling, but it had been a whole day
since the plate of hash I last ate,
and there was no ignoring it while

watching these men eat.

I put my camera back away and wished I were one of them.

A hand fell on my shoulder, and I jumped. "You must be new around here," the man said.

I turned to see a negro in rough overalls and a torn coat. He was maybe six foot one, with a pleasant face and a bald head under a frayed newsboy cap.

I tried to cover my surprise while I let my camera fall under the crook of my arm so the bulge in my coat wouldn't give me away. "And I suppose you know everybody living here?"

The man laughed and pulled a pipe out of the front pocket of his overalls. "Nope," he said, digging a pouch of tobacco out of another pocket. "Though I do know a fair deal. Just your suit is a little cleaner than most, and someone said, 'free food,' but you haven't jumped yet."

"Well you've got me there. I'm

not much of one for pushing my way to the front. How about you?"

The man filled his pipe and pulled the pouch closed with his teeth. "Let the others have their fill. Man said, they've got plenty for everyone, and one thing that seven years in a place like this will teach you, it's patience. Got a light?"

I said I did, and I dug around in my pocket until I found the fresh book I got from the pharmacy earlier. I handed them over, and he struck one, cupping his hands around the bowl of his pipe and puffing until it took. He shook out the match and handed the book back to me. "Come on. I think a couple spots are opening up."

He walked up to the table, and I followed along, carefully tucking my camera into my suit coat. He came up behind two of the men and laid his hands on their shoulders. "Ben, George, why don't you two give us a shot at that, hmm?"

Ben quickly shoveled another couple forkfuls into his mouth, but to my surprise, the two men got up and let us have their seats.

"I didn't catch your name," the curious man said, holding out a seat for me.

Getting caught sneaking around was bad enough, giving him my real name would just make things worse. The first name to come to mind was my brother's. "Jack," I said.

He stuck out his hand, and we shook. "Well, Jack, I'm Jesse. Let's see what we've got here."

Jesse? Was this Jesse Jackson, so-called Mayor of Hooverville? Jesse pulled George's plate closer, even though there was a stack of clean ones next to him, held down by a rock to keep the wind from pulling them away.

"Meatloaf! And boy, doesn't that look tasty," Jesse said. He set down his pipe on the edge of the table and lifted a forkful onto his plate. "What have they got down there in terms of sides, Jack? A little succotash, or maybe even some hot biscuits would just put me in heaven." He handed me the serving fork, and I put some on my own plate.

There wasn't any succotash or biscuits to be seen, but there were peas a little further along the table, and some grilled salmon and mash potatoes. I put a little of each on our plates, and we dug in.

The little guy came by and put a voter registration form in front of me and offered me a pen. I swallowed hard and said, "I'm already registered."

He picked the form back up. "I trust we can count on your vote." He moved on down the line to give forms to the rest of the men.

I leaned over to Jesse once the little guy had left. "So, what do you think? This isn't exactly usual, someone in politics buying us a feast like this. Is this guy for real?"

Jesse chuckled. "I thought exactly the same thing when he first came by and told me he wanted to do this. I told him, people 'round here got no use for false hope. What we need is jobs. He convinced me that jobs is what Seger is about. Even hired a few of us to make tonight's meal. They told me there would be biscuits." He stood up and yelled across the table. "Hey, Harry! You got hot biscuits down on that end?"

Harry yelled back that he had seen some earlier, but they were gone now.

"Damn," Jesse said, sitting back down. "I guess being mayor don't come with all the perks, huh now?"

"I suppose not," I agreed.

"So, Jack, what'd you do before all this?"

There was no way he was going to believe either soldier or boxer, and I sure didn't want to say investigator, so I gave him the next thing that popped into my head. "Writer."

"You mean, like newspaper reporter?" he asked.

"No, like novelist. Like Twain or Poe. Or London." Reporter sounded too close to investigator still.

"Uh-huh. I suppose you could fail at that anywhere, just as easy as Seattle. What made you come here?"

"I was born here." I hitched a thumb back behind us. "Just up there in Ballard. Couldn't pay the rent, though. I tried doing other things, but no one's hiring, so here I am."

Looked like he bought the lie.

"All I can say is, if you're gonna vote, and I hope you do, vote for change. Cause, staying the same ain't working."

The wind picked up, and rain started pelting the tables. Men lifted their plates and started running for their shacks. The rain became a downpour within seconds. The little guy ran after them with the remaining sheets clutched tightly to his chest. "Did everyone get their voter registrations? I can help you fill them out!"

Despite the fact that plenty more food sat on the table, and I could have easily devoured a second plateful, I used this as my own excuse to disappear. I felt damn lucky I hadn't gotten caught, and I wasn't going to press my luck any further.

The other two started shouting at the fleeing men, "Remember Lonnie Seger! Jobs! Not handouts!"

I was soaked to the bone by the time I got back to my apartment. I hung my suit up on the line above the

tub and towel dried. Sitting on the
edge of my bed, I stared at my camera.
I had some good photos now, but
nothing my client was going to care
about. Unfortunately, I was no closer
to discovering her husband's part in
all this.

Frankly, I didn't know what 'all
this' was. If it's just a
philanthropy club that's raising money
and feeding the destitute, that didn't
sound so bad to me. But it didn't
explain why my neck tingled around
that club, or why tonight just felt so
wrong.

Either way, I still had half a
roll to go. There was no sense in
wasting that by developing it now.
I'd go back to the club tomorrow
night, when with any luck, they
weren't having a party. I'd try to
get inside and see what they do behind
closed doors.

For now, I'd get a few hours'
sleep, then in the morning, I'd see if
Katie still worked for me. Your
typical clerical worker usually isn't
signing up to have a couple ruffians
pushing their way into the office.

I threw the towel over my chair and laid down, but it was one of those nights when my mind had no intention of letting me sleep. What united the Brothers of Unity? Why did it bug me so much? Were they into something shady? Nobody gives away good quality food like that, especially to hundreds of men, unless they had some motive.

Were they really just trying to tip the vote? I had never heard of this Lonnie Seger before. Was he really close enough that a few hundred more would push him into office? And wasn't the candidate usually the one to give stump speeches?

And what did all this have to do with Evan Noble?

I made a mental note to get all of this on the Dictaphone tomorrow, hoping that I could sleep after that, but instead, my mind went to Megan Bowerman.

She had been so frightened on top of that water tower. She hadn't even known about my part in this, and she already thought her husband might kill her. I hoped that Laslop was half the dick he thought he was. I hoped he did go with her, and he stood up to the man.

I wasn't very good at hoping.

Sleep wasn't coming for me that night, so I put my damp suit back on and headed down to Delaney's.

When I got to the bar, Brian Goldman was there. Brian rounded out my Sunday night poker quartet. He was a small guy with round spectacles and curly blonde hair in a trench coat that just about touched the ground as he sat on the barstool.

Brian worked at the P.I., that's Seattle's Post-Intelligencer, not Private Investigator. He had the occasional story make the nightly edition, but mostly he fact-checked other people's stories. This is one pony I could bet on, because when they did let him write, he was better than all the others. He would be editor in chief one day.

Now, I can hear what you're thinking. It's like all my friends are people that are useful to me, and I'm just mooching off of them. Well, it hasn't come up much in the story so far, but let me tell you, I give out as many favors as I collect. Some of those stories Brian has written came from photos I took. In fact, the one of the little guy waving registration forms around while feeding hundreds will probably go to him. Free of charge.

In the same way, if I ever found something in the course of one of my investigations that didn't relate to my client, I'd pass on a tip to Mike, and he'd get a collar. I'm not trying to claim I made him sergeant, but he might still be walking the beat if not for some of those tips.

Same thing goes for Betty over at the phone company, but I've promised not to tell her story, so forget I mentioned it.

I took the stool next to Brian, and Peggy brought me my scotch on the rocks. "Thanks, doll. Hey, Brian, how's the biz?"

Brian chuckled. "I spent most of the day calling grieving families to make sure we got the obits right. You?"

"Had to fight off my old client's goons, then I had to warn the gal I had been following about him, and to top it off, I rode a freezer truck from Queen Anne down to Hooverville. Just another day on the job."

We clinked our glasses and drank up.

"Speaking of, I took some pictures tonight that might interest you."

"Oh, yeah? Whad'ya get?" He turned in his stool toward me.

I lit a cigarette and took a puff before answering. "What do you know about Lonnie Seger?"

"Our own dark horse 'voice of Seattle?' A bit. Not a lot. Why?"

"Ever seen anyone campaigning in Hooverville before?"

Peggy refilled our drinks and set out an ashtray for me.

"You're kidding me! Lonnie was stumping in Hooverville?" Brian had a notebook out in an instant.

"Not Lonnie himself, no. But there's this club in Queen Anne, and they sent down a gourmet meal, along with a stack of voter registration

forms and a pretty little speech.
Ever heard of the Brothers of Unity?"

He wrote that down in his
notebook. "Can't say I have. Queen
Anne, you say?"

"Don't you go snooping around.
Leave that to the professionals. I'll
let you know if I find anything."

"And what about those pictures?"

"There was this little guy in a
suit. Polish name. It'll come to me.
He and two workers put a bunch of
tables together and fed all the
residents of Hooverville tonight. Any
idea how many that is these days?"

"There's no official tally, but
somewhere just south of a thousand, I
would imagine."

"And how many people in Seattle?"

"Census is in two years, but
ballpark? Three hundred thousand?"

I let out a big sigh and
contemplated my drink for a while.
That's what was bothering me. "That's
a drop in the bucket."

"What do you mean?" Brian asked.

"Well, let me ask you bluntly.
If you were going to spend all that
money buying votes, would you waste it

all on one-third of one percent?"

"You think he's buying votes?" Brian asked.

"Well, that's what it looked like to me."

Brian shook his head and traded his notebook for his drink. "Doesn't make sense."

"That's what I'm saying."

We sat in silence while I spun my shot glass, contemplating its scratches and trying to make the numbers fit in my head. Peggy poured herself a drink, and the three of us clinked glasses and threw them back.

"I'm still not sure you understand, because it's worse than that, Drake," Brian said. "The men of Hooverville weren't likely to vote before tonight. If you were going to buy a thousand votes, you don't make new votes, you want to take them from the existing pool. Hopefully, your opposition's base. They're worth twice as much."

"Maybe I'm not drunk yet, or maybe I was never good at math," I said, "but I'm not following you."

Peggy refilled our glasses.

"Get me one of those too, Peggy, will ya?" Mike showed up, clapping us both on the shoulders. Peggy poured him one, and Mike sat down on my other side.

"Hey, Mike," Brian said, then launched into his explanation. "Okay, let's say it was just the two of them running, and Seger had a decent shot, which he doesn't. But for the sake of argument and round numbers, he's got about 150 votes, and Dore's got the other 150. There's these people right in the middle that might go one way or another. You never know until the vote comes up. It could end up 148 to 152. Right? Now you're suggesting that Seger is buying someone from outside. So, it's 151 to 150. But you've still got those middle people. Just adding one person doesn't change that, and it could still go for Dore. What Seger has got to do is buy people out of Dore's camp. That way, it's 151 to 149, see?"

"Sure. I get it now. But I've got pictures to prove it. I ate the man's meatloaf."

"I'm not saying he wasn't there;

I'm saying he wasn't likely buying votes. So, what else can you tell me about this club?"

"It's the only finished mansion on an unnamed street off McGraw. Nothing but forest around it. They had a party there tonight. Lots of fancy cars and fancy dress. Everyone had these pins on them too. Wish I could have gotten a picture. Little round brass thing, with some sort of animal on it."

"You mean like a bear?" Mike caught me with my drink halfway to my lips.

I turned toward him. "Yeah, could be. Why?"

"Nothing much. The chief's been wearing one of those lately. Does it mean something?"

"I don't know yet. Could be. Describe it."

"It's like you said. Little, round, and brass. It's got a bear in the middle and says bou around the edge."

"Bow?" Brian asked. "That's ominous."

"No. B-O-U," I said, putting two

and two together. "Brothers of Unity.
The pin means you're in the club."

"So, what's that mean? The
chief's in some club."

I set my drink back down
untouched. "I'll let Brian fill you
in. I need to hit the hay. First,
though, what did you find out on that
plate?"

"Plate's not from Colorado. They
must have bought it somewhere along
the way. Idaho, Utah, Oregon? Who
knows. I can follow up if it's really
important, but I'll likely only get
prior owner info."

"No, forget it. It's a bust.
What about the guy?"

Mike dug a notebook out of his
jacket pocket and flipped it open.
"Evan Noble, age 31, married no
children. No tickets, no criminal
record. Did his taxes on time, kept
his nose clean." He put the notebook
back away. "Squeaky clean. Is he
involved with this club of yours?"

"He's the reason I'm looking into
it. Thanks, Mike. I'll see you guys
around. Looks like I'll be heading
back there tomorrow night." I put

some change on the bar for the drinks
and headed back home.

I had even more thoughts swimming
around my brain now than I did before.
Difference is, I had a couple drinks
up there swimming with them. This
time I managed to find sleep.

I dreamed all night I was running
from a big brass bear, and every time
I turned a corner or opened up a door,
it would be there.

When I made it into the office
the next day, Katie was already there.
I set a bouquet down on her desk.
Nothing much, a couple carnations and
some baby's breath, but her face lit
up. I guess I don't do it as often as
I should.

"What's that for?" she asked.

"For handling those two goons
yesterday, and for still being here
today."

"Oh, those trumped-up little
kids. If I had my broom, I would have
swept them out the door."

I smiled. "That's what I love
about you, Katie."

"Steady on, mad dog. Don't make me get my husband down here. How about you turn your attention to the lady in your office."

"Mrs. Noble is back?"

"No, it's not her. When it rains, it pours. She wouldn't give her name, though. Think you can take on another client?"

"The Bowerman case is over, except the billing. Something tells me it's going to be painful getting paid, but that's for another day."

I hung up my coat and hat and stepped into my office. Mrs. Bowerman turned to face me. Her lip was split, and she had a shiner like porterhouses were made to cling to. I picked up my desk lamp to see it better.

"I take it this is your husband's work."

She barked out a laugh. "My husband doesn't get his hands dirty doing things like this." The tears from yesterday were gone. There was a rage burning inside her like a California hillside in San Andreas season.

"So, either Laslop refused to do

anything, or he tried, and it didn't help." I set the lamp back down.

"Oh, Bill tried. And sure, he was quick to get his gun out, but he was outnumbered. Three on one, and he handed the gun over. Two of them walked him out of there with his hands up. Then Rudolph sat down in his favorite chair, and I got some alone time with Mickey. I want him dead, Mr. Glover, do you hear me? I want you to kill my husband."

"Listen, Megan. There's a reason the sign on my door doesn't read 'Assassin,' and it's not because I'm being discreet. Though I stretch things a bit on the subject of battery, I try to work within the law. Let me run some other options past you. I can try to convince him that having you hit isn't in his best interest -- And I can be very convincing. Option two: I can get you out of town. I know the sorts of people that can hook you up with new papers and a new name. Or, I can get you in touch with a grade-A divorce attorney. Let me get a couple pictures of you, and you tell your

story to a judge. Take Rudolph for
half of what he owns. Between you and
me, I'd take option three. Believe
me, for a man like Rudolph, taking him
down a peg publicly and getting half
his stuff in the processes will hurt
him more than breaking his fingers
would."

It didn't look like any of those
options were going to quell her rage.
She needed some time to calm down
before she could think rationally. I
gave her one more thing to think
about.

"Look, there's one other option.
I hesitate to bring it up because it's
an unpleasant thought, and it depends
upon your husband. What do you think
he might have done to Laslop? If they
just beat him all to hell and dumped
him off, sadder but wiser, there's not
much we can do. But if they put
stones in his pockets and rowed him
out into the Sound, coming back
without him, well, maybe I can link
him to that. If we find Bill's body,
we can maybe prove your husband had
him killed and send him to the
slammer."

"Oh, Bill," she said, and now the waterworks opened up.

I put a hand on her shoulder. "You two weren't together, were you?"

She looked up at me, shocked and offended at my assumption. "No! But if he's dead, it's because of me!"

"Don't beat yourself up, kid. If he's dead, it's because of him. You hired him to do a job, and he couldn't get it done, that's it. Now, that's if he's dead, and that can be a big if. Pointing a gun at a man is a whole lot easier than pulling the trigger. I don't know yet that your husband's the kind of guy who's willing to kill a man."

"I think you'll find, Mr. Glover, that it's much easier to order someone else to do it," she said.

"Did you hear him say to kill Laslop?"

"No. His exact words were, 'Get him out of here. Make sure he doesn't come back.'"

"Hmm. Threatening, but not conclusive. And there's always the chance that Bill fought them off once they were out of sight."

"He's not answering his phone or his door this morning."

I nodded. "Have you ever heard your husband order a kill before?"

She sighed, exasperated. "Not exactly. I've heard him threaten to kill people, to their faces, when he was angry. Business partners, accountants, and the like. But I don't think he ever killed any of them. Ruined them, sure. But it's different when he gives the orders. It's all, "Send him a message he's sure to understand,' or 'make sure he never crosses me again.'"

"And what happens to those people?"

She shrugged. "I usually haven't seen them before, and I don't ever see them again. I never thought until recently that he would have had them killed."

"Alright, Megan. Listen. I'll see if I can locate Laslop, dead or alive. Chances are, he's laying low or maybe even checked into a hospital. Either way, I'll do what I can to find him. I'll have a chat with Rudolph too, while his goons aren't around."

"They're always around, Mr. Glover."

"Call me Drake. I'm working for you now. My fee is ten dollars a day, plus expenses. I'll have receipts for those, and if anything's too expensive, I'll talk to you about it first. Don't worry about me, I'll find some way to make sure the hired help is elsewhere at the time. Now, come with me a moment."

I stepped around behind her and opened the door for her. "Katie, I know your skin tone's just about polar opposite to Megan's, but I'm hoping you've got something in that bag of tricks for her. Any chance you can help Megan out here with some makeup? She can't go outside like this."

"Mr. Glover, I'm surprised at you. I'm sure the lady has her own powder, but I can do the honors covering up those bruises, no problem. You just sit down right here, sweetie, and we'll have you fixed right up. I don't know about that lip, but we'll do what we can."

"Just a moment, doll. I need to get some photos first." I unfolded my camera and started getting shots from several different angles. "Megan, is it safe to assume anybody you might stay with is someone that Rudolph could get to?"

She nodded, biting her lip to keep from crying again. I think the tears this time were from relief rather than grief or pain.

I took a close up of that busted lip. "That's okay. I'll make a call. There's a place I know that will take you, and the doorman owes me a favor. If anyone suspicious comes by, he'll call me."

Maybe it wasn't miraculous, what Katie managed, but it was a transformation. You would have to look closely to notice her face was a little darker around the left eye, and her lip, well, it just looked chapped.

I borrowed Katie's car to drive Megan down to the Ben Franklin Hotel. Willis was there dressed as old Ben himself, complete with breeches, powdered wig, and tricorn hat. He started running to the car to open the

door for us, but I waved him off so
Megan and I could talk a bit first.

"Megan, when were you last at the
house?" I asked.

"I snuck out during the night.
Why?"

I pulled out my father's pocket
watch. It was half-past ten. "And
when does your husband usually get
up?"

"The markets open at six-thirty,
and he's glued to the ticker tape by
then. Why?" She was more insistent
this time.

"Because, by now, he's noticed
you're gone. Give me your checkbook."

"Mr. Glover--"

"Megan, your husband is a
controller. He knows you've gone, and
he can't allow that, so he's going to
do things to make you come back.
He'll enjoy the humiliation. By now,
he's canceled your accounts."

"He can't do that! I have money
that my parents left me!"

"He'll close the ones he
cosigned, and he'll report the others
stolen. If you show up at a bank,
they'll detain you, and he'll send his

men around. If you use a check in the
hotel, they'll call it in to verify
funds, and the same thing will happen.
Now, give me your checkbook."

She handed it over to me. "Good.
Now, what's your maiden name?" I
asked, sticking her checkbook into my
inside jacket pocket.

"Delphine. Why?"

"Because if he doesn't get you at
the bank, he's going to start checking
hotels next. They'll ask to ring for
Bowerman. You're going in there, and
you're paying cash. You do have cash,
don'tcha?"

"Not much..."

"Enough for today?"

"Should be..."

"Good. Here's another ten, just
in case. I'll find a way to get you
some money tomorrow. Have you got a
sister?"

"No, a brother, but he lives in
New York."

"Never mind that. What's your
mother's name?"

"Prudence," she said.

"That'll have to do. Your name
is Prudence Delphine. You sign in

under that name. If I need to call,
I'll ask at the desk for Prudence, but
when it rings through, I'll ask for
Marcy. Got it? If your phone rings
and they don't ask for Marcy, I want
you to disguise your voice, say 'wrong
number,' and hang up. If they call
back, don't answer. Call my office.
If I'm not in, Katie will know what to
do. Now, repeat that back."

"My name is Prudence Delphine. I
pay in cash. If the phone rings, and
it isn't for Marcy, I say 'wrong
number--'" Her voice turned gruff,
and her accent French. "-- And I hang
up."

"Good," I said. I motioned for
Willis to come over. "Will your
husband be home tonight?"

"Probably not until late. He's
been hanging out at the club every
night lately."

A chill went down my spine.
Somehow, I knew the answer before I
asked the question. "Which club is
that?"

"The Brothers of Unity," she
replied, her nose wrinkling. "I went
with him the first time, but it was

just a bunch of men smoking and
telling fish tales. I didn't like the
other wives, so I refused to go after
that, but he went along happily
without me. That's where I think he
meets his women."

"Swell," I said. "I was planning
on heading that way tonight, anyway.
I should probably just apply for
membership and have it over with."

Willis opened her door, and she
got out, thanking both of us. He
closed the door after her, then ran to
get the hotel door.

Chapter Five

Back at the Brothers of Unity club that night, I waited with my camera, determined to find some sort of evidence to either allay my suspicions or confirm them. The partially constructed house continued to be my base of operations, and I used it as cover until I saw what was up. I didn't want to run into any more parties, but if what Mrs. Bowerman said was true, there was a good chance that there would be more than a few people there still. And any time you've got too many rich people together, that means security.

I snuck through the house-to-be and peered over a stack of two by fours. There were a couple of men at the front door again, and it looked like someone strolling around the back.

I moved to a cement mixer further back on the property so I could see in through the windows. Lights were on all over the ground floor, and I could make out some movement but couldn't see much.

I watched the guy in the back for a while, then crept up on the hedgerow. I waited until his pacing brought him back close to me, then a few more moments for him to turn and head the other direction. As soon as his back was turned, I hit him as hard as I could at the base of the skull — the area my dad used to call 'the knockout spot.'

The man went down. I caught him and dragged him back through the hedge. I quickly tied his hands behind his back with his own shoelaces, and I stuffed his cap in his mouth, then I ran back through the hedge and up to the house, peeking into the first window. It looked like the smoking room that Mrs. Bowerman had mentioned. There was a group of five men in there, not Bowerman though, and not Noble. The next one was the large bay window I had spent so much time at last night. I risked a quick peek. No one was in the immediate room, but I could see into the far room, where a group was sitting on a chaise lounge, talking and laughing. I vaulted the rail to the kitchen door and peeked in there as well.

There were only two cooks in the kitchen this time, but both had their backs to me. I snapped a quick shot anyway, who knows? Claire might recognize him by a freckle on his neck or something.

I went down the ramp to the driveway and took a look at the far side of the house. There was a balcony on the second floor, and the trash cans sat below it. That was going to be my entrance.

I consolidated the trash, so I'd

have an empty to turn over, then I placed it top-down as quietly as possible. I could just imagine the two brutes at the front door wondering what that metal scraping sound was. I paused for a few moments. If anyone came now, I could still run for it. Once I was standing on top of the bin, I would have some explaining to do.

No one came, so I put one foot on top quietly, then did a little hop, landing with my other foot on the opposite side of the rim. Barely a noise.

I reached up as high as I could and could barely scrape the stone of the balcony with my fingertips. I was going to have to jump. If I didn't make it on the first attempt, I was going to wish I'd had my running shoes on. I crouched down low and took aim at the spaces between the stone slats above me.

I jumped. The can went over below me, clanging on the concrete driveway like a drunken drummer. I managed to grab the balcony, but I had only seconds to climb it and get over before someone was there to see me. I shimmied up the rail and tumbled over, landing hard on my shoulder.

"You see anything?" I heard someone say below.

"Naw. What do you think, raccoons?" was the response.

"Probably. Do you think we'd get in trouble for shooting them next time?"

The other guy chuckled, then someone set the can back up. I waited another minute like that before I dared to move. Then I slowly stood up and looked over the rail. Whoever owned those voices were gone, but with the can moved like that, there was no way this was going to be my exit. Not without breaking a leg anyway.

I turned toward the window and the room beyond. The lights were off, but I could make out the white tiles on both walls and floor, and the fixtures evenly spaced along the wall. A shower room? The windows were set in a pair of French doors with a simple latch in the center. Finding the doors locked, I popped them with my penknife.

Stepping inside, I quietly shut

the door behind me. I crept across the humid and slippery room to the door on the other side and pushed it open a crack. The room beyond was dark and musky. Moonlight trickled in, illuminating long rectangular shapes at around knee height. That would be a changing room. I pushed through to the next door and repeated my cautious investigation.

This door opened onto a brightly lit hallway with a red carpet. There were doors to my immediate left and right, and halfway down the hall, it opened up into the grand staircase I saw the bottom of yesterday. There were muted voices coming from below.

I tried the right-side door first, which turned out to be a closet. So, I tried the left one and found a darkened bedroom. After giving it a moment to make sure no one was sleeping inside, I stepped in and closed the door behind me.

The wardrobe was first on my list, but both the drawers and the cabinet were empty except for bare wire hangers. Next to it was a washbasin and a pitcher, some hand towels were laid out on a shelf beneath it. Both bedside tables were empty, and I ran a hand between the box spring and mattress. Nothing there either. It looked like the room was set up for guests, not for regular use. On a hunch, I pulled the painting off the far wall, but there was nothing but wallpaper behind it.

I entered the next room. There was a drafting table on one side, and some rags laying out on a workbench. The place smelled of paint thinner and linseed oil. On the far end of the room was what looked like a printing press of some sort. There were rollers and a mechanism that was operated by a crank. It looked like the top came down with a turn of the crank to press down on whatever was below. It was well oiled and looked to be in general usage, but I couldn't see where the typesetting went. I didn't know much about this kind of equipment, though Brian would. So I screwed my bulb back into the camera and took a couple shots.

The drafting table was likewise bare, but I could feel impressions on its surface, so I turned on the desk lamp and tried to view it from an angle. If I had paper and pencil, I could have gotten a rubbing off it, but there were none in sight. Pretty weird for a drafting table not to have paper. While I was thinking about it, the printing press should have had some too. I looked through all the drawers and cabinets, but I only found bottles of chemicals I didn't recognize and a pantograph, if I remembered the name for that thing correctly. I turned all the bottles so that the labels were facing forward, then got a shot of those too. Time pressed on me. Someone was bound to come in here eventually if this was an active workroom, so I left.

I got back to the hallway and listened again. There were still voices coming from below. I snuck up to the next door and eased inside.

It was somebody's office. A comfortable-looking swivel chair sat behind a large mahogany desk. Most of the remaining room was taken up with filing cabinets. I checked the one closest to the door, but it was

locked. I had my lock picks with me,
so it wasn't a concern, but that could
wait for after a cursory search of the
place.

There was a map of the United
States on one wall, and on the other,
a painting of a man fly-fishing in the
bend of some river. I pulled down
this painting as well, and behind it,
there was the wall safe. Just in
case, I tried the handle, but it was
secure. There ended my thievery skill
set. The safe would remain secure
unless I happened upon the combination
lying around somewhere. I returned
the painting to its hook and turned my
attention to the desk.

Moonlight streamed in through the
window behind the desk, so I didn't
need the lamp. The desk had the
standard ink blotter front and center,
a phone, a desk calendar, a small
American flag sticking out of a pencil
tray, and some framed pictures. On
any other desk, the photos would be of
a wife and family, but these were all
of various locations in and around
Seattle. No people in any of them.

I checked the calendar, going

back a few days. On each date, there
were times listed, and some scribbling
I couldn't decipher, but enough to
tell me, whoever's desk this was, he
was busy.

I looked forward a few days as
well. A couple days from now, there
was one bit of writing I could read in
among the rest of the scribbles.
12:00pm, something, something, 'Dore.'
A meeting with the mayor. I flipped
forward a couple more sheets, but they
were blank until next Tuesday. No
times and no scribbles, but a big
circle in red ink around the date. I
returned it to today's date.

The two side drawers held
unimportant items. Most of them
seemed to be building supplies, most
likely for this place. The center
drawer was locked, and this time, I
pulled out my lock picks.

I slid the chair out of the way
and knelt to work with them better.
It was a pretty serious lock for a
desk drawer, but after a few moments,
I got it open. Inside was a ledger.
I pulled it out and laid it on the
desk. There was a ruler acting as a

bookmark, and I flipped it open to the ruler. Dates, names, and dollar amounts. Now I'd hit the goldmine. I got a photo of it, then turned back a page and got another. I was going to go back a third, but I suddenly realized the sound of voices was louder. The floor creaked in the hallway outside.

I closed the ledger and threw it in the drawer, closing that as well. I ducked under the desk, the only place to hide. Just as I pulled the chair back in, the door opened, and the light clicked on.

"No! It can't just be close, it has to be exact!" A voice barked. He spoke like he had something in his mouth, a cigar maybe. "Someone needs to take the initiative, and to do so now! Go! And take Seeley with you in case you run into trouble. Now, Kowalczyk, let's get some more pins on that map. Read it off to me again."

After clearing his throat, a familiar voice spoke. "Well sir, there's San Antonio, so that's good. Then there's San Diego and Santa Barbara, we expected those though."

I tried to get a look at who was talking but only managed to bang my head on the drawer.

"What was that?" a new voice asked.

I froze. The back of my head ached, but I didn't even breath. The room was perfectly silent. The slightest noise would have pinpointed my location.

"What was what, Phillips?"

Silence again, for a moment, then Phillips spoke again. "I don't know. I just heard something. You didn't hear that?"

"No, I didn't hear anything, you dumb clod. Now, will you go and do your job? We only have a few days left, and our victory isn't yet assured."

"Alright. I'm going." In the dead still room, I could hear the whisper of footsteps on carpet, then the door closed, and the spell was broken. Kowalczyk and 'Sir' went back to discussing the map.

I let out a quiet breath and rubbed my head with a glance at the offending drawer.

There was an envelope taped to its underside. Scrawled across it in big letters, were the words, "Hey, Gumshoe!"

I lost track of what the men were saying. I wanted to peel the envelope off immediately and read whatever was inside, but that would make too much noise. It couldn't possibly have been put here for me. But then, why was it there? I would have to get it after they left. I tore my attention away from the envelope and forced myself to listen to them.

"That's swell, Kowalczyk. Real swell. How about the polls. What do they say?"

"It was a good week for us, sir!" Kowalczyk said. "Dore, forty-one percent. Langlie, thirty-two percent, and Seger, nineteen! The rest are undecided."

"Marvelous! Simply marvelous! You did good work today, Kowalczyk. Come downstairs with me and have a drink before going home."

"Oh, thank you, sir, but I don't drink."

"Really? Alcoholic?"

"No, sir, I just don't --" The light clicked off, and the door closed behind the two of them, muffling the rest of Kowalczyk's response.

I tore the envelope free and flipped it over, but there was nothing else written on the outside.

Pushing the chair out of the way, I stood up, staring at it. "Hey, Gumshoe!" The envelope was sealed, and I debated opening it up right then and there, but I decided 'Sir' might be back any minute, and I had pressed my luck enough already. I slid it into my jacket pocket.

I risked taking a picture of the map, though. After lining up the shot, I discovered all my bulbs were blown. I turned on the desk lamp, swung it toward the wall, and took the shot. Not ideal, but it would have to do. I put the lamp back, turned it off, and went to the window. There were bushes outside to break my fall if I jumped, but the two mugs at the front door were within reach. I would have to go back into the hall.

I pulled the door open a crack and listened. There was a piano

playing distantly, but over that, I
heard sir's voice again. "Are you
still here, Phillips?"

"Take it easy, boss, I'm just
waiting for Seeley."

They didn't sound close, so I
poked my head out and looked up and
down the hall. It was deserted. The
voices were coming from downstairs. I
stepped outside and pulled the door
closed with a click.

"You must have heard that!"
Phillips said.

Damn, that kid had some ears on
him. I wasn't going to make it out of
the house the way I'd come, so I
pussyfooted it down the other end of
the hall.

"Heard what, Phillips?" Sir's
voice was impatient.

"There's someone upstairs!"

I heard footsteps on the
staircase below me and hurried to get
out of sight. The first door on the
left would have to do. It was another
bedroom, and empty, so I ducked
inside. I ran to the window,
unlatched it, and pushed it open. The
hedge didn't extend quite this far,

but I could make it if I tried. Only problem were the two goons at the door would be there in an instant if I did.

I went back to the door and put my eye to the crack. There was a man opening the door to Sir's office, and he had a gun drawn. The moment he stepped inside, I made my move and crossed the hall. Throwing caution aside, I opened up the door. It was the only choice I had left.

It wasn't a room at all, but a spiral staircase. The walls at the top were just shelf space filled with cleaning supplies. It must be used by the servants to go about the work of resupplying the guest rooms without being seen.

I quickly closed the door behind me. The iron staircase was carpeted so the servants could be unheard as well as unseen, which suited me just fine. I quickly made my way down the stairs in near darkness. At the bottom of the steps, there were doors both front and back. From what I saw looking in through the windows, the back door would lead to the smoking room, so I pushed the front door open a crack.

There was a man at the far end of
the house playing piano, and a woman
sharing the piano bench resting her
head on his shoulder. Nobody was
looking this way, so I stepped out and
closed the door. There was a window
just next to me with a view of the
partially constructed home I've come
to think of as my base of operations.
I unlocked the window and slid it
open. I looked over my shoulder one
last time, half-expecting to see
Phillips pointing a gun my way.
Phillips was nowhere to be seen, so I
dove out the window, and I was gone.

I wanted to get some distance
between myself and that club, just in
case anyone found the unlocked window.
By the time I got under the first
functioning streetlamp, though, my
curiosity got the better of me. I
leaned against it and ran a finger
under the lip of the envelope.

There was a single sheet of paper
inside, folded in thirds. On it was a
typewritten note.

To Drake Glover, P.I.

Yes, I knew you would be under
that desk to read this note. Come
find out what else I know. Meet my
associate in Post Alley behind the
newsstand tonight at midnight.
     - X.

I had to read it three times
before I could believe it was real.
It was one thing when it just said
gumshoe, but to actually see my name
on the note...
     According to my father's watch
held under the streetlight, it was
nearly 11:30 already. I would have to
beat feet to get to Pike Place in
time. I folded the paper back up and
put it in my pocket.
     Cutting across some of the empty
lots to save time, I headed south,
down the hill. Of course, I wanted to
meet. There was a new player in town,
and they knew where I'd be. They knew
who I was, and I needed to know what
their interest was.
     If they were members of the club

and they knew I'd be there, they would have just told those three that were up in the office, and I'd be wearing cement shoes by now.

Who else could have put it there? Maybe Megan got in touch with Laslop after we spoke, and it was him. Or maybe Bowerman's goons got out of him that I warned his wife. Maybe Bowerman even saw me nosing around the club the night before, and he just put two and two together. But there was no way he'd know I'd be under that desk.

It could have just been an ambush. Post Alley would be a great place to get someone alone and disappear him.

On the other hand, if they were interested in this club and whatever it was up to, then this meeting probably meant they hadn't the grift to act directly.

I got to the Pike Place newsstand, and my instinct kicked in. Immediately, I started looking around for any signs of a trap. There were

several cars parked nearby, but I
couldn't see any silhouettes inside
any of them. Same thing with doorways
and stairwells -- everything seemed
kosher, but I was having trouble
trusting much of anything recently.

I lit a cigarette and checked my
watch again by matchlight. It was
12:08.

Across the street, lights still
blazed in a few apartment windows, but
there were still no suspicious
silhouettes or conspicuous rustling of
curtains. I wasn't going to feel any
safer by waiting, so it was time to
meet this mysterious 'X'.

I went behind the newsstand and
took the ramp down into Post Alley.
The Alley runs first under, then
behind, the Pike Place Market. Right
at the corner was an area by the
theater that was completely unlit.
And me without a torch. There was no
chance of turning back at this point,
so I just went in with all my other
senses straining.

I got through without incident,
and once on the other side, I looked
for my contact. Post Alley does go on

for the rest of the block and beyond,
and the note didn't actually specify
where along it we should meet, but
this was the spot people generally
thought of. I looked back the way I
had come, into the shadows there.

It wasn't so late that whoever I
was meeting would have given up yet.

I heard a match strike up behind
me and turned to see the end of a
cigarette glowing in a darkened
doorstep, and not much more. "You
came," said a voice out of the
darkness. "Good." He spoke with the
sort of rasp you only earn from
serious contributions to the tobacco
industry.

He stepped out of the doorway,
but just one step. The light sources
were all behind him. All I could see
was a beige overcoat with the collar
turned up, and the brim of a hat
pulled low over his face. Whoever he
was, he didn't want to be seen.
Maybe, that meant I knew him, or just
maybe, it wasn't me that scared him.

"Alright, so I came. What's your
interest in this?"

"If you knew what I know, you'd

realize how important this job is.
I'd rather play a part in it than sit
on the sidelines."

"That doesn't tell me much of
anything. Are you a member of the
Brothers of Unity? Are you working
for them?"

"What? No. Of course not.
We're on your side."

"Who's this we, then?"

"I'm talking about X, and anyone
that works for X."

"So, you're not X? You didn't
write that note for me?"

He took a drag from his
cigarette, casting a glow around his
eyes. Something struck me as
familiar, but I couldn't place him.
The voice meant nothing to me, but
maybe, he was putting that on. "No, X
wrote the note, not me. And it wasn't
really for you, it was for the author.
You just had to read it so that it
would enter into the narrative."

"I don't get it. I don't know
anything about any author."

"Look, pal, you're not very quick
on the uptake, are you? Haven't you
noticed the tropes? The seedy bar you

spend your time in? All the rich folk
with bodyguards? The constant chain-
smoking? It's a wonder this city
still has a liver to go around, the
way everyone here drinks."

None of this had anything to do
with the club. I was beginning to
think he was a crazy person without
any information for me, after all. I
gave him one last chance to start
making sense. "A man's gotta have his
vices. You still haven't told me how
you're involved in all this, or how
you or this 'X' is planning to help
me."

"X figured out what was going on,
and then explained it to me. It all
makes sense -- in fact, it's obvious
when you look at it. I can't come
right out and say it, so pick up a
clue. If you know how the railroad
tracks are laid down, you can predict
where the train is going and get ahead
of it, see?"

Christ. The man was insane.
What does that say about this 'X'
person? Hell, maybe, there isn't even
an X at all, just a voice in the man's
head that tells him to murder puppies.

I was starting to put together how he had gotten the envelope there. I bet he just saw me taking photos at the party last night and figured I'd be back. I tried to think back to the young man just inside the window holding the two champagne flutes. Was it possible he saw me at some point? Were these his eyes?

"You still aren't getting it. Look, ask yourself how we knew where to put that note? Is it likely that someone was following you, managed to get ahead at some point, plant that envelope in the club, and then arrange everyone's schedule so that they would come into that room right when you were searching it? Of course not. When you hid under the desk, escaping discovery, the reader didn't question it even though this doesn't happen in real life! Because it *is* consistent with the tropes of a detective novel That's how we knew you would be there. It was predictable!"

Suddenly, I had some insight into this guy's particular brand of madness. Did he think this was some sort of movie he was living in? He

was the guy in the third row shouting
at the screen to warn the damsel
before she opened the wrong door. I
had more pressing things to work on
here in the real world, and I nearly
told him so, but then I remembered
this X fellow. Could I really risk
that he wasn't real? What if I ran
into more of them doing stupid things
like leaving notes lying around the
club? Instead, I decided to humor
him, see what more I could find out.

"Fine," I finally said. "Let's
say for the sake of argument that I
believe you. Why contact me? What
does X have to gain by having you
here?"

The man chuckled sarcastically.
"You ever hear that saying? 'No one
is ever truly dead while someone
remembers them?' What if that's true?
What if it's even true for characters
in a story? You close a book, you put
it down, and the story's over. But
you remember the hero, the bad guy,
maybe, a quirky sidekick, and they
live on. What if you're just a bit
part? No one remembers you. But if
you can make yourself more

important... Even integral to the plot..." He let it trail off.

"So, you're insinuating yourselves into my life to get a better role in the story. But, the way I read it, you don't get to be the hero by skulking about in dark alleys and passing cryptic notes. The hero is the guy who swoops in at the end, defeats the bad guy, saves the day and gets the girl."

"You still don't get it, do you? It has to fit the narrative! You introduce the subplot and work your way up. You can't have some schmo from chapter one show up at the end and kill the bad guy! No, once we knew it was a crime drama, it had to be cloak and dagger."

"I hate to burst your bubble, sunshine, but this crime drama is my life. I'm the detective here. If anyone's telling this story, it'll be me."

"Don't be ridiculous. The point of view character isn't the same thing as the writer."

This guy may have been nuttier than a squirrel in a sack of almonds, but he was starting to get to me, so when I heard a loud bang behind me, I realized he could have been just a distraction. I swung around, getting my fists up to defend myself, but it was only a cat trying to get inside a garbage can. By the time I looked back, the madman was gone.

I ran to where he'd been. There was a short fence next to the doorway he was standing in. He must have jumped the fence and run down between the two buildings.

Now that I looked, I could see a hat and coat laying on the ground at the far end. There were a number of waterfront dives down there, and they would all be busy at this time. He could have disappeared into any of them, and I'd never know him.

I may have lost my contact, but I was still going to collect any clues he had left behind. I never knew what might lead me to him again.

On the pavement, just this side of the fence, there was the stub of a cigarette, still smoldering. He must

have flicked it away before jumping
over. There was a pile of them in the
doorway where he'd been standing. I
bent down to collect one and stood
under a nearby streetlight. I rolled
the butt around between my fingers.
The man smoked Morleys. A common
enough choice, but I'd keep an eye out
for everyone's brand from here on out.

I vaulted the chain link fence
and followed the track down between
the buildings to where the hat and
coat lay. There wasn't much chance
that he'd left anything identifying in
his pockets, but I could always use
another coat. I checked the pockets
anyway. He'd left a matchbook behind
from the Silver Hotel bar. Maybe, he
was staying there, but more likely, he
just stopped in for a drink. I
transferred it to my pocket, then
checked the rest of the coat. The
label was cut out, so no tracing it
back to a recent sale.

The hat was a different story,
though. It was brand new, and
underneath the band was the name
Byrnie Utz, the haberdashery where it
was sold. As I examined it, a small

piece of paper fluttered out. The
number seventeen was stamped on it.
It could be the number of this hat in
the production run, I suppose, or it
could be the number of the sad sack
whose job it was to make this hat.
Then again, I might get lucky, and
it's something identifiable.

I knew the shop, and it wasn't
far away. I made mental plans to stop
by tomorrow and see if someone knew
something about number seventeen.
There's even a chance they'll remember
the nutcase they sold the hat to. If
he was ranting about authors, he'd
have stood out. Then maybe, I can get
a better description than "I've seen
his eyes before."

I looked around the corner, up
and down the street for anyone
standing in the shadows and smoking
Morleys. Instead, I saw a woman with
pro-skirt written all over her,
leaning against the bricks, quietly
humming to herself.

"Hey, doll," I said to her.

She looked at me and smiled.
"Hiya, boyfriend," she said.

"That ain't it at all," I said.

"Did you see anyone come out of this alley a minute ago?"

"Sure, boyfriend, but if you're looking for some company, I could keep you warm."

"You're barking up the wrong tree, doll. Did you see him, or not?"

She looked more annoyed than disappointed. She went back to leaning against the wall and watching the stars come out from behind a cloud. "Sure, I seen him. He was in a hurry to get out of here, though."

"Which way did he go?" I asked.

She looked back over at me and shrugged. Then she indicated with a nod of her head. "That way."

South. "Not into one of these clubs?"

"Look, pal, I'm not your babysitter, and I didn't know I was supposed to look after him. He ran past me that way, and I didn't pay him any more mind. Now, if you're not looking for some company, then beat it. You're scaring away the other fish."

I looked up and down the street for the rest of the fish, but it didn't matter. "Alright. Thanks."

I started heading back up toward Post Alley, then a thought occurred, and I turned back.

"Blonde or brunette?" I said to the girl.

"What?" she asked. Clearly, I was really annoying her now. Putting myself in her high heels, I would probably be annoyed too. I'd feel better about myself if I could at least offer her a buck or two, but here I was, broke again. Maybe if someday I kicked the coffin nails, I could afford more information. But that day wasn't today, and if I was being honest, probably not ever. I needed some sort of information on the man though, so I pressed my luck.

"He dropped his hat just before coming around this corner. So, you must have seen his hair, you must have noticed at least that. Was his hair long? Short? Curley? Blonde or brunette?"

"I thought you knew this guy," she asked, beginning to get wise.

"Never mind that. What was his hair like?"

"Take off your hat," she said.

It was my turn to be annoyed, but I took the hat off anyway.

"It was blonde. And a little shorter than yours. Not much. Good enough?"

"Yeah. That's great. Thank you again." I got what I was going to out of her, and I was lucky to have it. I put my hat back on and started heading for the office.

It was time to take some notes. This case was getting too complicated, and the more I went over it in my head, the more jumbled it all got. I had to laugh. My usual case was so simple. I followed someone, and when I found out what they were up to, I took some pictures, and I got paid. I had to remind myself that the paying gig involved looking after a woman's husband. All she wanted to know was what he had gotten involved in, and whether it was either dangerous or illegal.

I hadn't managed to discover any of that yet, and I didn't know if I'd even managed to get a picture of the man. I couldn't even say for certain that he was in that kitchen either of the times I was at the club.

All I knew for certain, aside from the way the back of his head looked, is that he went to that club with a load of fresh seafood, and that evening, a fantastic salmon dinner went to the men of Hooverville. Suspicious, for sure, but not illegal in and of itself.

I also didn't know if he was involved because he was a part of whatever it was that club was planning, or simply because he was being paid to cook for them. In the end, that bit of knowledge might make all the difference.

Chapter Six

I got to the office and set up the Dictaphone, but it took me the longest time to figure out where to start. In the end, I decided to keep it simple and start with Bowerman, but then I got to the part where he belonged to the Brothers of Unity, and simple turned complicated, really fast.

I started over with Claire Noble. Once I did, everything that had happened over the last few days poured out of me. My first meeting with her,

and then following her husband that
first morning. Returning that night
with the camera and ending up having
dinner in Hooverville. I brought in
Bowerman and setting his wife up at
the hotel, and I linked him back to
the club. Then I remembered Chief
Sears of the Seattle P.D. wore the pin
too, and I brought him in. I detailed
the rooms in the club and Kowalczyk's
conversation with the unknown man.
Why were they so excited about the
polls when their candidate was losing
so badly? I finished up with my
bizarre meeting with Mr. X's lackey.
I wondered aloud about X's motives in
this and started coming up with a
suspect list. It occurred to me that
I'd mentioned where I was going to
Brian and Mike when we were all at
Delaney's. Could one of them be this
'X'? Just having a go at me?
Suddenly, the night made a lot more
sense. It was probably one of Mike's
buddies down at the station, maybe
even a member of the club. That would
explain how he got the note in there,
as well as how he knew where I was
going.

Come to think of it, Brian had his sources too, and this kind of joke would be just the sort of thing he'd come up with.

I find it's often this way. Just saying out loud what's been swirling in my head, I started to make connections that weren't entirely obvious before.

In the morning, Katie would come in, and she'd type it all up. Then I'd have the chance to read it all again. Who knows? After a few hours' shuteye, I might see even more of the picture. Sometimes, I can be a bit slow that way.

I put the Dictaphone back on Katie's desk and left her a note. Then I went home for some dreamless sleep.

My breakfast was courtesy of Sir Thomas Lipton again. I used the time while the water was boiling to iron my shirt. It was looking a little too slept in, even for my tastes.

I also decided to develop my

film, even though I hadn't used up the whole roll yet. There was always a chance that Brian would be able to pay me something for that one in Hooverville, and it wouldn't hurt to get him looking at the partygoers at the club. He works the society column from time to time, and there's every chance he'll recognize somebody.

I made it into the office closer to 9:30 than to 9:00, with an envelope full of photos, a new coat, and a shirt that, if it wasn't exactly clean, was at least well pressed. Katie was there as usual, but rather than her normal greeting, she paused the Dictaphone and lifted one of the earphones. "You had a real live one last night, didn't you? Think he's right?"

I paused in the middle of hanging up my coat. "Don't tell me you go in for that nonsense?" She had another one of her bodice rippers lying on the desk. This one looked to involve pirates and the girls that loved them.

She clicked her tongue dismissively and covered up the book with the pages she had typed so far.

"I was joking, of course. But the idea isn't that unusual, you know. Certainly not the strangest world view I've run across."

"How's that?"

"Well, there's something comforting about the idea that there's some almighty author guiding your existence. Especially if you're the subject. Then you know you have a purpose."

"Doesn't say much about the argument for free will, though, does it?"

"It looks like it at first, but I've heard authors talk before about discovery writing. They 'discover' things like character motivation as they are writing the book. Sometimes, the character surprises them."

"What do you mean, 'surprises them?'" I asked.

"As they're writing, they realize the character would never do or say what they had planned, and it takes the story in a new direction. Sure, the author knows how your story ends, but how you get there... Maybe that bit's up to you."

"It's too early for this deep and meaningful philosophy. How is that not the strangest world view you've ever heard?"

"Well, after the war, my husband got stationed all over, and I went along. In the Philippines, there are people who believe the entire universe is some creature's dream, and one day, it will wake up, and we'll all be gone. Some spiritualists have suggested the only thing holding the world together is the fact we all believe in it. If enough people stopped believing in reality, it would fall apart."

"Well, I like my reality just fine the way it is. Besides, it's almost certainly either Mike Benson or Brian Goldman just yanking my chain. Any calls?"

"None so far. You going to be here a while?"

"I think so. I want to have another go at those notes once you're done with them. I'll get the phone if it rings."

She nodded and set the headphones back in place. "I'll bring them in soon as I'm done."

As I sat down at my desk, I glanced over at my phone and suddenly thought of Betty over at the phone company. At this point, I probably had all the information that she was likely to give me, but she's also an invaluable contact to have, so it was in my interest to call her back and gab a bit.

Slamming my fist on one end of the receiver and catching it as it popped up into the air, I dialed zero and spun around in my chair to look at the view outside the heavy wooden blinds.

"Operator," she said.

"Hi Betty, any chance you or the girls got anything on that line I asked you about?"

There was an unexpected pause on the line, and when she spoke again, her tone was uncharacteristically formal. "Yes, sir, I'll connect you. Please hold."

"How'zat, Betty? Do we have our lines crossed?"

"Sorry, Drake," she said in a quick whisper. "Can't talk now, the

boss is in the room." She switched
instantly back to formal. "I'm sorry,
sir, you said 'KL511?' That number
isn't picking up, sir."

"If this is a bad time, Betty, I
can ring back tomorrow," I said.

She was back to whispering. "No,
we should talk. I've got a lunch
break in ten minutes, meet me at the
park near Union Station."

That wasn't in my plan for today,
but before I could think of a way to
beg off, she said, "Yes, sir, try
again later. Goodbye." I was
disconnected.

Well, it looked like I had lunch
plans. It was going to be a little
early, but breakfast wasn't exactly
filling. The only problem was, I'd be
buying, and I barely had two quarters
to rub together.

I knew the park, and it would
only take me five minutes to get
there, so I went through the paper
that was sitting on my desk. Mostly,
it was the usual sort of local fluff
and international misery. I kept
thinking someone would surely do
something about that Hitler, but no

such luck.

Closer to home, it looked like Joe's favorite pony won the day before. He would be thrilled that it happened on a day he wasn't there. Mayor Dore was holding a rally the next day for his re-election campaign. At noon too. Now I knew what that note in the calendar was about. Some Brothers of Unity presence was likely, but what for? Seemed like I was getting into local politics whether I wanted to or not. I decided I might just go to that, and see what he had to say about Seger if anything.

The phone rang, and I picked up before the bell finished its first ring. "Glover," I said.

"Mr. Glover, I'm getting desperate here!" It was Claire Noble. "Tell me you know something!"

This was the lunch date I had wanted for today, and I'd come prepared. It occurred to me that this wasn't all bad. I just might eat twice today. "I know a few things. I've also got some questions and some photos. How about I let you buy me lunch? Do you know where the Dog

House is?" It was almost as far from Union Station as you could get in Seattle, but it was closer to where she lived.

"I'll find it," she said.

"Denny and Aurora. I'll meet you there in --" I pulled out dad's pocket watch. Half an hour for my meeting with Betty, a little longer to checkout Laslop's flat, then another hour to get up north to the Doghouse. "Let's say 12:30. Sound alright?"

"Sure, I'll be there. Thank you, Mr. Glover."

I had a sudden thought of Mrs. Bowerman. She was going to need more rent. "I'll need another couple of days on this, and I had to buy some film, so bring some cash."

"Alright. I will."

I got to Union Square amidst a refreshing mist of rain. The park across the street was just a triangle of land that the city had no other idea what to do with, so they bolted a few benches to the sidewalk and left the trees standing. Around this time of day, food merchants started pushing their carts up to the park, and office workers descended like termites from their towering nests of concrete and glass to pick them clean.

Betty was there. I'd never actually seen her before, but I knew a few things about her. She always seemed to think my job was a lot more exciting than it actually was. I always got the impression that she retold my stories like I was some sort of international spy, maybe with a French accent and a military uniform, and they would all sigh and flutter. So, when I walked up to the park and saw the dame in the trench coat and dark sunglasses clutching a manila envelope to her chest, I knew it was her.

I wasn't much of one to talk, though, with my rumpled blue-gray suit and fedora, I probably looked the part -- even without the long coat I'd be wearing if the weather were truly inclement.

"Hello, Betty," I said, removing my hat.

She turned, and a smile filled

her face to beat back the clouds.
"Drake! How'd you know it was me?"

"Easy doll, I just looked for the
prettiest gal in the park."

She blushed instantly, and if
anything, her smile widened. "Oh,
you," she said.

It started to get awkward, the
two of us just smiling at each other,
so I pointed to the envelope. "Is
this for me?"

"Oh!" she said, holding it away
from herself and looking at it as if
just noticing she had it. "Yes --
It's not much, though. I just had the
girls scribble down some notes. Date,
times, and numbers. But that's not
the important bit."

She got distracted as a man
passed between us pushing a sandwich
cart. I signaled him to stop. "Here,
let me get you a sandwich while we
talk."

She had a ham on rye, and I got
egg salad on white. We took our
sandwiches to the nearest bench and
sat to unwrap them. She looked both
ways as if she thought we might be
watched and placed the envelope on the

bench between us.

I suppressed a smile and picked the envelope up to peek inside. Lots of different handwriting, but the same number over and over.

"Any idea who it is keeps calling?" I asked.

"Nuh-uh. He never identifies himself." She sat back and gave me a knowing look over the top of her sandwich.

"So, not much help there then." I put the paper back in the envelope and wedged it under my thigh while I went after my sandwich.

"Oh, I didn't say that. Not by a longshot." She picked up the envelope and pointed at the number. "This letter here? That means it's assigned to District Fourteen. That's Queen Anne if you don't work for Edison. And this one here?" She slid her finger over to the next one. "This one is really high. That means it's a new number. The line couldn't have been installed more than maybe four or five months ago."

"I think I know the place. Can you tell me any more about it?"

"I'm just getting warmed up, Drake," she said, flashing that smile again. "I listened in on one of these calls. The man on the other end spoke with an accent."

"Let me guess. Polish?"

She seemed surprised by that. "Well, now I wish I'd listened closer. Could have been, I guess. I was going to say he sounded like my brother-in-law. My sister married a Russian man named Ippolit, but Polacks are pretty close to Russians, ain't they?"

Poles, I thought to myself, but it wasn't going to help me any to correct her. "Yeah, I suppose they are. Did he say anything interesting?"

"Well, he wasn't threatening or anything, like you told me to look out for, but weird. He kept calling someone 'Sir.' Not like regular, though, he said it like it was someone's name. He wouldn't talk until he had the husband on the line, and it was like he was talking in code." She put on a deep voice and a cheesy accent. "Another four blocks for tonight. Sir wants to see the plates."

Four blocks? Four city blocks,
maybe? Did they have someone out
canvassing and collecting votes for
Seger? That could be, but if so, why
did they want to inform their chef?
Butcher blocks, perhaps? But why
would he need four? And what did that
have to do with plates? Maybe
nothing. The two statements might be
completely unrelated.

"Yeah, crazy, huh?" She said,
reading my face. "But that's not even
the weirdest part."

"Really? What else did he say?"

"No, that was all he said. BUT."
She paused for effect. "Lindsey, one
of the girls on the night shift, she
left a note out about that number."
She tapped the envelope as if I
wouldn't know what number she meant.

"Yeah?" I asked, hoping to lead
her to the point. I was going to have
to move things along if I was going to
get to Laslop.

"Well, our manager, Mr. Alcott,
he came in that night, like he
sometimes does, but he saw the note on
the line, and he picked it up. He

went bonkers! He wanted to know why
she was checking on this number.
Lindsey just told him that she was
doing a favor for me, but he told her
to stop or he'd fire her. He tore the
paper to pieces and threw them into
the trash."

I hadn't seen that coming. I
knew there was a risk of getting her
in trouble, but I never figured I was
putting her in danger. "You didn't
get in any trouble, did you?" I asked.

"Well, he was there at the
beginning of my next shift and called
me into the office the moment I came
in. He was furious. He wanted to
know what it was about, but don't
worry, Drake. I lied. It was a good
one too, it just popped right into my
head. Wait until you hear what I
said."

"What did you say?"

She leaned forward
conspiratorially. "I told him that
the man at that number was complaining
about an echo on the line. I put a
note on it so the girls could check."

"Did he buy it?"

"You tell me. He told me the

line was fine and that I'd better stop
it. But he watched us girls all
yesterday, and he was back today, just
pacing back and forth."

"Okay, Betty, you did great.
This is real good stuff. But you're
done now. I don't want you risking
your job or anything else, you got it?
Just leave that number alone from here
on out, and things should go back to
normal."

"But what about the calls she's
getting, Drake?"

"You got me everything I need,
doll. I was already looking at a
Polish guy up on Queen Anne Hill, and
you confirmed that. But think about
what might have happened if he went
through your purse and found that
envelope. His friend might be
dangerous, and I don't want anything
happening to you. I've got it from
here."

I looked down at my sandwich, or
as it turns out, the empty wrapping
paper. I'd somehow managed to wolf it
down without noticing. I balled it
up. "Speaking of which, I've got to
meet with the client about this."

I stood up. She was giving me a disappointed look. "Thanks again, doll. It was good to finally put a face to that lovely voice of yours." Her look softened, and she smiled. "You'd better get back in there. Your lunch break's almost up."

I walked across the park, checking my pocket watch. Good, I still had time to quickly look in on Laslop. If it turned out he was home and okay, I could set Megan's mind at ease. A win would feel good today.

I glanced back once, and Betty was still on that park bench, watching me go.

I made my way to First and Spring and pressed the button next to the label, 'B. Laslop.' There was no response. I looked at my watch again, trying to decide how much time I could spend waiting for him.

A woman tapped on the glass of the door, wanting to get out past me. I lifted my hat in apology and stepped back. I held the door for her while she passed, then let go of it. I returned my attention to the doorbell panel, pressing Laslop's button again. The door slowly closed on its pneumatic brake. But the moment the lady passed out of sight, I caught the door and let myself in.

Pulling the door shut, I made for the staircase. Laslop's apartment was up two flights.

The sound of big band music as played through the speaker of some unseen radio greeted me on the third-floor landing. I listened at the door of 3A, but Laslop's apartment wasn't the origin of the sound.

There was a copy of the Post-Intelligencer lying on his threshold. It was just past noon, and this was the morning edition, guaranteed on your doorstep by six. Unless this guy was the king of the morning people, he should have picked it up by now. The fact that he hadn't pointed to something foul. I knocked anyway.

Silence greeted me, so I tried the handle. Locked. I knocked again. "Hey, Laslop. Open up. I want to be able to tell your client you're alright."

Still no reply. I reached into
my pants pocket for the small leather
wallet that held my lock picks. I
looked both ways before starting in on
it and noticed a woman and her little
boy standing on the threshold of 3C.
The woman was locking the door behind
them, but the kid was just standing
there staring at me.

When the woman finished what she
was doing, she turned to the kid, and
then followed his gaze. I knew enough
not to get caught looking, so instead,
I acted like I was pulling the door
shut. I bent down with my back toward
them and picked up the paper. With
any luck, she would mistake me for
Laslop, if she even knew who lived
here.

I went straight for the stairs
and headed out. I had to leave
anyway. I was supposed to be halfway
across town in a bit under thirty
minutes, and I couldn't afford a cab
ride. I'd make a call to Laslop's
office after lunch. Who knows? Maybe
he'd be there or maybe his secretary
would know a thing or two.

I was at the Dog House, watching
the ice slowly melt in our glasses for
a good ten minutes before Mrs. Noble
showed. After the first five minutes,
the waitress started to get
suspicious, and so I ordered a BLT and
a Coke. After the sandwich came and
she still wasn't there, I started to
worry that I'd have to find a way to
pay for my own meal.

I was winding my pocket watch for
probably the third time when she came
through the doors. She lowered her
sunglasses long enough to locate me,
then pushed them back onto her face
and made a beeline for my table.

She sat right down at the booth
and blurted out, "What do you know
about my husband?"

"Take a deep breath, Mrs. Noble.
Have some water. So far, there's
nothing to get so worked up about.
Okay?"

I made it clear that I wasn't
going to say a word until she had done
so, so she grabbed her glass of ice
water in both hands and drank half of

it in one go. "Alright. I'm calm.
Can you please tell me something now?"

I leaned forward and looked
around to make sure no one was getting
too curious. "I followed him that
next morning. He stopped by the
Ballard docks, where he met with some
men in a freezer truck. He picked out
a bunch of seafood from the fishermen,
and they loaded it onto the truck.
Then he bought some produce and met
them up at a club in Queen Anne."

"A club? What club?"

"It's called the Brothers of
Unity. Does that mean anything to
you?"

She thought for a moment. "No...
No, I don't think he's ever mentioned
it."

"How about a pin? It's brass and
has a bear on it. He may have been
wearing it on his lapel."

"No, I haven't seen him wearing
anything like that."

"And you do the laundry?"

"Don't be ridiculous. That's
what the Chinese are for."

I closed my eyes for a moment.
Luckily, the waitress came by and

asked if Claire wanted anything besides water. The last time I made judgments about paying customers, it didn't turn out so well.

"Oh, I'll have what he's having."

I paused until the waitress was out of earshot again. "What I mean is, when you're sending the laundry out, naturally, you go through the pockets. You would have noticed if you ever saw a pin like I described."

"Oh. I see. No, like I said, I've never seen a pin like that."

"Alright. I'm going to mention a few names. Just let me know if any of them sound familiar, okay?"

She narrowed her eyes suspiciously. "Okay..."

"Bill Sears. Maybe William."

She thought for a moment. "No," she said.

"Rudolph Bowerman," I tried.

"Who? No, I would remember that name."

Okay, here goes the big one. "Lonnie Seger."

"Lonnie Seger, oh my dear, yes. Don't bring him up in front of my husband, though!"

"Oh yeah? Why's that?" I asked.
I was going for nonchalant, but I'm
not sure I managed it.

"Well, you must understand, back
in Colorado, Evan was never much into
politics. Like most couples, we would
agree who we were going to vote for,
usually on election day, and we'd go
to the polls together. It wasn't
really a big deal. But we had some
friends over around a month ago, and I
casually asked them who they were
voting for."

She gave me a look as if to say
it was an innocent enough question.
"Well, Nancy said they were both Dore
supporters, and Frank agreed, saying
that Dore's been great for businesses
during this lean time. That he's
helped protect them against the threat
of collective bargaining or some
such."

She placed her palms on the table
and leaned forward. "Evan flipped
out," she said. "He went off about
how businesses wouldn't be in this
tight spot if Dore didn't let the mill
fail. It's his policies that lead to
worker unrest, so he was only saving

businesses from a problem he created."

The waitress came by with Claire's BLT and Coke. Claire glanced up and gave a quick "thanks," and the waitress tore off our tab and set it on the table. I slid it over to Claire's side, but she paid it no mind.

"The Andersons were shocked, of course. Evan is usually so even-tempered. I've never known him to get so upset about anything, especially politics. And you know what's the kicker? We've only been in Seattle six months. The stuff he was talking about was a couple years ago. Well, dinner was both quiet and tortuous after that, and the Andersons left early. I haven't heard from them since."

"Alright. Let's move on. I want to show you some pictures." I pulled out the envelope and picked through them until I found the right one. "Is one of these men Evan?"

I passed across the picture I took of the two cooks in the kitchen.

"Yes!" she said, tapping on the darker-toned one. "That's him."

"This is the kitchen in the club. He was there last night." I pulled out a couple more pictures. These two were from the night of the party. Most of the shots I took were useless, but you could make out faces in a couple of them. "Do you know any of these people?"

Again, she tapped the photograph. "That's Faye and Russel."

"Faye and Russel what?"

"Denmeyer." I flipped the photo over and wrote their names on the back of the dancing couple.

"None of the others in that shot looked familiar?"

"No. Nuh-uh." She started eating her sandwich. I looked down at my plate, but all I had left was the garnish, and I didn't want to be seen eating that. I drank some of my Coke instead.

"Alright. It's hard to make out the man in the next shot, but look at his lapel. I know I asked you about this already, but maybe it'll spark a memory. Maybe you saw it on someone else, one of your friends, maybe?" I passed across the picture I tried to snap of the trio right by the window.

She took it from me and looked at it closely. After a few moments, she passed it back to me. "Nope, sorry. I really haven't seen it."

I tapped on the picture with Russel and Faye dancing. "He's wearing one. See? Right there."

"I get it, Mr. Glover. I just don't remember seeing one."

"Alright. I've got just one more. Have you ever seen this man before?" I passed across the photo of the little guy waving registration forms at the Hooverville feast.

She took the photo and stared at it closely for quite a while. "No," she finally said as she passed it back.

After Claire left, I collected the sixty-five bucks she gave me, as well as my photos. I put them back in the envelope and grabbed the half of her sandwich that she hadn't finished. Shoving it in my pocket, I left the Dog House and stopped at the corner payphone. I dialed Mike down at the

station, and he picked up on the
second ring.

"Hey, Mike. It's me again. I
got some shots I'd like your opinion
on. You know that park, down by the
water near the Post-Intelligencer?"

"Look, Drake, I'm real busy, and
I'm still dealing with the ribbing
from when you were here last. Can't
it wait until Sunday?"

"No, Mike, I don't think it can.
Something fishy is going on here, and
I think it has to do with the
election."

"Exactly," Mike said. "There's
an election coming up, and a lot of us
are working double shifts around here.
That's why I don't have time to deal
with your problems."

"A-huh. Who're you voting for,
Mike?"

"What's that got to do with
anything? Look, I've got to go."

"Look, Mike, all I'm saying is
you've got to eat lunch sometime. Why
not eat it in the park behind the P.I.
building?"

"Okay, okay. Will you get off
the line if I say I'll be there? Just

give me two hours."

"Alright, Mike. You won't regret it."

"I already do," I heard him say as he hung up the phone.

I held down the cradle switch for a few moments, then dropped another nickel in the slot and dialed up the Ben Franklin asking for Prudence Delphine. They put me through, and I waited as the line rang. It kept on ringing, and I began to worry. She shouldn't have left the place... I was pretty specific.

Finally, it picked up. "Hello?" said a timid, childlike voice.

"I need to talk to Marcy," I said.

"Oh, Drake, thank God!" she said loudly enough that I held the receiver away from my face.

"Hey, Megan, it's alright. I just wanted to be sure you were staying put. Listen, I've got a little time to kill, and I've got some more cash for you. Can you meet me in the lobby so I can hand it off?"

"Yes, absolutely. I'm going nuts here by myself!"

"You'll have to put up with it a little while longer. I can't stay long. I'm meeting with some people."

"Is it Bill? Did you find Bill?"

"No, I didn't find him, but I'm going to ask some people I know about him."

"Okay. It's just --"

"Yes, Megan?"

"Could you stop by a dime store? Maybe if I had something to read, I wouldn't be so lonely."

"Sure, I can do that. You like romance or adventure?"

"Westerns are my favorite. Or crime novels."

Crime novels. Made me think about my meeting with X's lackey in Post Alley last night. She would have loved that. "Alright. I'll grab a couple on my way. See you in a bit."

There was a Bartell's on the way to the Franklin, so I stopped by and managed to pick up a couple Zane Greys, along with another roll of film and some flashbulbs. When I got to the hotel, she was waiting there in the lobby. I'd actually meant to ring and have her come down, but it was too late now.

I gave her the books, along with a twenty-dollar bookmark. That would be enough to keep her in room and board for a few more days if necessary. She was starved for company, and I had some time to kill, so we had coffee in the hotel bar and talked for a bit. Not a lot of it was relevant to my tale, though, so I'll leave it off from this account.

When I had to go, it was all too soon for her, but I promised she wouldn't be confined to the hotel for long. We'd resolve this situation soon. Sometimes, I don't know where I get that confidence from, but it seemed to work.

I put her in the elevator and sent her back up to her floor.

Chapter Seven

I spent some time on the payphone outside the Post-Intelligencer building. First, I tried Laslop's home number, which I'd gotten from Megan, but I got no answer, so I tried his office number. The gal that picked up offered to take a message for me, promising that he'd be back shortly. I asked her if she really believed that, and she went silent. I told her that I knew he had gone to confront his client's husband, and I asked if she had seen him since then.

Her only response was to break down in
tears. I had too much to do without
comforting another crying woman, so I
hung up and tried the hospitals.

I dialed Seattle General,
Swedish, and Harborview Hospitals
checking to see if a William Laslop
was brought in. After each of them
came up negative, I asked about any
John Does matching his description.
Bupkis there too.

I gave up on the phone calls and
went inside the Post-Intelligencer to
ask the lady at the desk for Brian
Goldman. A few minutes later, he
joined me on a walk out back of the
building and to the park. We found a
bench with room for three and waited
for Mike. I pulled out my sandwich
and offered Brian half.

"Kosher, remember?"

"Right." I shoved it in my mouth
to get it over with quickly.

"You said you had something I
might be interested in?"

"I want Mike here for most of it,
but here's a teaser." I pulled out
the picture of the little guy with the
registration forms and handed it to

him. "I remembered his name.
Kowalczyk. Mean anything to you?"

"The name sounds familiar." He
adjusted his glasses and peered
closely at the picture. "I like the
picture, though. Mind if I take it?"

"Be my guest."

"And you have the negatives if
they do decide to publish this?"

"Sure I do. You gonna be able to
give me more than 'familiar' with this
guy Kowalczyk?"

Brian smiled. "Tit for tat, eh?
Yeah. It's got to be in one of the
articles I was working on recently.
I'll go over them again, and if I
can't find it, I'll ask my editor.
Can I go now?"

"Not so fast, Brian. Mike's
still coming."

"Mike's here, actually," Mike
said from behind us.

"Hey, thanks for coming. Have a
seat," I said. I stood up and began
pacing. Now that we were at this
point, I wasn't sure how to say any of
this.

He came around and sat on the
bench. "This better be worth it,

Drake."

"Maybe I just owe you one," I suggested.

"You already owe me one. You said something about the election?"

I stopped pacing and faced them. "First off, who do you like for mayor?"

"I got no problem with Dore. I say give him a couple more years."

"You, Brian?" I asked.

"I'm more of a Langlie man myself," he said. "I voted for him last time."

"And which one of you is X?" My eyes darted back and forth between the two of them, watching for any little hint of an expression that would give them away, but they both looked back at me with confusion. Brian's lip curled just a bit as if he were about to make a joke, or maybe he thought I was going to. Mike just looked impatient. Whichever one was X must have expected the question and came prepared because he was hiding it well.

"Drake, maybe you should stop stomping out the grass and just tell us what you brought us here for?" Mike asked.

I nodded and squeezed back in between the two of them. I took a moment before I began. "It's this club I was talking about. They're backing the underdog, Seger, but they're up to something shady." I quickly gave Mike the gist of my Hooverville dinner story. "But according to Brian, that makes no sense. The votes aren't enough to matter. Now, last night, I was inside the club, and I overheard --"

"Drake, damn it, what the hell did I say about breaking and entering? You ever heard of accomplice after the fact?"

"I didn't break into anything, don't get so excited. Now, I overheard this Kowalczyk talking to another guy, someone who sounded like he was in charge. The guy was through the roof over the poll results, but his guy is losing badly. Dore's got forty-one percent to Seger's nineteen, so what's he so happy about? And his plan is apparently national. They were putting pins in a map, here, let me show you." I dug the photo out and passed it around.

Brian grabbed it and held it close to his face. "Looks like America to me. Can't see much else."

I took it from him and handed it to Mike. "I was out of flashbulbs. Point is, there are pins in it, all over. They were talking about San Diego and Santa Barbara, and a few others. They were real excited."

Mike handed the picture back to me. "I don't know what to tell you, Drake. This isn't exactly evidence."

"Police Chief Sears is in the club, my former client Bowerman, my new client's friends, the Denmeyers. Here, maybe you'll recognize some of these." I pulled out photos from the party and passed them around. Brian knew several of them, and I added the names to the backs of photos.

"So far, all we know is that a mayoral candidate cares about the destitute and has some wealthy backers. That's not much to go on." Mike was still playing devil's advocate on this one.

"Well, how about this?" I dug

through the photos for the ones I wanted. "They've got this room in there, with a drafting table, and a pantograph. Then there's this weird little printing press and all these chemicals. Here." I handed the two photos to Brian. He looked at them for a bit and then passed them to Mike.

"What's wrong with them having a printing press?" Mike asked.

"That's not a printing press," Brian said. We both looked at him, waiting for his explanation. "Well, the pantograph is a giveaway, isn't it? That's a minting press. They probably used that to design and then print those pins that everyone is wearing."

"You see now? You're all worked up about nothing. There's usually a simple explanation," Mike said. "Now, if you don't mind, I've got to get back."

"Damn it, Mike, I'm telling you, this club is trying to rig the election, and the chief is a member! Doesn't that worry you?"

"That's the difference between

you and me, Drake. You never seem to
get it. I need evidence. I can't
just go around accusing the police
chief of being involved in a
conspiracy to rig an election without
it. That's called slander, and I'd be
out of a job quicker than you could
ruin toast."

"That's what I'm saying, I do
have proof. Maybe not enough for an
arrest, but it ought to be enough for
a friend to pay attention to!"

"What, a picture of a map and a
minting press? That's not evidence,
it's conjecture. And pretty slim at
that."

"And an eyewitness account of
their conversations, and whatever it
is they were doing down at
Hooverville. But I've got more than
that! Look at this. There!" I said.
I put the photograph in his hands and
pointed. Brian slid in and looked
closely.

"What is this?" Mike asked.

"It's a ledger they had in that
office. You've got names over here,
and payments over here. Lots of
numbers, right? But you can ignore

most of them. I figure that's just
members making payments. It's the
negative numbers that got my interest.
See? Here, here, and oh, look here,
doesn't that say Sears?"

That got Mike's attention. He
stared at it for a bit, his mind
almost visibly whirring. "That
doesn't mean anything, that could just
be a mail-away catalog," he finally
said.

"Come one, Mike. Don't be
obtuse. Eight thousand dollars? What
were they buying? Don't answer that
because I'll tell you. They bought
themselves a police force!"

"Keep it down, would you? Okay,
maybe. But that's still a dangerous
accusation, and it means nothing
unless we get someone to testify
that's what this means."

Brian took the photo. "Even
circumstantial evidence could be
convincing if you have enough of it.
Look at some of these other payouts.
McBride? Could be Judge McBride.
Five thousand dollars. I wonder who
certified Seger to run? Or there's
this one. Pettus. The editor in

chief of the Washington New Dealer is named Pettus. Valburg? The Paramount director Valburg? Thirty thousand. It costs more to buy a theater than a police chief and a judge."

"Alright, both of you. Shut your yaps. Maybe there is something here. Can you get me a copy of this?"

"And one for me?" Brian added.

"I brought along copies of that one just in case. But what I need is information. If I call, you guys have to answer, you got it?" I held out the copies, one to each of them, but I held on until they agreed.

"Yeah, I got it. But now, I've got to go. I've already been away too long."

I let go of the photo. "Just one more thing, Mike," I said, collecting the other photos and putting them back in the envelope. "I'm looking for this guy. His name is William Laslop."

Mike shrugged. "Never heard of him."

"That's odd, see, because he's a P.I. I thought you cops made it your business to know us."

"No, Drake, just you. On account of your history and all."

"Well doesn't that make me feel all rosy inside. This Laslop guy paid Bowerman a visit a couple of days back and hasn't been seen since. Seeing as how Bowerman tried sicking his goons on me, I'm thinking foul play. Only none of the hospitals have him."

"I'm telling you, I've never heard of the guy. What do you want me to do? Send a uniform to talk to Bowerman?"

Brian spoke up before I did. "Hey, what about that John Doe, washed up on Alkai?"

"What did he look like?" I asked.

Brian shrugged. "I don't know, the notice just came across the obits desk, that's all."

"Well, Mike, did you get a body or what?"

"It's not like they put it on my desk or nothing, but yeah, we got a body. It would be down at the morgue."

"Do you know what he looked like?"

"Six foot, blonde hair, brown

eyes. One hundred seventy pounds.
Gunshot wound to the chest. Sound
like your guy?"

"Yeah, that could be him," I
said. "Any way I could get a look at
the body?"

"Jesus, Drake! You won't be
happy until you've put me in
Hooverville, will you?"

"Come on, Mike. Someone's got to
I.D. the body, right?"

"Fine. I'll give you a ride, and
get you in. But then, you're on your
own."

The morgue wasn't in the same
building as the precinct, but it was
part of the same block of buildings.
There was a decent chance I could get
in and out of there without any of the
other cops seeing me. Even still,
Mike was silent during the entire car
ride. One day, I'm going to have to
straighten things out at the precinct.
Maybe I could live with the scorn, but
it was causing Mike troubles, and I
didn't want that. It's not exactly
friend-like behavior.

When we got there, he signed me
in, and we waited for the coroner.
Then he handed me off and left. The
coroner, whose name was Boris, led me
down the stairs to the morgue proper.
If you've ever wondered why the morgue
is always in the basement of
buildings, he told me, so I'm telling
you. It's because it's naturally
colder there. It helps keep the
bodies from deteriorating and with the
overall smell of the place.

I'm glad he started the
conversation because the only thing I
could think to say was, is your last
name Karloff?

"How well did you know the
deceased?" Boris asked.

"Assuming it's him, of course.
We were business associates."

"Aha. You should prepare
yourself. It's probably him."

"How would you know that?" I
asked.

"Seattle may be the biggest city
around, but it's really not that big,
and we don't get a lot of John Does.
Maybe one or two a year. If someone
goes missing, and someone else comes

looking because a body's been found,
ninety-nine percent of the time, it's
them."

"Did he have anything on him when
his body was discovered?"

"All his effects will be up in
evidence. You can see them, I'm sure.
But there wasn't much, and nothing
identifiable. His clothes, a soggy
pack of cigarettes, and some loose
change. His wallet, assuming he had
one, was gone."

I knew going up to evidence meant
dealing with the cops, and if Boris
said there was nothing to identify
him, it probably wasn't worth my time.

We pushed through swinging doors,
and Boris turned on the light. There
were four-wheeled tables in there with
sheets over them. The oddly
disturbing shapes of dead people were
clearly visible through the sheets on
each of the tables.

I've seen dead bodies before, and
once, I even saw a man draw his last
breath. I thought I was pretty well
hardened to the sight by now, but
something about being in a room where
they stored you when you died was

giving me the creeps.

"One a year, you say?" I asked,
looking at the four shapes under the
sheets.

Boris was examining a clipboard.
"Hmm?" he said, looking up. "Oh, we
know who the other ones are. They
still come here based on the
circumstances of their death. We've
got a stabbing, a lynching, and a
suspicious fall down the stairs," he
said, pointing with the back of his
pen at each in turn. He set down the
clipboard and went to the second table
from the left.

"This should be your guy." He
lifted the sheet around the feet and
examined the toe tag. "Yep, that's
him."

He covered his feet back up (so
he wouldn't catch cold, I thought) and
came around to the other side of the
table. I joined him there. He held
the sheet before pulling it back. "He
isn't going to look the way he did in
life," he said.

"I understand. Go ahead."

He pulled up the sheet and laid
it across the man's chest.

It was Laslop, I had no doubt.

Funny thing is, he looked exactly like he had in life. When I'd seen him last, he'd had a gun pointed at me, and a sarcastic sort of smile that the body wasn't currently wearing. But it was him, only a bit paler. He just looked like he was sleeping there. At peace. "It's him. William Laslop, private detective. Lives over on Spring Street and First. Well, did." I reached for the sheet.

"Allow me," Boris said and started to cover the face back up.

I grabbed his wrists. "No. Not yet." I pulled the sheets down lower, exposing the tiny round hole in the center of his chest. I put my pinky finger up to it, but Boris stopped me again. This time I let him. He covered the body back up.

"Did it go clean through?" I asked.

"No, I'll be retrieving it later today."

"Any idea what the caliber was?"

"The wound is consistent with a .22, but I'll know for sure later. Why?"

"Because I'm going to be looking for the gun that fired it. And I've got an idea where to start."

Another one of the things that people don't know about Seattle if they aren't from around here is the tides. Puget Sound is a massive body of sea water, but for the most part, it's pretty shallow around the cities. That means that twice a day, as the moon exerts its influence on the oceans of the world, the Sound fills up. And all the water that's hanging out around Seattle starts heading south toward Tacoma as fast as any river.

That's going to seem like a real swell thing to anyone trying to dispose of a body. You drop it off Pier 57 and watch it steam away like a fleshy ferry.

The thing that such gruesome businessmen don't realize is the same thing that industrialists didn't account for when they started dumping their waste into Seattle's waters. That same tide comes roaring on back

at the same speed just a few hours
later.

Whatever you dump into Elliott
Bay comes right back to haunt you.
Bill Laslop was no different. I'm
sure that when Bowerman had his men
dump the body, he thought he had seen
the last of it. But instead, Laslop's
body had simply gone on one last
victory lap before hitting the finish
line on the beach outside of Salty's
in West Seattle.

There was one more thing I did
when I was at the Ben Franklin Hotel
bar with Megan Bowerman. I had her
sign a check out to cash. Now I was
standing outside the Wells Fargo
branch on Capitol Hill. Kids were
walking home from school, and I
selected one, a toe-headed boy around
nine years old, carrying a backpack
half his size. His main
distinguishing feature was that he was
there by himself.

"Hey, champ. Want to earn a
quick dollar?" I asked him.

"Would I!" he shouted with a big
old grin on his face.

I knelt and held out the dollar.

"Okay, kid. Take this and stick it in your pocket. It's all yours." The dollar quickly disappeared, and I held out the check. "Now, here's what I want you to do. Take this check into the bank here. You'll have to wait in line for a bit, but that's okay. When one of the tellers calls you over, slip him this check. It's for forty dollars, and it's made out to cash, see? That means anybody can get the money. If they give you the money, that's yours too. Go ahead and keep it or give it to your mom. I'm sure she'll find a good use for it."

The kid took the check and was looking it over, eyes wide as dinner plates.

"Alright. Now, this bit's important, so listen up, okay?" He looked back up at me, and I continued. "If they ask you where you got it, you need to say, 'Some lady,' then I want you to point at this alley, right over here. Can you point to it?"

The kid pointed to it. "Okay, you can put your arm down. Now, who gave it to you?"

"Some lady," the kid said. He

lifted his arm back up and pointed at the alley again.

"Perfect. Now, you're probably going to get a bit bored in there, so remember. Forty dollars is a lot of money, and it would really help your mom. So you've got to make sure you do this, okay?"

"Okay, mister."

"Alright. Go ahead now." I watched the kid go up to the bank. He had trouble with the heavy doors, but then someone else was coming out, and he ducked in.

I turned and went across the street to catch the bus.

The bus dropped me off at the end of Bowerman's street, but I remembered that big bay window he likes to sit in front of, so I took the next street over instead. As I said before, in this area, the lots they built these houses on are tiny. They stacked them side by side and back to back, then they ran a row of fencing down between them with barely room for a walking path on the side of each house.

I walked up the street behind Bowerman's house and noted nobody home at the place that would otherwise be his back yard. I took the walkway between that house and the next one, then looked over the fence onto Bowerman's property. I couldn't see much through the small windows in the back of his house, but I could see that his Chrysler was still there. That meant one of two things. Either I got here before the bank got in touch with Bowerman, or that kid was walking out of that bank one rich third grader.

Moments later, I got my answer when a door slammed, and those two nice men who visited me at my office got into Bowerman's car and took off in a hurry. I gave them around two minutes, then I hopped the fence. There were three of them who stayed with Bowerman, according to Megan. That meant I had one more to deal with. Well, Chasly too, but he didn't count.

Bowerman had a line of trash cans along one side of the house. I picked one of them up, took a couple paces backward, then hurled it at the other ones.

The cans made a fantastic clatter, but I was already crouched by the far side of Bowerman's back door. Three seconds later, the last of Bowerman's goons was barreling out the door to see what was up. Of course. It was the big guy from the water tower. I slipped in the door behind him and locked it, then wedged a chair from the dining room under the knob for good measure.

I pulled the phone cord out of the wall and went past the front door on my way to see Bowerman. I made sure it was locked, then dropped the coat rack across it.

"What the hell was that noise?" I heard Bowerman say from the depths of his chair. I came up behind him and grabbed his jacket by the lapels, then tipped the chair backward until we were face to face.

"Raccoons," I said.

"G-Glover!" the old man said, his face going red. "What the hell do you think you're doing here? Rocky!"

"Don't bother calling for your men, I've made sure they're all off on errands just now. It's going to be

just you and me, you fat chump. You
might want to give Chasly a holler,
though. I'd hate to have him sneaking
up behind me and proving his loyalty."

He didn't say anything, and
instead was flailing to get upright.
I let the back of the chair drop an
inch or two. "Call him, or I'm going
to get nasty." I raised a hand as if
to slap him.

"Chasly!" he called. I liked the
sound of desperation in the fat man's
voice. Just as long as it didn't
sound a warning to his manservant. It
didn't last long. "Whatever you're
thinking of, you won't get away with
it! I can make it so you never work
in this city again! You know I can!"

"Yeah? But you won't, and do you
know why? Because now you know I can
get you alone. And if you act against
me, I'll do to you exactly what your
boys did to Megan."

His eyes widened in a satisfying
example of terror. Bingo. Now he was
ready for what was coming. Behind
every bully is a coward. You just
have to figure out how to get past the
façade.

Chasly appeared at the bottom of the staircase. His eyes widened when he saw me.

"The muscle outside is going to want in," I said. "Only you're not going to let him, see? Otherwise, something unfortunate might occur. Now, how about you fix Rudolph here his favorite drink? Help calm his nerves. Come to think of it, maybe you should have one too. Then get back here before I worry."

I watched Chasly move in his arthritic way toward the kitchen, then I returned my attention to Bowerman. "You've been making a lot of mistakes lately, Bowerman. A man in your position only stays in that position by being careful, and you've been sloppy, and you're going down for it. You never should have knuckled up that wife of yours, and you never should have killed her detective." Then I ran one hand up his lapel until I found the pin. "And you never should have gotten involved with this club," I finished, pulling the pin off his jacket.

"Wh-what?"

"You heard me. The Brothers of Unity. They're up to no good, and you're going to spill what you know."

"No, before that. I didn't kill the detective! I didn't have anybody killed!"

The acrid smell of urine reached me through my rage, and I looked down to see the stain spreading across his pants.

"You gotta believe me, Glover! I yell, and I threaten, and I've even had people beaten up, but my men don't kill people, they only hit them. The gun's just for show!"

"He's telling the truth, sir," Chasly said. He was standing a couple paces away with a drink in each hand. "Mr. Bowerman is dead frightened of his enemies. They're here for his protection, not to kill anyone."

"They took the detective's gun away, then they threw him down the stairs! They told him they would kill him if they ever saw him again! That's it!" Bowerman looked like he was going to cry, and I just about believed him, except then I saw Laslop lying on that cold metal table with the hole in his chest.

I shook him again. "That story's bull and you know it! I just came from the morgue where Laslop's got one more hole than he needs. But you know what? Maybe I don't feel like going to the cops with my story. You know what I do feel like? I feel like a man is going to come by here in the next few days. He's going to have divorce papers with him, and you're going to sign them. Your soon to be ex-wife is going to ask for half of everything you own, and you're going to give it to her. And as you're signing your name, you're going to count yourself lucky. Because if you don't, I will go to the cops, and I'm going to make sure they put you away for good."

"Okay! Alright! I'll sign. Just let me go." He really did start crying now.

"Not until you tell me what I want to know. Chasly, he's going to need that drink now."

Chasly came over and tried to give Bowerman his drink, which was difficult to do in this awkward

position. I didn't make it any easier
on him. "You gonna drink the other
one?" I asked.

"No, I thought you might like
one, sir."

"Forget it. I'll take this one.
He can have mine." I put the pin in
my pocket and took Bowerman's drink,
letting the carefully balanced chair
do most of the work of holding
Bowerman up. Chasly continued to try
to hand Bowerman his.

I finished the drink, which
turned out to be brandy, in one quick
gulp, then I pushed the glass back on
Chasly. Bowerman finally managed to
get a hold of his. I took pity on him
and let his head up so he could drink
some without spilling it up his nose.

Somewhere in all this, a pounding
had begun at the back door. "Wave him
away, would you Chasly? He can come
in when I'm done."

I lowered the head of the chair
again. "Now, tell me about this
club."

"It's a club! There's nothing
special. You pay your dues, and they
throw parties. I've found a lot of

like-minded people there. We have intelligent conversations!"

"And you work to elect like-minded people too, is that about right?"

"There isn't any work involved! It's like I said, it's just parties and talk. We're all Seger supporters if that's what you mean, but it's not like we go door to door or make signs!"

Was it possible he didn't know? "And you feed the hungry too, right?"

"What are you talking about?" Bowerman asked. He seemed genuinely ignorant.

"Exactly how are you like-minded?"

"We worry about the direction this country is headed, of course. The sort of thing that's happening to society. And we agree that electing the right kinds of people is the way to solve it."

"And who runs the club? What's his name!"

"Oberman! Kenneth Oberman!"

"Sirs, it's about Rocky," Chasly said. "He says he's going to bust down the door if I don't let him in."

"You tell him he's fired if he does!" Bowerman yelled. He downed the rest of his brandy. The bully was back in Bowerman's eyes. "It's alright. Mr. Glover will be leaving now, won't you, Mr. Glover?" It was amazing how quickly he recovered, now that there was someone he could boss around again.

I'd probably stayed as long as was safe anyway. The other two would be returning from the bank any minute. "Yeah. I got what I needed. You just remember the man with the papers. Sign them." I set his chair back on all four feet and straightened my tie. "Thank you for the drink, Chasly."

I set the coat rack upright and went out the front door. A crazy idea was formulating in my head as my hand went to my pocket.

Chapter Eight

I arrived back at the club by cab
that night. This time I let him drive
me all the way to the porch. There
was a party going on again, which was
good. The other guests will help to
complete my camouflage for the
evening.

One of the bruisers opened the
back seat of the cab, and I paid the
driver. Between that and the suit I'd
rented, I was spending money too fast
for my tastes. It was hard to watch
that money go, it was supposed to be

paying for my rent.

I stepped out, dressed better than I had since high school graduation, and with pomade-slicked hair and a carnation at my lapel to boot. Also on my lapel, in a place of honor, was a small brass pin of a roaring bear and the three letters, 'BOU'. Thank you, Rudolph Bowerman.

The bruiser took one look at the button and paid me no more attention. I walked in through the front door this time, while he shut the door of the cab behind me.

A waiter was standing just inside the door with a tray of champagne flutes. I've never developed a taste for champagne, but I took one just the same. More camouflage. I sipped it and found it was actually quite good. I guess cheap champagne is like cheap liquor. No comparison to the good stuff.

The piano was playing, and there were couples nearby, deep in light conversation. I wandered over, under the pretext of listening to the piano, but instead, I wanted to hear the sorts of things these people talked

about. Snippets of conversation came
to me; college sports, mostly football
and rowing. Apparently, UW was doing
well in both this year. I've always
been partial to hockey, another sport
where they underestimate the little
guy, and where fighting teaches you
useful skills.

Another group was talking markets
and futures. There was no way I could
keep up with that kind of talk, so I
steered clear. I grabbed a few hors
d'oeuvres. If I had to risk eviction
to be here, I may as well leave fed.
I paced myself so as not to be a
spectacle, but I ate plenty more than
my share. One of the conversations
made its way toward the table, and
before I could move, it sucked me in.

"I don't think I've seen you
around here before," said a pale, thin
woman in a shapeless, yet highly
fashionable dress. She had earrings
dangling to her shoulders, and a
haircut shorter than mine, yet deeply
feminine. "I'm Phyllis, and this is
my husband, Calvin. This one's Dinah;
she's with that boorish fellow, Peter.
And you are?"

"Jack," I said. I had my alias prepared since my last encounter. I kept my brother's name, but now I had a surname and a job. "Jack Major. How do you do?"

"Well, Jack, I see you're here alone, and without a wedding ring. Perhaps you're in the market, so to speak?"

"Pay no attention to her," her husband said, leaning in to shake my hand. "Phyllis can never resist an opportunity to play matchmaker. What do you do for a living, Jack?"

"I'm an author and wildlife photographer." I flashed open my coat to show off my camera hanging from the neck strap.

"Simply marvelous!" Dinah said. "Anything we may have read?"

"Oh, mostly ornithological texts, but I'm working on a sort of coffee table book." I figured that was safe. The chances of running across a birder seemed slim, but it was the sort of thing that these people might go for.

"I'm a member of the Audubon Society," Peter said.

"I'm sure Jack didn't come here

to talk shop, Peter," Phyllis said,
then to me, "Pay Peter no attention at
all. No one else does." She
twittered a little laugh. I'm pretty
sure it was intended to be attractive,
but it wasn't. I've spent enough time
on the other side of a laugh like
that.

"Have any of you seen Oberman?
I've been looking to thank him for the
invitation."

"He's usually in the smoking
room. Boys only, you know. I can
introduce you if you'd like," Calvin
said.

"But you mustn't call him
Oberman," Dinah said, clicking her
tongue. "It's either Ken or sir.
There's no in-between."

Phyllis added, "And your place
here can be determined by which one
you dare to call him."

"Come on, Jack," Calvin said. He
grabbed my champagne flute and passed
both his and mine off to his wife and
Dinah. "Let's go see Ken. Peter, you
can handle the womenfolk while we're
away, can't you? That's a good man."

I'd actually only wanted to put a

face to the name and the voice, and maybe snap a few photos if possible. It wasn't anywhere in my plan to be stuck in a closed room with Oberman, much less to be the subject of his attention. But stuck I was.

Calvin led me through the doorway to the back of the house. I caught a fleeting glance into the kitchen, hoping to see whether Evan Noble was there. You remember Evan? I was supposed to be following him. A few people said hello to Calvin as we passed through, and he waved back, but we didn't stop. We approached the double doors on the far south side of the room, and Calvin pushed them open.

Smoke billowed out from between the doors as the two of us entered. The sweet smell of cigar smoke impregnating leather-bound books was the first thing I noticed. The room was taller than I expected, taking up the second story as well, with bookshelves lining three of the walls. One of those rolling ladders serviced the shelves, and below those were glass cases filled with cigar boxes stored at a precise humidity. The rest of the room was taken up by overstuffed leather chairs, and some of the hardiest ferns I've ever seen in my life. One small, low-hanging chandelier and several gas lamps on reading tables provided the only light.

Two dozen men were standing or sitting around the room, with only a few isolated conversations going on. Each man had a lit cigar and was contributing to the cloud that hung just above head height.

Calvin and I weaved our way through the group to the biggest of the chairs. I had to do a double-take because it looked like Fatty Arbuckle was sitting there. Red hair, jolly dimpled face, short little legs not quite reaching the floor, and enough room in that belt to fit five of me easily. The little guy standing next to him, the only man without a cigar in his mouth, was definitely Kowalczyk, though, so the big guy had to be Oberman.

"Ken," Calvin said, "I don't know if you've met Jack Major yet. He's an author."

Oberman took the cigar out of his mouth and pointed it accusingly at Calvin. "Cal, you know the rules around here, and yet you shamelessly flaunt them. No business before you've had a decent smoke." He laughed and put the cigar back in his mouth. "Major, you say? What will you have?"

"Pardon?" I said.

Kowalczyk waved one arm toward the humidors lining the walls. "Do you have a preference?"

"Cuban," I said. "Partagás if you have it." Now here, I did know my stuff. I may not be able to afford them, but I was raised to appreciate them. My father had one after every match, win or lose. And he didn't let a little thing like throat cancer slow him down.

"If we have it?" Oberman said in a fit of laughter. "Give the man a cigar!" he added, mimicking a boardwalk barker's voice.

Kowalczyk left. "Never gets old, sir," he said. He returned shortly with two cigars and handed them out. He offered us a heavy lighter from a nearby table.

"An author, eh?" Oberman said, once our cigars were going.

"And a wildlife photographer, Ken," I added deliberately. I handed back the lighter, then flashed the camera again. I figured if they knew I had it, and thought they knew what it was for, it would go better for me than if they found it on me and suspected rightly instead.

Oberman's eyes narrowed momentarily when he saw the camera, but his face was that same jolly mask a moment later.

"Wildlife?" Kowalczyk asked. "What kind, if I may ask?"

"Birds mostly. That's what I write about."

Kowalczyk was positively gleeful. I may have guessed wrongly about there being no birders here. "Perhaps I've read something of yours?"

I quickly made up something that sounded plausible. I hoped it wasn't a real book. "Waterfowl of the Puget Sound?" I said.

"Sounds delightful," the little man said, laying the stress on the word 'sounds' like grease on an axle, then laughing at his own little pun.

"Hmm. Yes," Oberman said. "Well, welcome to our little club. I hope you like it here. Any friend of Calvin is a friend of mine, so long as he's paid his dues, right?" Now he was laughing too. My jaw was starting to hurt from forcing smiles.

I was just about to wander off, when Calvin had to say those fatal words. "Oh, we've only just met tonight."

"Is that so?" Oberman asked. The smile was still on his face, only now it wasn't so friendly. "Who recommended you for the club then, Jack?"

"Bowerman," I said, doing my best to keep my own smile friendly.

"Rudolph Bowerman?" he asked. "And, is he here tonight?"

"I haven't seen him yet," I said.

Kowalczyk raised a hand, signaling to someone behind me.

"Well, Jack, what say we take our little meet and greet somewhere a bit more private?" Oberman said, pushing forward and rising from his chair.

I turned, but my space was suddenly limited by three large men standing around me. One of them plucked the cigar from between my fingers. There was no way I was fighting my way out of this room, so I graciously accepted his invitation instead.

He led the way out of the room, with Kowalczyk at his side. I followed along, closely watched by my three new best friends. We went up the grand staircase and back into his office, where we had all been the night before.

Oberman went around behind his desk, and two of the goons flanked me while the other one closed the door. Kowalczyk stood in the corner by the map, looking smaller and less significant than ever.

"You couldn't have picked a worse person to claim to be their friend. Rudolph Bowerman hasn't got a single friend in the club, and in all the time he's belonged, he hasn't once recommended anyone. We also have a policy that first-time visitors come with their sponsor. My top drawer was

mysteriously unlocked this morning,"
he said, showing me a key and then
unlocking it. "Tell me, Mr. Major, do
you have any idea why that would be?"

"Nosy cleaning lady?" I
suggested.

"I assume the same cleaning lady
left the window open downstairs. Do
you suppose this devilish woman also
attacked one of the guards out by the
property line?" Oberman picked up the
phone on his desk and waited a few
seconds before saying, "Get Ryder up
here." He hung the phone back up.

The two of us locked eyes for a
moment. I could feel him sizing me
up. "Get his camera," he finally
said.

One of the goons came around
front and pulled open my jacket. He
reached for my camera. That camera
was my livelihood. If they took that
camera, whatever else happened to me
tonight, I was out of a job.

I knocked his hand away and put
everything I had into a left hook.
The man's jaw went sideways, and I
felt a crunch that told me he just
lost a tooth. He staggered backward,

a look of shock on his face.

The man behind me grabbed me by the shoulders. I tried to twist around, but his grip was like a vice. The third goon approached with his fists raised, and I held mine up defensively.

"That's enough of that, Mr. Major," Oberman said. He had a gun pointed at my head.

I unclenched my fists and held my hands up. Goon number three opened up my jacket and grabbed my camera. The camera was an antique, the leather strap ancient and worn. He gripped it in both hands, snapping it.

I tried to wriggle free from the second goon's grip, but it was no use. I looked up at him instead. "Easy on the suit, big fella, it's a rental."

"Check him for I.D. too," Oberman said.

The first goon, recovered from the unexpected punch to his jaw, came back up to me and hit me hard in the stomach, bending me in two and knocking the breath out of me. While I was bent double, he pulled out my wallet and threw it to Oberman.

"You can have your fun with him later, Henry. For now, I want him able to answer some questions." He set the gun down on his desk while he went through my wallet. My eyes fixated on the gun. If I could get to that, it might change how things ended here.

"Drake Glover, private detective. Very pleased to make your acquaintance, Mr. Glover," Oberman said, that childlike smile back on his face. "Bring me the camera," he said to goon number three.

The goon handed my camera to Oberman, who took it by the broken strap, swung it around in a great arc, and brought it crashing down against the edge of his desk. The case popped open, and the billows unfurled.

I stood back up, barely breathing, but still staring daggers into him. "You..." I started, voice quaking. Henry gave me another shot to the belly, a little higher up this time. I felt a couple ribs break. Oberman gave my camera another spin, and this time, when it hit the table, the back of the camera broke off, and

the lens shattered. To add insult to
injury, I hadn't taken a single
picture on that strip.

He dropped the remains of my
livelihood in the trash bin next to
his desk. "Now then, Mr. Glover, who
do you work for?"

It took me a while before I could
breathe again, and even longer before
I shoved my temper back down. "I was
just looking for some decent food, and
saw the light on," I said.

"Yes, very droll. You seem to be
able to take a punch, but perhaps it's
a case of 'Iron stomach, glass jaw'?
Henry, if you don't mind?"

The guy behind me still had my
arms locked tight. Henry lifted my
chin up to fist-level and gave me a
shot across the jaw. I knew how to
take a blow to the face too, so I
managed to keep my teeth. But man,
that kid could hit. I was seeing
double and tasting blood. Another
shot like that, and I was going down.

I barely registered it when the
door opened behind me. "Ryder!"
Oberman said. "You're just in time.
We got the guy who clocked you one

last night. How would you like a shot
at him?"

"I'm already registered."

I didn't know who said it at
first, but Oberman looked over at
Kowalczyk in the corner. "Come
again?"

"Yes, I'm certain of it now.
I've seen this man before. He was
there in Hooverville the night of the
voter rally!" The little guy came
over and studied my face, which must
have been swelling up into an
unfamiliar configuration by then, but
he still recognized me.

He turned back to Oberman. "He
was sitting there next to Mr. Jackson.
I gave him a voter registration form,
and he said, 'I'm already registered.'
The suit threw me at first, but he
said it's a rental. This is
definitely him."

"Son of a -- You're telling me
this is one of Jesse's boys?" Oberman
said, face going red.

Kowalczyk looked back at me for
just a moment and said, "Yes. Yes,
I'm sure he is."

"Damn it! If I didn't still need

that --" He went on to use a phrase I don't care to relate. "Henry, Ryder, you take this Glover back to Jesse and see if he still wants him. Otherwise, you do as you see fit. I don't want to see him back here, though, is that understood?"

"Yes, sir." It was Ryder that spoke that time. He had a rather thick accent, I would have placed as Mexican, except the name didn't fit.

"Get him out of here," Oberman said, turning toward the window.

Henry smiled. I could briefly see the space where I had taken a tooth from him, then he hit me again in the left eye, and I didn't see anything.

When I woke up, I was being jostled back and forth, lying on a cold hard floor. My head was resting on my aching eye, and my lips were pulled back tight by the gag in my mouth. My hands were tied behind my back, but my legs were free. I pulled my knees under me and got to a kneeling position. I was in the back

of the freezer truck again, making my
way back to Hooverville. Something
told me there wouldn't be a gourmet
meal at the end of this trip.

The cold air hurt my lungs, as
did the broken ribs. Two, I decided,
on the right side. I struggled with
the bonds, but whoever tied these
knots knew what they were doing. I
looked for something sharp, and
finally settled on the corner of one
of the ice boxes right where the door
rolled down. I had to sit on the box
while I worked the ropes, and I
couldn't feel my legs within minutes.

Pulling the ropes across the tiny
edge of exposed metal was enough to
get my blood pumping, and I started
sweating from the exertion. After a
good ten minutes, I ran a finger along
the spot where I had been attacking
the rope. It was frayed a bit, but
the progress wasn't encouraging.

Keeping my body temperature up
was good enough incentive, though, so
I kept going. There was always a
chance it would do some good.

The truck eventually came to a
stop, and I heard the doors close on

both sides. I moved away from the corner so they wouldn't know what I was doing. I hadn't made enough progress to get excited about, but some. Unfortunately, it was hard to move now, my legs were so cold.

The door rolled up, and the two men were standing there. "Come on out," Henry said.

I stood, but with my first step, I nearly fell over, so I stopped again. "What? You going to make us go in there?" he said.

I gave it another shot. Both of my legs were numb, but I slowly put my weight on each and shuffled toward the back. When I got there, Henry pulled my legs out from under me, and I sat down hard on the lip of the truck. I grunted in pain, which only seemed to delight them. They each put a hand on my back and pushed me off the truck. I landed on my feet but wasn't able to support myself, and I went sprawling in the mud. There went my deposit on the rental.

Ryder and Henry shared a laugh and picked me up. Ryder shoved me in the back and walked after me.

It was the tail end of a good rain. Thick globs were falling, not in any hurry, and without any wind to accompany them. The men of Hooverville were inside their shacks, and smoke poured out of pipes sticking through their roughshod roofs.

Ryder continued shoving me as we moved in between the piecemeal construction until we reached one shack no different from any of the others. It was made of broken wooden beams poorly nailed together, with a door made of old license plates and flattened soup cans. A light came through the cracks between boards. Henry knocked on it, and the tinny sound reverberated through the silent night.

The door opened a crack, then widened when he saw us standing there. "We found him at the club. Sir thought maybe he was one of yours," Ryder said.

"Oh, no, no, no, no, no," Jesse said, shaking his head as he looked at me. "You boys don't get it. The very tenets we are fighting for is that everybody deserves fair and equitable

treatment! What does it say about us
when we beat a man down and throw him
in the mud? Come on in here, son. At
least get out of the rain."

I went with him back into his
little shack. There wasn't enough
room for Henry and Ryder, so they
huddled in the open doorway. The rain
was passing anyway.

"Well, sit down! I can't offer
you much, but that crate makes for a
good enough seat." Inside his little
hovel, there was an orange crate for a
stool, a group of crates pushed
together with a mattress and one thin
blanket laying on top; a stove was in
one corner made from an old fridge,
and a table made from a wooden spool.
Under the stool was a pickle jar that
I guessed was his bathroom, and on top
of the table was a gas lamp, a pad of
paper, and a pencil.

"Bet you didn't even think I
could read," he said, following my
gaze. "But I do. I write too. I've
told my story of Hooverville, from
where we started to where we are now.
Maybe, the right person will read it
and do something about all this. Or

just maybe, the right person already did. Well, sit down already. Don't you worry about me, I got a spot here on the bed."

I sat down, and he joined me. He watched me silently. I wasn't sure what would come next, but I sure hadn't expected this.

"I do know you. It was hard to tell at first, with the eye going all shut like that, but I only saw you from the other side anyway. We sat together the other night, didn't we? Jack, right?"

He looked at me as if expecting me to answer, and only then noticed the gag. "Oh, let's get that fool thing off you." He leaned across and started untying the knot from behind my head.

"His name ain't Jack, it's Drake," Henry said.

"Is that a fact?" he said, still working the knot. "I felt sure you said it was Jack. Were you lying to me? Or maybe it was a different guy."

He got the handkerchief undone, and I exercised my mouth before saying, "Thank you."

"You're welcome. Now, which is it? Jack or Drake?"

"It's Drake," I admitted. I sized him up. I wasn't sure whether he was really a way out of this, but I tried to determine what would be the right answer to get him on my side. I opted for the truth. "I lied before because I wasn't sure what they were up to. It seemed like no good."

"Oh, these boys mean well. You can't help who you are. A man's got nothing in life but a pair of big fists, he's gonna hit things with them. It's up to other men to point them at something useful. The men they're working for have the best of intentions. Only sometimes, they need to physically knock a cog back into place to make sure the machine keeps working properly. Understand?"

"He's a detective," Henry added.

"My word. I suppose it would be hard to get far as a detective without lying once in a while. Let me tell you a thing or two so's you'll understand. What we've got going on here isn't just an election. We're changing the world! Seattle is going

to be a shining city by the sea. A
beacon to Washington, the whole USA,
and maybe beyond. A place where every
man who's willing has a job and can
hold his head up high and say, 'I'm
worth something.' Sure, it's been
tried before, but this time, we've got
lawyers and judges, doctors,
policemen, and newspapers, and we've
got the votes. So, we can really make
this happen! And everybody's going to
be treated the same. There aren't
going to be any more lines where you
stay on that side, and me and mine
stay on this side. This is the way
the world is supposed to be. Now, in
the end, isn't all that worth a few
knocked skulls?"

"Sounds great, yeah," I said.
"But my father used to have a saying
about anything that sounded too good
to be true."

"Uh-huh. I think I heard that
one myself. The thing is, no one
actually knows because no one ever
tried! And even if everything doesn't
turn out all peaches and cream, we're
all going to at least have work. And
that's a mighty fine thing."

He played with the handkerchief, winding it around his fingers, then pulling it through. "Only thing is, somebody gets in the way of all that, somebody has to stop them. And that's where these boys come in."

Somewhere in the time we were inside, the rain had given up completely, and a mist had now followed it in off the bay as it often does in the Spring. Jackson stood up and spoke to the men outside. "No, gentlemen, he isn't one of mine after all, which I suppose makes him one of yours."

Henry leaned inside the shack and grabbed me by one arm. He pulled me to my feet and out the door.

"But you remember the rules. There's no fighting in Hooverville, and there sure ain't no killing. That's how we maintain the peace. I let you all start hurting people, and it won't take even hours, only minutes. It's gonna devolve into anarchy. Go on, and get your detective Drake far away from here, and do what you got to do. I've got to look out for my people and make sure things run smoothly around here, so I don't want any part of this. Goodbye, Mr. Drake. It seems your fate is to be on the receiving end of these boys' talents, and I'm sorry for that. But that sure was a nice meatloaf we shared."

With that, he closed the door to his shack.

Ryder got back to shoving me. I think we were heading back toward the truck, but I couldn't honestly say I was paying a lot of attention on the way down there, and the fog was getting too thick to see more than a dozen feet ahead.

"What say I just jump into the bay, and you guys can say you threw me?" I tried.

"Hold him for me, Henry," Ryder said in his odd accent, "I want to get some payback for the other night."

Henry grabbed me by the arms, his thick fists taking up the entire area from shoulder to elbow. Ryder looked around for something to use. His fists were half that size if not smaller, and they didn't look so used to being used. He spotted a lead pipe bracketed across somebody's window and pried it off. "Who's out there?" came a voice from within the shack, but nobody answered him.

Ryder took a couple practice swings, then it was batter up. He pounded me repeatedly in the stomach, then decided to mix it up. He clocked me one good one in the head, and I could see that the end of the pipe came away covered in blood. He got me in the shoulder with the next one, though I don't think he was aiming for that. Finally, he hit me in the knee. That was too much for me, and I cried out in pain.

Ryder got a big smile on his face and gave it a few more practice swings, then took careful aim at my injured knee and twisted back for a big swing.

A harsh whistle broke the silence of the night. Ryder's smile turned to a look of fear. "The cops!"

"I thought we own the cops," Henry said. The whistle continued to blow, and men started complaining from inside their shacks.

"Maybe not all of them. Hide!"

Ryder tossed the pipe back over next to the shack.

"Over here!" I yelled. Henry shoved me in the back, and my injured knee went out. I fell to the ground for the second time tonight. Now I could see the beam of a flashlight bouncing through the fog.

"No time for that now, Henry! Hide!" Ryder said, and he was gone into the fog. Henry ran past me on his way after Ryder.

"Over here!" I shouted again. I did my best to stand, but I couldn't get my right knee under me. I don't think anything was broken, it was just in too much pain.

I heard the sound of running feet approaching, then someone was kneeling by my side. "Let me get those ropes," the man said. "Can you stand?"

He didn't sound like any cop. I turned as well as I could to get a look at him. He wore a dark suit, with a light-colored hat and coat. He looked like any ordinary Joe.

"Who are you?" I asked.

"I saw you go into the club, and when they dragged you back out. I've

been following you since then. When
they started beating you, I had to do
something."

"Thanks. Now, who are you?"

"Never mind that now," he said,
sawing through the ropes with a
penknife. I like to think he made
such short work because of all the
effort I put into it back on the
truck. They came undone, and I got my
arms in front of me.

I pushed myself into a sitting
position and examined my knee. "Do
you live here in Hooverville?"

"I work for X," he said
impatiently.

"X, again? Who is this X?"

"We've got to get out of here.
Give me your hand. I'll help you
walk." Unlike the guy in Post Alley,
I got a good look at this one. I'd
never seen him before. Dark hair,
blue eyes, two days' worth of stubble,
and a pimple in the corner of his nose
like his teenage years were back for
revenge.

I gave him my hand, and he helped
me to my feet. As soon as I got up to
his level, I grabbed him by the lapels

and gave him a good shake. "Tell me
who you are! Who is X?"

He knocked my hands away.
Through gritted teeth, he said, "Look,
you figured out I wasn't a cop pretty
quick. These guys are a bit dim, but
they're gonna get it sooner or later!"

"Now you look. I don't know
whether X is a friend or an enemy.
All I know is he's taken an interest
in me and has me followed everywhere.
You're gonna tell me who he is before
I let you take me into the dragon's
den."

He took off his hat and held it
to his chest. He looked at me
earnestly and said, "If I tell you --"
There was the sound of a gunshot, and
this guy's face exploded right in
front of me. I watched in shock as
his body hit the ground. Inside my
head, I was shouting at myself to run,
but I still stood there looking down
at him. There was a second shot, and
a hole appeared in the shack next to
me.

Whatever spell held me there
broke, and I took off. My right leg
hurt too much to bend, but I ran with

the other leg and swung the right one
stiffly forward, like one man running
in a three-legged race.

I took a turn around the shack,
and zig-zagged, always trying to keep
one of the buildings between me and
the two guys following. In the fog, I
wasn't sure where I was going, but I
had some hope that it was working to
my advantage. I was sure that first
shot that hit X's man was aimed at me,
but they couldn't tell who was who in
the fog.

I broke into an area where I
couldn't see the shadows of any more
shacks looming ahead. It must have
been where the banquet had been set up
a couple nights back. I stopped and
took a rest with my back pressed
against a shack.

"Did I hit him?" I heard Ryder's
voice. He was whispering, but it
carried oddly in the fog. I couldn't
tell for sure which direction it came
from.

Footsteps somewhere nearby. "I

don't know. He can't run far on that
leg anyway."

"The boss isn't going to like
this."

"He's gonna like it even less if
he gets away. We should call and get
everyone down here looking."

I still couldn't be sure, but it
sounded like they were getting further
away. Waiting here for more searchers
to arrive was a bad idea, so I took a
right and ran along the row of shacks.
I stopped again after the third one.
My knee was throbbing with pain.

I gave it a few seconds and tried
to put it out of my mind. Footsteps
came from close by, but trying to
figure out where they were was just
making me paranoid. Better to be shot
trying to get away than cowering in
the dark.

I rushed across the vast open
space. There was gravel under my
feet. Anyone who knew the area and
was paying attention would have heard
the difference in my footsteps and
known where I was. I hobbled faster
so as to get back to the more
ubiquitous sounds of muddy ground.

When I saw the shacks on the other side loom ahead of me, it was a relief. I zig-zagged through them again and took another rest against a pallet-wood shack. That was too much exertion for a guy with two cracked ribs. Every breath ended in stabbing pain.

A flashlight beam illuminated the shack next to mine and swept away. Either they picked up the one that X's man dropped, or there were more than just the two of them searching now. How long had I rested for? I probed tenderly at my knee. It was now swollen and stiff as well as pulsing with pain.

I looked up. The fog was obscuring things at ground level, but the clouds above had moved on. I could make out a few of the brighter stars, and ahead of me, I could see part of the big dipper. That meant I knew which way was north, and better yet, which way was northeast. Because that's where Pioneer Square was, and from there, I could find some place to lay low.

I took off again, with a

direction this time. Purpose drove me despite the pain. I limped on until I got to asphalt, then I crossed the street and used the warehouse wall as support. Once I found a doorway, I leaned against it for another rest.

I wanted to slide down and sit or even lie down, but I knew if I did, I might not get back up. So I stood on my good leg and let the other one just throb while I thought. Where could I go? Oberman had my wallet, so he knew where I lived and worked. If he knew I had escaped, surely, he would send someone there.

Every time a car's headlights came by, I flinched. Jesse said they owned the cops. At least some of them. Were they out looking for me now? Anyone could be one of them. I had to rest up and heal, but not here. Not in the open. The only safe place I could think of was Delaney's. I might be able to make it, but I would sure look a fright. With all the attention on my leg, I had forgotten about my cracked skull. I put a hand to my head and found my hair caked in drying blood.

I heard footsteps on the pavement somewhere nearby and knew I had to move again.

I did my best to walk normally, so the sound of my odd gate and one scraping leg wouldn't give me away, but I couldn't keep it up. My only hope was that whoever else was out there was having just as much trouble locating sounds in the fog.

I ran. Their advantage was that I didn't know how many of them there were, but my advantage was that nobody knew the city better. I've made it my business to know my way around Seattle. So now that I knew where I was, I could take all the back alleys.

Every time a door banged open, or heels clicked on pavement, or a car passed by, I hid. But I got there. I could see the word 'Delaney's' writ large in neon even through this pea soup. Suddenly, the feeling possessed me that they would know I'd come here, and they would be waiting. I gave it a moment, leaning against a car parked across the street. No sound of footsteps came this way. There were no telltale glowing cigarette ends in

any of the dark shadows that
surrounded me.

I picked my moment and crossed
the street. If they came and got me,
it would be with cheap scotch warming
my belly.

Once inside, I shot past my usual
spot at the bar, and instead, took a
booth at the back of the room. I
didn't want my back to the door
tonight.

I thanked Providence for the dim
lighting back here and put my right
leg up on the seat of the booth. I
assessed my overall state of health,
touching anything that was sore,
starting from my head on down. There
was a split on my head that was going
to need stitches. There was no way I
was going to a hospital, though. I
just about laughed, picturing myself
at home with the sewing kit in front
of the mirror. By the time I was
drunk enough not to feel the pain of
the needle, I wouldn't be able to sew
straight. Before that, I would need a
good wash. There was no mistaking

this blood for Dapper Dan pomade.

Lower down. My eye would likely be bruised, but it didn't seem cut, and I could still see out of it fine. Next was my jaw. It crackled a bit when I moved it side to side, but all my teeth were still where they ought to be. It was puffy and tender on the left side, but I'd live.

The shoulder was going to ache in the morning, but I could move it okay, and miraculously, my collarbone seemed fine.

I poked a couple fingers into my ribs. That was a bad idea. I ran my finger along one side to the sternum, where it ended abruptly and painfully. Didn't look like they caught my lung on that side, but they weren't where they ought to be.

With all the other pain I had, my stomach muscles were almost a delight. Finally, I rolled up my pant leg to look at my knee. That was also a mistake because I wasn't sure I'd get the pant leg back down over it. It was easily double its normal size and a bright red and purple. It would need ice and a week without walking, which it wasn't going to get.

Peggy came by and sat a scotch on the rocks in front of me. "Rough night?" she asked.

I drained the drink and pushed it back across to her. "Another," I said.

"Maybe I should leave the bottle," she said.

"Better not. Someone else is walking around with my wallet right now. I got nothing to pay you with."

"Alright. One more. On the house." She turned to go.

"Thanks, doll," I said. "Hey, hold up. Could I get some ice for my knee?"

She looked over the table at the raw meat I had on display and winced. "Be right back."

The door opened, and I jumped. I looked around for anything I could use as a weapon, but the only thing in reach was the candle on my table. I supposed in a pinch, hot wax could be a deterrent, but not as good as hot lead.

A sailor walked in with a working girl and took a booth by the door.

They looked drunk already. I relaxed a bit.

Peggy was back. She set another scotch in front of me, then handed me a bundle of ice cubes in a dishtowel. She made a move to sit down beside me. "Not right now, doll. I'm not glad company, and I need time to think."

She looked offended, of course, paused there, halfway to sitting. I didn't tell her, but I didn't want her hit by any stray bullets should the wrong person step through that door. Finally, she shrugged. "Suit yourself." She walked over to the sailor's table and took their order instead.

I watched the door for the next few hours, certain that at any moment, it would fly open, and gunmen would start spraying the place Chicago style. I nursed the scotch all night, and despite what Peggy had said, she kept refilling it way past the first.

Who did the club have working for them? Was it really the whole department or was it just the chief? And how strong a hold was that, really? I've known him for a long

time, and even though I don't like him
much, he's always been straight with
me. I never suspected he would take
grift. Maybe he'd be willing to look
the other way over zoning or
something, but attempted murder? Of
course, eight thousand was a lot of
grift. I might be on the run until
this whole thing goes one way or the
other.

　　And who else? He mentioned
judges and lawyers. What do they need
them for? Ruminating on that one for
a while, I couldn't come up with much
besides the usual need for a lawyer.
And newspapers. It was definitely
plural. I got a picture of a payout
to the editor of the Washington New
Dealer, but there were a lot more
pages in that ledger, and the Post-
Intelligencer could have been on it.
Even if I got this information to
Brian, would his editor publish it?

　　And who was this damned X?
Coming away from Post Alley, I had
thought it was a joke played by either
Mike or Brian, but not anymore. We
had people dying because of him, and
whether he's helping me or not, I

couldn't side with that. If it was one of them, that scared me because it meant I didn't really know them like I thought I did, and I needed to rely on them both. And if it wasn't them, I had no clue who it could be as they were the only ones I told about the club. On the other hand, maybe X has been following me for longer than that. Bowerman set me on this course originally, and he certainly had the resources, but I couldn't figure out the motive. And something told me X wasn't as yellow as Bowerman turned out to be.

I kept getting interrupted by the thought of people tossing my apartment. I had a thing or two hidden away, and maybe that was safe, but all those negatives were still hanging over my bathroom sink. If that's all I had that they would consider proof, then I was nowhere. Not to mention, I didn't have a camera to get more with.

Somehow, I missed last call because Peggy came over and sat down with me. "Time to kick you out, Drake." It was time to kick everyone out.

"Give me a few more minutes, Peggy. I can't go home. I've got to figure this out."

"I can't let you stay here, Drake. It's the law."

"You didn't care much about that law when it was the Eighteenth Amendment, did you?"

She gave me a look that could peel paint off walls.

"I'm sorry, Peggy. That was rude. I don't know why I said it. I'm just desperate."

"Don't you have anywhere else you can go? A friend? Maybe Mike?"

"No, not Mike." The more I thought about it, the more it seemed he must be X. "Especially not Mike. Don't ask me why."

"Geez, Drake, you don't even have a car to sleep in." She leaned forward for a good look and reached over to touch the wound on my head. I pulled away, and she put her hand down.

"You should be in a hospital. Tell you what. Why don't you let me drive you to Harborview?"

The club had doctors on the take too. Maybe they were there to stitch up their own, no questions asked, but just maybe, they were there to inform someone if a guy like me came in. "No, Peggy, I can't trust the hospitals either right now."

"Whatever you stepped in, you sank up to the knees, didn't you, Drake?"

"You could say that, Peggy. You could definitely say that."

She finished off my drink for me, then got out of the booth and stood up. She looked me up and down, but this time, she wasn't looking at my injuries, she was looking somehow deeper than that. "You know, I haven't had a man stay over since Pete died?"

"No, Peggy, I couldn't ask you to--"

"You didn't ask. And you're not saying no, either. You can't stay here, and I can't send you out there knowing you might not make it back. You still owe me for that bottle, after all. Come on. You can help me lock up.

She drove me to her apartment in her old beater pickup. She had the same one since her husband and she first drove out here from the Midwest. They were barely even kids and freshly married. Pete and Peggy had all the hope in the world, and all their lives ahead of them. They sank what little money they had into the bar, and did okay for themselves, even talked about starting a family. But most of all, they had both just fallen in love with the Emerald City.

All that had been before the draft.

I knew all this before, of course. My father used to bring my brother and me here back in the day. Pete started me off on soda water and cherry syrup. Even Jack had been too young for the hard stuff by the time they shipped him and Pete off to war. I was a young man in the academy, having moved on to scotch and coming to Delaney's on my own when my father died. I practically grew up in the place.

The regulars in her bar like to talk though, and even though I was barely walking when the war broke out, and still in my early teens at armistice, I've heard the war stories a hundred times since then.

All the men that came back from the war when Pete didn't had something to say about him. When they found out who I was, most of them had something to say about my brother too. It wasn't possible, of course. Jack and Pete served on different fronts entirely, but to hear the stories, every man in that bar fought with both of them.

Strangely enough, anybody much younger than me assumed that I fought in the war, and they would ask me for stories when they got drunk enough. I guess the new generation isn't any good at math, just like the old men say.

Still, Peggy felt like talking about Pete while we drove. That was fine by me because I could do my thinking uninterrupted and still nod and laugh and comment at all the right parts.

When we got there, she wouldn't let me in until I'd taken off my shoes, and even then, she made me stand in the entryway, holding my muddy jacket inside out while she went off looking for something I could wear.

She came back holding a man's night clothes, neatly folded, as if they had been there in that drawer next to hers for the last twenty years. She pointed me toward the bathroom. "You can wash up and change in there. Just leave the muddies in the tub. I don't plan on being at the bar until eleven. I'll see if I can do something about it in the morning."

The shower felt incredible. Getting all the caked-on blood off me, and the smells of mud and shack and food truck... I put the water on nearly searing, and let it pummel all the painful spots. I left that shower nearly a new man.

I'd managed to get my split skull bleeding again, and I had toilet paper stuck to the cut when I emerged from the bathroom wearing Pete's gray pajama suit. It appeared that he and

I were a near-perfect fit.

Best case scenario as I'd imagined it was that when I would come out, she would have the couch made up to sleep on, with a blanket and a pillow, but that's not what happened.

Peggy was standing just outside the bathroom door in a white nightgown. She breathed in deeply and bit her lip when she saw me standing there in her husband's clothing, lit from behind by the bathroom fixture. I couldn't say for sure if she really saw me there, or maybe just Pete, but I'm pretty sure she had been waiting for this view for twenty years.

You'll forgive me if I skip forward a bit. You either know what happens when a man and a woman find themselves alone in a stressful situation, with nothing but each other for comfort, or you're too young to be reading this anyway.

In retrospect, I also feel I have to say that this isn't the sort of thing I do on a regular basis. I'm not trying to say it was my first time, but I had always been in a relationship with the girl before.

This time, it just sort of happened.

I had a dream worth mentioning, though. I was back in the morgue, but I was alone this time. I approached the second table on the left and pulled back the sheet.

There was Laslop, peacefully resting on the cold metal slab. I came around the table to see him better. His eyes opened, and I jumped back, banging into the next table. Laslop sat up and turned toward me.

The room around me grew dark and cold. The light grew dimmer until I couldn't see anything. I was close to panic, but I felt there was a reason for all this; that he wanted to tell me something. I remembered something my grandmother used to say: "The dead don't speak in words."

I put my hands out in front of me to ward him off in the darkness, then I heard the sound of a match head striking against sandpaper.

It lit up, just a spec of light. Just enough to show his fingers. He brought it up to his face to light a cigarette. The only thing I could see of Bill Laslop was his eyes.

I sat up in bed, heart racing in the darkness, but absolutely certain who had been in Post Alley with me that night. I needed to break into his place, see if he had anything there that would lead me to X.

I couldn't say for sure whether it was the dream or what Peggy and I had just done, but I suddenly had hope again.

Chapter Nine

Peggy sewed my head up in the morning. Ironically, the bar owner didn't keep any alcohol in her apartment, so I was without anesthetic. She did have a bottle of aspirin, though, and I took about ten of those once she was done.

She cleaned the rented suit as well. It was still damp when I put it on, but the sun was bright that morning, and it would dry. I couldn't bend my right knee, but it could stand some pressure. I could walk okay.

We didn't talk about what happened the night before. She made breakfast for one, and I understood what that meant. She was talkative on all sorts of other subjects, so I didn't get the impression that she regretted anything, just that whatever it was, it was done.

I left her place, heading toward my apartment, but thinking about Laslop. It turns out, Bowerman must have been telling the truth. His goons weren't the last ones to see Laslop alive, I was. He was alive when he left Post Alley, and the B.O.U. wasn't after me at that point. The only other person who knew he was there was this mysterious X. He had done the job he was hired to do, but he knew too much about X, so he had to go.

I was getting near my place, so I got my mind on the immediate job. After my escape last night, the BOU would probably have all its resources looking for me, and they had my wallet with my address. There was a good chance someone was there now, and a near certainty that they had been. I

crossed the tracks and cut up
alongside St. James Cathedral instead
of turning on Ninth.

It turned out I was right to be
nervous. There was a sedan across the
street with two men inside watching
the entrance. I went around the back
instead and climbed the fire escape.
I keep the window locked, but I also
keep a handy tool nearby for unlocking
it. It looks just like a label for my
potted oregano, but pull it from the
soil, and it will slide between the
panes nicely. Better than any
switchblade and leaves no marks
behind. Instead of putting it away
when I was done, I stuck it in my
pocket. I might need it to get into
Laslop's.

Once inside, I found the place
ransacked. The butcher paper was torn
from my bathroom window, and all my
photos were ashes in the waste can.
Whoever hit the place was thorough.
I'm guessing a cop did it because they
knew all the little places to look.
They had pulled the lid off the toilet
tank and searched under the flapper.
Everything was pulled out of the oven,

and it was pulled away from the wall. That part was okay. I never used it for cooking or storing secrets in. It was there more for ambiance.

The vent cover was torn out of the wall too, and that one did bother me. Would it have killed them to use a screwdriver? There was one in the top drawer in the kitchen, though I could see that someone had kindly spilled those out onto the floor. Pillows and couch cushions were everywhere, and they had taken a knife to both the couch decking and the mattress.

I picked up my screwdriver and dragged my chair, which had mercifully been spared the knife, over to the center of the room. I stood on the chair and unscrewed the overhead light fixture. I pulled it out of the ceiling and let it dangle from the wires, then reached inside the hole and retrieved a bundle wrapped in chamois. After putting the bundle in my jacket pocket, I screwed the fixture back into place. I carefully positioned both the chair and screwdriver exactly where I'd found them, then pulled the bundle back out of my pocket and unfolded the chamois.

The barrel of my brother's service revolver glinted in the light, as pristine as the day I had put it up there. They say that metal doesn't have a smell, but that's baloney. And gun metal has a particular scent that's part cold iron and part warm oil. I've always been both attracted to and afraid of that smell. It makes you feel stronger. It makes you want to use it because the smell is missing something. Because the smell of spent gunpowder completes it. I pulled back the catch and flicked out the cylinder. Five bullets, and one empty chamber. The gun hadn't been fired since I'd inherited it. I had no replacements either. If I had to shoot more than five times, I was going to be out of luck.

I flicked it back into place and rolled the cylinder across my arm. It spun freely and clicked invitingly. I wrapped it back up and jammed it into my pocket. I didn't need it now, but I might later. The next time someone pulled a gun on me, I wanted to return the sentiment.

After changing into my own clothes, I slipped back out the window and used my little tool to replace the window catch. Climbing down the fire escape with a stiff knee was harder than climbing up, but I managed it. I went east a block, then south another before heading west toward Laslop's place. The two men were still out in front of the apartment in their sedan. Only now, one of them was sleeping with his mouth hanging open, and his hat pushed forward over his eyes. The other one was still watching the apartment entrance and didn't notice me crossing in front of them a block away.

Laslop's apartment was all the way down on First Ave, and there was a lot of open ground between my place and his. In the daylight, and possibly because of the heater in my pocket, I felt braver than I had last night. That being said, I was still exposed. There were too many cops who had paid too much attention to me over the years, and if any of them were in the club's pockets, this would be a much shorter walk than I intended.

The street I was on ran past the station, so I cut over to the next. I continued my zig-zag route until at Spring Street, I went around to the back of Laslop's apartment. I should have known. The street behind his place was Post--a few blocks further north it turned into Post Alley, the last place I had seen him alive. I'm not usually one to put too much stock in information that comes to me in dreams, but this clinched it. Without a doubt, it was him.

I went in the back entrance and climbed the stairs to the third floor and Laslop's apartment. There were a couple newspapers in front of his door. I picked them up and got out my little tool. Wiggling it up and down, I slid it in between door and jamb until the lock popped, and the door opened. The hall remained empty, so I stepped inside and closed the door behind me.

Aside from being a better part of town and closer to the office, his apartment was just plain nicer than mine. He had a closet just off the front door that was about the size of my bathroom. Inside, he had several coats and an umbrella. I went through the pockets, but the only thing I found was a used handkerchief. The kitchen was also bigger, and his fridge had a freezer on top instead of just an inset icebox like mine. It looked like maybe he used it once in a while too. The countertop had a ceramic vase filled with spatulas, tongs, and a spaghetti spoon. His sink was on a little island that separated the kitchen from the living space.

I looked through all of it, pulling out the drawers and checking for anything taped behind or under them. He had an ancient tub of ice cream in the freezer that I nonetheless opened and checked inside. His utensil caddy held nothing of interest either. Either he was a lot more creative than I am, or he used his kitchen as a kitchen.

He had a bright blue couch and a coffee table in the living room, with

a newspaper spread across the table.
I tossed the two papers I brought with
me onto the table with the first one.
Two rooms connected to this one, the
bedroom and the bathroom. One wall of
the bathroom was a large mirror,
beneath which, a counter ran the
length and contained two sinks. I felt
along the edges for any loose spots
and unscrewed each bulb to check
behind it. Opposite was a bathtub
that was built into the room. A shelf
above the tub was covered in soaps,
shampoos, and cologne bottles.

Either Laslop had someone else
develop his film, or he had a lab
somewhere else because his bathroom
was bright and clean. Everything mine
wasn't. The space beneath the sinks
was filled with towels of various
sizes and a tin of tooth polish. I
checked every one of them and the
toilet tank as well, but no dice.

I made my way into his bedroom.
On the nightstand, he had a lamp, a
phone, and a picture of himself with a
woman. She had her head covered in a
kerchief, and her face was turned in
toward his chest, but I could see the

tail end of a smile on her face. He
seemed happy as well, but his eyes
bore into me. I caught myself making
the sign of the evil eye before
putting the picture back, face down,
and went through his bed. Between the
cushions, he had a switchblade and a
roll of bills. Tempting though it
was, I put the money back. That felt
a little too much like thievery, and I
wasn't robbing a dead man. Who knows
what he had in the way of next of kin,
but I didn't want the man's ghost over
my shoulder for eternity while some
kid somewhere went hungry. I put his
switchblade to good use, though,
peeling away the base of the lamp and
the back of the picture before
unscrewing the ceiling fixture. I
decided to keep the blade. Maybe it
would stop me from ending up like him.
And besides, kids shouldn't play with
knives.

   The nightstand had a drawer that
came next. Inside was a pad of paper
and a pencil. Setting the pad on the
nightstand, I turned on the lamp and
laid the pencil at an angle, gently
rubbed at the top sheet of the pad.

Slowly, a message revealed itself.
"Post Alley, Midnight." Tell me
something I didn't know.

I put the pad and pencil away and
turned off the lamp. Hopefully, the
closet would hold more answers. The
man had six suits. All of them clean
and pressed. I worked above a laundry
and usually looked like I'd been in
the tumble drier wearing my clothes.
His suit pockets were entirely empty.
This trip was a bust. All I got out
of it was a deflated ego and a
switchblade knife.

I crossed the living room to
leave, when I noticed something about
the paper he had out--an article had
been circled in red. Leaning in to
get a closer look, I saw it was about
Mayor Dore's re-election rally. With
everything else going on, I'd
forgotten I wanted to go to that, and
it was at noon today! I pulled out my
father's pocket watch. It was almost
noon now.

I hurried out of my dead rival's
apartment, making sure to lock the
door behind myself.

I still didn't know why the club preferred Seger to Dore, especially when he was so far behind in the polls. But as it was on their calendar, I felt I ought to see Dore's speech anyway, and now that I knew Laslop was interested as well, I had to.

Of course, that's not the sort of place you want to go carrying a gun. I had to stash it somewhere. My first thought was the office, and suddenly I thought of Katie standing there with it turned upside down as badly as my apartment was. No, I couldn't go to the office. It was certainly being watched if it hadn't been burnt to the ground.

What I could do was make sure Katie was okay. I found a payphone in the lobby of the Grand Pacific and dialed the office. "Drake Glover, private investigator," came her voice, high and sweet.

"Katie, it's Drake. Listen, things are going from bad to worse on this Brothers of Unity case. They tried to kill me last night, and now they're looking for me. Aside from the usual thugs, they have cops on the payroll. I'm not coming in, maybe not until I figure this all out."

"Don't you worry, I'll hold down the fort," she said.

"No, that's not what I mean. I want you to make yourself scarce. If they haven't tossed the office, they're going to soon, and I'd rather not have you there when they do it."

"Drake, if two palookas like Bowerman sent aren't going to scare me, you think they get scarier when you squeeze them into a uniform? No, I'll be here. Otherwise, who would answer your phones?"

"Alright then, just don't get in their way. There's nothing in that office worth getting hurt over. If they want my rotgut, you tell them it's in the second drawer."

Katie rang off, saying, "You take care of yourself, too, Drake."

I left the hotel, knowing what I had to do, and not wanting to at all. I briefly considered hiding the gun in some alley, but I couldn't risk a kid finding it and shooting his own eye out. No, it had to be Delaney's.

After last night, and now this, though, Peggy was liable to think that nothing meant something. But I was out of people I could trust, and Delaney's was between here and the rally.

I pushed open the door. The noontime crowd was there, as well as Peggy, of course. She looked surprised to see me, but I motioned for her to join me at the end of the bar, and she played along.

"I've got something for you," I said.

She put a hand on her hip. "Now look, don't go thinking that--"

"I don't. It's not that. I just need you to hold something for a while. Hide it somewhere."

Now she was suspicious. "What kind of something?"

I took the chamois bundle out of my pocket and dropped it in her open palm. The weight and shape of it hit her hand, and her eyes widened. "Is this what I think it is?" I think she intended to whisper it.

"Shh. Yes. Don't worry, it's not a murder weapon or anything. At least, not yet. I'm going to go see the mayor, and I can't have that on me. You've got a storeroom back there, right? Just hold on to it for a couple hours. I'll be back for it."

"You presume too much, Mr. Glover," she said. Her lips had grown thin, and for a moment, I didn't think she'd do it. "I don't want this thing in here a second longer than I have to. Understand me? You come back for it soon, or you might have to chase the garbage trucks to get it."

"If I don't come back for it soon, I probably won't be coming back at all." As soon as the words were out, I wished I could take them back. The look in her eyes was one I could go without seeing for the rest of my life. It was done, though, and I didn't have the words to make it better, so I left. I had somewhere to be.

When I got to the courthouse, I had to push through the crowds of

people already there. A brass band
was playing some rather patriotic
music to get the voters primed for the
mayor's message, leaving me an
opportunity to squeeze ever closer.

I finally got to a position where
I could see the band. Their heads
were visible above the crowd, arranged
around an open area with a microphone
in the center. The microphone carried
the KOMO logo of a local radio
station. It turned out I could have
avoided all this walking if all I'd
wanted to do was listen to the mayor's
speech.

But that was only part of what I
was here for. I wanted to see who was
here with him. If there were any cops
on stage when the mayor arrived, those
were probably men I could trust. I
wanted to get a feel for the crowd
too. There were a lot of people here,
and he still enjoyed a sizable lead in
the polls.

I turned in place while the band
played, mainly looking for any
familiar lapel buttons. Oberman had
this time and the mayor's name circled
on the calendar for a reason. So I

expected, if not Oberman himself, then at least a number of club members.

The crowd was mostly men, a mix of negroes and whites. Some looked like they'd been jobless for a while. I recognized the gaunt frames under suits a size or two larger than they needed. I became aware again that without my camera and my P.I. license, I was technically one of them.

Lots of campaign buttons, 'Two More for Dore' and the like, but I didn't see any of those small brass pins I was looking for.

The tune changed, and I turned back around toward the musicians who were playing the mayor onto the stage. Some folks, mainly toward the front, began cheering. While the back of the room was more of a mix of yelling and cheering. I glanced back to see a number of policemen removing protesters from the foyer.

The mayor approached the microphone, holding his hands up in acknowledgment of the crowd. He smiled and waved a bunch, pointing at various people in the crowd. The usual. The band finished playing its bit, and after another minute or so, the crowd died down, and the mayor could speak.

"I'd like to thank you all for being here today. In these hard times, it means a lot to have the support of the people behind me. When you look around the nation, you see the same story repeated in city after city. And when you look at it from that angle, Seattle is doing pretty well."

It was about then I tuned him out and started watching the crowd again instead. If someone were to ask me my opinion of the speech, about all I could say was the band was pretty good.

Still no Brothers of Unity pins. Maybe they just wouldn't be wearing them to the rally, or maybe they really weren't there. That seemed odd, though. There were a number of cops present in and around the constituents. They looked like crowd control, though they weren't doing anything to keep the people back. We were pressed in like sardines.

Then I noticed a man three down

from me. Sweat was forming a sheen
across his bald head despite the chill
in the early Spring air. His coat was
dirty and frayed, and I could see bare
skin underneath. Either he didn't
have a shirt or it was in even worse
condition. I caught a glance at his
feet, and his shoes were more
cardboard than leather.

He had to be a resident of
Hooverville. While Dore's policies
weren't directly opposed to the
interests of the unemployed masses,
this man still stuck out like a corn
stalk in a strawberry field.

He seemed to jump every time the
crowd swayed and someone touched him.
He was mumbling something to himself,
and his eyes kept darting around the
room. I switched places with the guy
beside me, hoping to hear what the man
was saying. He was still too far
away.

There was only one guy between me
and Mr. Sweaty now. I tried to push
past him, and he pushed back
impatiently. The man had his neck
craned to see the mayor and wore a pin
that read, 'Re-elect Dore.'

Mayor Dore must have said something inspiring because a cheer went up through the crowd. Mr. Sweaty continued to mumble and only put his hands in his pockets, but the man between us joined the crowd in clapping, and I tried to get behind him this time. He turned toward me, putting a palm on my broken ribs, and shoved me backward. "Buzz off!" he said.

Just as the crowd noise had died down, and before the mayor started speaking again, Mr. Sweaty yelled, "Sick center tyrannosaur!" He pushed the person in front of him out of the way, but he was struggling to get his right hand out of his pocket. I could now see the shape of the gun in there, and the hammer was catching on a tear in the fabric.

Ignoring the pain in my chest, I shoved hard against the man between us and dove for Mr. Sweaty. The crowd gave way, and screams filled the air as the gun came out.

I grabbed his arm with both hands and pushed downward. I got my shoulder in his chest, and the two of us went down.

The gun went off.

It was still pointed toward the floor, and the bullet dug a gouge out of the marble. I looked along its path for where it might have ricocheted. People were diving for cover everywhere, and the crowd was pushing for the exits, trying to get away. Up on the stage, a couple of the mayor's aides were rushing him out the back.

The shooter kept trying to raise his arm off the floor, and he was winning. I switched tactics and lifted it up. Once it was pointing at the ceiling, I figured it was safe. I caught his arm in the crook of mine and wedged his elbow in place so he couldn't move it. He fired again, right next to my ear, deafening me on that side.

Next thing I knew, four policemen were there. They pulled me off the man forcibly. I went sprawling on the floor and watched them start beating the man with their clubs.

They broke his arm, and the gun went spinning across the floor. After

a crack to the head, the man was
entirely submissive. He screamed and
begged for them to stop. After a
second wallop, he was out like a
light, but they kept on beating him.

I regained my feet and yelled for
them to stop. "I have questions for
this man!" I said, reaching out for a
cop's shoulder. The cop turned and
gave me one across the skull.

There was a moment there where
the world tilted, and I couldn't hear
anything but the ringing in my left
ear. The cop went back to beating the
other guy in slow motion. I think I
yelled something, but no sound was
coming out. The floor was coming up
toward me.

Mike was there, holding my
shoulders and shouting something at
me. I thought I was imagining it
because he was in uniform, which I
don't think he's worn in a decade.
Perhaps I was seeing things because of
the blow to the head.

He pulled me away from the scene.
It looked like the foyer was filled
with cops now, running back and forth,
while those first four continued to

beat the unconscious man.
    The world went black.

Chapter Ten

I woke up in the back of Mike's car. My head was pounding, and it took me a moment to realize I was even awake. I sat upright and looked around. We were parked in the lot overlooking Alkai Beach.

Mike was staring at me from the front seat of the car, and I looked questioningly back at him, holding up my handcuffed wrists.

"They're saying you had something to do with that," he said.

"Yeah, in case you didn't see, I

stopped him killing the mayor," I said. I put a hand to the side of my head. It was tender there, but the stitches weren't broken. My ear still felt like it needed to pop, and I exercised my jaw, trying to fix it.

"So, what was it then, Drake? Cold feet? Second thoughts? You just couldn't go through with it?"

I paused what I was doing. "What are you talking about, Mike?"

"Oh, come on, Drake, you're smarter than that! You've been obsessing over this guy Seger for the last several days, and now you show up at the mayor's speech, and there's a shooting! Drake, they're calling you an accomplice. I'm supposed to be bringing you in!"

"You don't believe that, do you, Mike? We've known each other for a long time. I may be a lot of things, but I'm not an assassin!"

"Are you, Drake?"

That was a slap to the face. Of all the cops on the force, he was the only one who vouched for me, but it turns out even he didn't believe me.

"This is about my father's

murderer then, is it? Well, if you
don't believe me, saying it again
won't change things, but I did not
throw him in front of that trolley."

"I don't know what to believe!
You were talking yesterday about
rigging the election. Is that why you
showed up at the rally today?"

"Yes, but I'm not the one rigging
anything, I came to stop it! To find
out what they were up to! It's this
club!"

"Oh, there you go with that club
again! If there even is such a club."

"What's that supposed to mean?" I
asked.

"It means, I can't find any
'Brothers of Unity.' I had someone
check the records. There's no
registration with the city, and it's
not a local non-profit."

"And what does that mean?"

"It means it doesn't exist!
Drake, I'm worried about you. If
you've been making all this up while
getting involved in a plot to kill the
mayor, and you try to blame it on this
non-existent club, they're gonna lock
you up in the looney bin."

I sat forward in the seat. "No, you've got to believe me. I was there because I was worried this club might try something in public. When I saw the shooter, he was sweating like the groom at a shotgun wedding, and he was mumbling something to himself. That's why I was looking his way when he drew the gun, that's how I got there in time to stop him!"

"What was that he shouted just before shooting?"

"Sic Semper Tyrannis. It's Latin. 'Thus, always to tyrants.' Or at least that's what he was trying to say--but that's more proof! Someone told him what to say and gave him the gun, but he got it all wrong. He'd never shot one before -- he had no idea what he was doing! And all that mumbling was just him trying to remember the words, but he screwed them up! He had no idea what those words meant."

I realized by Mike's lack of reaction that he had no idea what it meant either. "It's what Brutus said after the Roman Senate killed Julius Caesar. Then John Wilkes Booth said it after shooting Lincoln. But that's not important. What's important is this guy is a patsy. You've got to let me talk to him."

"Even if I wanted to, there's no way you're going to get to him."

"Oh, would you forget the ribbing you get from the guys for the moment? This is serious! They tried to kill the mayor, and no one even knows they exist except for the members!"

"It's not that. I was listening to the police radio on the way over here. The guy's been taken to Harborview in a coma. He's probably not going to make it through the night."

"Damn it!" Of course, they had to make it so he wouldn't talk. The hope was probably that after he killed the mayor, one of the cops would just kill him. Nice and tidy, but I got in the way. Then I remembered the ricochet. "He got two shots off. Did anyone get hurt?"

"A tuba took one between the eyes." He shrugged. "Other than that, a bit of plaster needs to be replaced."

"Okay, good. You've got to at least find out who he was. I'd bet my life savings he lived in Hooverville. Maybe someone saw how he got the gun."

"I know how to do my job, Drake. If I end up with the assignment, I'll get to the bottom of it."

"Alright, sorry. Then I'll talk to Bowerman. I might be able to get him to turn on the others. He wouldn't have the guts to take part in an assassination."

"Bowerman's a dead-end too. He's lawyered up. He sent a high-price suit to the station, threatening to sue the city. He says you broke into his house, caused some property damage, and threatened him."

"That, I did do. A bit. But only after he beat his wife. And I left him a fair deal better off than he left her."

"If I put men in jail for laying hands on their wives, I'd be locking up half the city."

We locked eyes in silence with only seagulls interrupting before Mike finally spoke. "Here, let me get those cuffs off. But you lay off

Bowerman."

"Whatever you say."

"Get out," he said as soon as the cuffs were off.

"Here? It'll take me forever to get somewhere useful."

"Exactly the point. I'm going to have to say you got away. They're going to be looking for you, but probably not way out here."

I reluctantly got out of the car.

He leaned across and rolled down the passenger window. "You'd better be right. And you'd better wrap this up quick. If anyone suspects my involvement with you, it'll be the end of my career."

A stroke of genius occurred to me, and I dug the club pin out of my pocket. "Here. Put this on your lapel and see what that does for your career. It will be interesting to see what people start saying around you, especially the chief."

He took the pin but didn't immediately wear it. "Be careful, Drake. All the boys know you, and some of them have been gunning for you for years." With that, he drove off,

leaving me to a long walk back on a
stiff leg.

I was in a real jam, and that
wasn't even counting the long walk
back. It was one thing to have the
resources of the club after me, now,
even the cops that have nothing to do
with the club were out to get me, and
I had nothing to defend myself with
but a dead man's switchblade.

They burned my negatives, the
only proof I had, and without my
camera, I wasn't going to get more. I
had to figure out another way to prove
this conspiracy. And if I didn't find
a way to implicate the chief, I would
have a hard time clearing my name.
That was going to be a much harder job
now. There was no way I was going to
get anywhere near the club, and even
if I did, I'm sure they've hidden the
ledger, and probably the map as well.
What else would they have of value?

No, that line of thinking wasn't
doing me any good.

I found myself standing on the
street corner looking across the West

Spokane Street Bridge. There were
only two ways out of West Seattle, and
one was a couple hours walk south.
Since I needed to get back north,
let's call it number one option.
Spokane Street had a bridge over to
Harbor Island, and a second one off
the other side and onto the mainland.

If anyone had spotted me, all the
cops needed to do was block off either
of these bridges, and that would be
that for me. If one of them even
spotted me out on patrol while I
crossed the bridge, I would have
nowhere to go but over the side. I
took a look over the railing,
preparing myself to make a jump if I
saw any squad cars. There was no
chance of survival though. It was a
thirty-foot drop to low tide on the
Duwamish River, and the muddy bottom
was only a few feet below the surface.
Anyone who fell in there would stick
in the mud up to their waist, with the
water rising to just over their head.

I had to quell the instinct to
hurry across too. My stiff leg meant
that my walk would tend to grab
attention. It was best to take it

slowly and casually. I wished I at least had Joe's coat and hat. I lost my own hat somewhere along the line, probably when that cop brained me, but they would be looking for my coat.

I considered tossing it into the Duwamish but decided against it. There was a bitter wind, as there often is along this stretch, and the clouds looked like they could open up at any minute.

There was nothing to do but push through, so I steeled my nerve and made the crossing.

When I reached the other end, I realized I'd been holding my breath the entire time. I didn't see any cops, and it didn't look like anyone was paying me any particular attention. Still, I was real nervous, and now that I was on Harbor Island, I could get off Spokane Street. I took side streets around the southern point of the island, coming back up to Spokane right at the east side bridge.

It was a longer stretch, so a bigger risk. On the other hand, the bridge was closer to the water's surface, and the river didn't look so deep on this side. If I jumped, there was at least a chance I'd make it. I still wouldn't want to be stuck in the mud with my head just above water, waiting for the cops to come collect me, or the tide to come in, whichever was first. I decided that would be a last resort, and a desperate one at that.

Just as I steeled myself and stepped onto the bridge, I spotted a squad car at the far end, coming this way. I quickly turned north instead toward the Duthie Shipyard, where a group of men was gathered seeking work for the day.

The moment the squad car passed, I headed back for the bridge. Having seen one bull in his bucket, what were the chances there would be another before I managed the span?

Halfway across, I found out they were pretty good. Another one heading into West Seattle. Maybe Mike figured I'd be gone by now and had let them know where I 'escaped.' Maybe I would have been if not for my knee. Either way, turning around at this point would probably be worse for me. I glanced over the side, but a dip in the drink had little appeal. My best bet would be to play it cool and hope he didn't notice me.

As we approached, I kept my head angled toward the ground ahead of me, but I watched that driver like a hawk. When I saw his eyes widen in recognition, I ran, bum leg or no.

He angled the car in and came up onto the sidewalk. I hopped over the fender while he was still opening the door. I recognized the bull driving -- a Johnny, or Joey or something. Always standing near the water cooler with a story to tell, mostly involving leggy blondes. He also joined the other cops in looking down his nose at me, even though he didn't know me. I didn't like him. His passenger was a stranger to me, but by the looks of it, he wanted to be a cop mostly for the doughnuts. I slammed into his door, forcing it back shut on him as I sped past.

"Stop where you are!" I heard Joey yelling from behind me. That was good. It meant I had a few more seconds. He would either have to draw

his heater or come around the car to
give chase, while his partner was
still wrestling with the door.

"Stop or I'll shoot!" My time
was up, but I'd made it across the
river. Over the side of the rail was
the steep incline of the riverbank,
and I dove for it. I heard two
bullets ring off the truss behind me
as the ground came up to meet me. I
rolled onto my side and crashed into
the scrub brush. The idea was to
spare my throbbing knee, but I ended
up reminding myself about the broken
ribs.

The brambles tore at my clothes
and skin as I scrambled up the side.
The abandoned buildings of the old saw
mill were ahead of me, and my best bet
was to get to them before the shooting
started back up.

The seconds wore on me. It was
taking me too long to get behind a
building. My leg just wasn't capable
of taking this much use, and I was
limping hard. But the bullets never
came. I realized Joey had opted to
call in for backup rather than chase
after me. It wouldn't be long until

every squad car in the city was at the
Elliott Bay Saw Mill, and I had to
keep moving to stay ahead of them.
Still, I needed a moment before basic
biology failed me.

I finally got around the corner
of the closest building, and I put my
back to it so I could massage a bit of
life into my swollen knee.

It turned out I didn't get more
than a moment to rest.

The mill closed down in 1930, but
people, probably the men of
Hooverville, had broken in and stolen
the door off one of the pulping vats
and a number of other large pieces of
metal, so they sold a lot of the
equipment to another mill. Kids and
vandals took over next, broke most of
the windows and painted graffiti all
over. So the owners hired a few men
with a penchant for cruelty, gave them
some heavy clubs and declared them
guards.

Two such fellows came upon me
leaning against the wall of the drying
house and started running at me from
opposite directions. One of them was
blocking my way east, so I had to run

north instead.

My knee screamed at me, and I did my best not to rely on it too much. But I had to get around the next corner before the closer of the two men caught up with me. I made it okay and came to a stop in the shadow of the building, then put out my arm to clothesline my pursuer. He ran straight into it, and crashed down onto his back, dropping his bat. I picked it up and gave him one to the stomach that knocked the wind right out of him. Then I limped off again at full speed.

The second guard stopped for a bare moment when he ran across the first one, but it wasn't much of a lead. Then a third guard came into view ahead of me, and I had to swing back toward the north again.

Now I was out in the open, with two men twice as fast as me coming up fast, and in the best-case scenario, I still had to climb a chain link fence with a busted knee. At the rate they were gaining, though, I wasn't going to make it.

Then a shot rang out, and a chunk

flew up from the tarmac a good ten
feet from me. Joey had started
shooting again, but he'd never hit me
at this distance. The guards giving
chase pulled back at the sound of
gunfire, though, and started looking
around for the source.

A second shot hit the ground way
off to my right, but I never stopped
running for the fence. The guards
started after me again, but by then, I
was going to make it. I leaped up
onto the fence as high as I could, and
I got my bad leg up on top, then I
pulled myself up and rolled over. I
managed to land on my good leg, but I
still felt the pain shoot up my bad
one.

The guards crashed into the
fence, banging their clubs impotently
on the chain link and yelling at me to
stay away. They said they would
remember me. I bet they would.

Joey came running down the
tarmac, no sign of his partner,
though. "Police!" he yelled. "Get
out of the way!" He was still trying
to get a clear shot at me. Made me
wonder whether taking me alive was

even on the table anymore.

The two guards moved in opposite directions. When one of them went toward the east, I went too, using him for cover and following the fence line down behind Kilbourne & Clark's, also abandoned, but without the money to afford guards.

There was a set of tracks just past their manufacturing plant, and a train was coming in at just that time. It was slowing down to stop at the shipping yards north of here, and the opportunity to take a rest and keep moving at the same time was too tempting. I caught a handrail and swung onboard to collapse on the open bed.

I sat up and watched Kilbourne & Clark's recede into the distance. There was no sign of Joey or the guards trying to follow. Even if they did, the train ended a couple cars behind me, and they were unlikely to catch up on foot.

I turned my attention to my leg, which had swollen and badly needed icing. It was tender to the touch and wasn't going to take much more running. I tried to massage a little life back into it and happened to glance up as the train was passing the Hanford Street Pier.

A group of workers was standing around on the dock, a job which paid better than most. A couple of them were pointing at me, and I could just make out someone shouting. One of the men started running toward a small booth that had telephone lines coming from it. They were calling the cops.

I didn't know if they recognized me from some news report, or whether they accorded the same treatment to any old bindlestiff riding the iron. But I did know that half the force would be there when this train came to a stop. I was in no hurry to put weight on this knee again, but it had to be done.

Just past the docks, some sickly bushes grew, and I rolled off the train using them as cover. I got carefully to my feet and pushed through the bushes to the open area on the other side.

I was back in Hooverville once again. I had done my best over the previous several years to avoid this place at all costs, but here I was again, for the third time in a week. Still, it was better here, where I could cross a lot of territory without scrutiny, than on the streets where every cop on the force, except for Mike, was out looking for me. I wondered idly, whether the chief had ordered the men to arm themselves, and if so, how many of them would shoot me without a second thought?

I carefully wound my way through the trash heaps, the cattails, and the makeshift houses. I took my time. With any luck, I'd have a plan before I came out the other side.

I wasn't going near Queen Anne again. That much was decided. Maybe it was time to look into this Lonnie Seger. Was he strictly the beneficiary of the club's actions here, or was he in cahoots with them this whole time?

It was hard to believe the club was going to these lengths, trying to get the man elected, and he had no

idea of their nefarious methods. No,
I'd never met the man, but I was
pretty sure he stank.

So I had a plan, or at least the
framework for a plan, and I wasn't yet
through most of Hooverville. Things
were looking up already.

Now it was just the simple matter
of figuring out where Seger lived,
breaking into his place, finding
damning information, not only on him
but also on Chief Sears. Then exposing
that information to papers, getting
them to print it even though they're
probably somewhere in that ledger, and
Bob's your uncle. My name would be
cleared.

Okay, I wasn't buying it either.
Since when did things go so right for
me?

I suddenly I felt eyes on me.
Spinning around, I didn't see anyone.
It wasn't Joey because he wouldn't be
hiding, he'd be shooting. Was it
another of X's men, following me?
They seemed to always know where I'd
be before I did.

So far as I could tell, I was
alone out there, but the feeling

didn't leave me. I stood in place, peering into the tall grasses, and into the shadows on the North sides of shacks. There was no movement, other than the wind through the weeds. Many of the shacks had small windows cut out of them. Anybody could be watching me from inside one of them, and now I was behaving suspiciously.

Or maybe it was nothing but my nerves running wild with me. No one could blame me; I'd had a hard couple of days.

I got back to walking, trying to put that feeling out of my mind, but despite my better intentions, I kept succumbing to instinct. I would pass by close to one of the shacks and make a sudden left turn to go down the next row. I even stopped a couple of times, pressed into the shaded area on the side of a shack, and waited to see if anyone would come wandering past.

I was hiding in one such shadow when the door to one of the shacks burst open, and none other than Kowalczyk came backing out of it, hands up defensively.

"Our relationship hasn't

changed," he was saying in his thick accent.

Jesse Jackson came storming out after him. "Like hell, it hasn't! You think I'm stupid? I see what's going on! You and your folks are using us! We had an agreement!"

He kept pressing forward, and the little man kept backing up. He held his hands up to protest, and he kept stammering, looking for a space to get his words in. But Jesse wasn't having it. "There are rules in this place! You didn't respect that, and two men got killed! There's no violence in Hooverville! But you shot a man dead right here on my doorstep!" Doors to many of the shacks were inching open as the residents of Hooverville listened in to the commotion. "Then you get one of my men, and you promise him a job, and what do you do? You make him try to kill a man! And then you beat him to death for doing what you told him to do! Now, you tell me, what kind of influence you got, is gonna bring him back now, huh?"

"The club is ready to offer his family a large sum of money to offset-

_"

"He didn't have no family! That make him any less of a man? And his name was Owen. Owen Miles. He didn't have a violent bone in his body either until you laid your hands on him. Now you take your reparations and get the hell out of here! You tell your masters that the deal is off! Not one man of Hooverville will be voting Seger!"

Jackson spotted a brick lying nearby and stooped down to pick it up. Kowalczyk turned and ran. Jackson stood watching him for a while, then dropped the brick, retreated to his shack, and slammed the metal door behind him.

As soon as Jackson was gone, I left my hiding place and went limping after Kowalczyk. I wasn't sure what I was going to do when I caught up, but I had the sudden urge to talk to him.

He had a head start on me, and I could only see the vague direction where he had gone to, but I hurried to catch up. I came skidding around one of the shacks, then jumped back behind the corner.

There was Henry from last night, with another big bruiser. They were waiting by a car as Kowalczyk approached.

"Boss ain't gonna like this," Henry said. He was standing with one hand on the door latch but didn't open it yet.

Kowalczyk waved it off. "Sir will be fine. We were going to dump Jackson after the election anyway, and we just saved some money."

"But now we ain't got their votes," Henry said, still not opening the door.

"We never needed their votes, you ignoramus. We only ever needed their names."

The big lout opened the door for him then, and Kowalczyk climbed in the back. Henry and the other ignoramus got in the front and drove off.

I stayed where I was for a while, adding this piece to the puzzle that was beginning to take shape in my mind.

Chapter Eleven

I finally made it back to familiar territory and sought out a payphone. I wanted to make sure Katie was alright. After recent events, they had both urgency and legitimacy on their side, and if they hadn't ransacked my office yet, it was only a matter of time.

She picked up on the second ring. "Katie, it's me. You alone?"

"Sure, I'm alone. Why wouldn't I be? I'm glad you called though, I --"

"Hang on," I interrupted. "This

time you've <u>got</u> to get out of there,
alright? It's not just that club's
goons now, the cops are after me as
well." I looked back over my
shoulder. The entryway to the Polson
building was all glass, and the phone
booths were clearly visible from the
street if anyone was looking.

"Geez, Drake, what did you get
yourself into?"

"There was an assassination
attempt on Dore. I stopped the guy
that tried it, but they managed to
spin it around, so the story is I was
there to help him. The cops beat the
gunman to death, so I have no
witnesses to say otherwise. I've got
to get to the bottom of this thing,
and I've got to do it now."

"Okay, Drake, I'll be careful.
But I've got to tell you, Mrs. Noble
has been calling for you. Four times
today -- she's absolutely frantic.
The last time was about an hour ago, I
got her to leave a message with me.
She wants an answer from you. Should
she be worried, yes or no? She also
left her number. She said call her,
no matter what."

She read off the number to me,
but it was the same one Claire had
given me before. I turned and watched
the street as I spoke. I'd already
been there too long, and any cop
heading down to Meridian would pass
right by here. "Alright. I'll call
her. But you get out of the office,
alright? Take a couple days off, in
fact. Call up your son and see what
he's doing, maybe." Another thought
occurred to me. "Hey, just before you
go, could you ring up Mrs. Bowerman at
the Franklin? Tell her I've made some
headway regarding the divorce, but
it's going to take a bit longer.
Remember, you've got to ask for
Prudence Delphine at the desk, then
Marcy when she picks up."

"You've got it, Drake."

We hung up, and I immediately
dialed Mrs. Noble. While the phone
was ringing, I spotted a police car
cruising slowly outside, and I turned
my back toward it.

She picked up the phone. "Noble
residence," she said.

"Hello, Claire, it's Drake
Glover. I understand you've been

calling me."

"Yes, Mr. Glover, I have been, but never mind that now. I would like to thank you, but I won't be requiring your services any longer. You see, since you never phoned back, I had to take matters into my own hands. And I straightened everything out, no thanks to you."

I had a bad feeling about this, and not because I was fired either. "You mean, you confronted your husband, and he told you everything that was going on?"

"No, Mr. Glover, nothing so simple as that. My husband continues to be the soul of discretion, operating under a veil of complete secrecy. But Mr. Mysterio called again, and this time, when I was sent out of the room, I went to the bedroom. And I brought a glass of water with me.

"I drank the water, then put the glass to the wall and listened in. I heard the entire conversation."

"What exactly did you hear, Mrs. Noble?"

"Never you mind that, Mr. Glover,

it's no longer any of your concern."

"Indulge me, please. I want to hear what a good sleuthing job you did." In my previous encounters with her, she talked about dinner parties she would throw and described how fickle her friends were when her monetary status was in question. This summation of her social life had led me to conclude that she rather enjoyed gossiping. She may be holding back at the moment, but inside, she was probably just dying to brag. She should also tend to be susceptible to a bit of ego stroking.

"Well, if you must know, he's going to be out late again tonight. But I found out where he will be, and it's all above board. None of the danger I was worried about. If you were half as good as you claim to be, you would have figured that out by now too."

"And what is your husband going to be doing tonight?" I asked.

"Well, when he picked up the phone, he called the person on the other end, 'sir,'" she started. So, he's the sort to call him sir and not

Ken. "He went on to say, 'Yes, of course I'll be there, I'll bring the plates.' You see, Mr. Glover, he's catering. For huge numbers too. It's a fundraising event for our next mayor, Lonnie Seger. One of those thousand-dollar-a-plate things. Nothing dangerous, wouldn't you agree, Mr. Glover?"

"You say huge numbers. How huge?"

"Well, I must have heard him wrong. I <u>was</u> listening through a wall after all," she said.

"How large, Mrs. Noble?" I persisted.

"Well, at one point he said, 'One hundred thousand people, tonight?'-- but that's not possible, is it? A thousand, I would understand. Or maybe, just a hundred. But the next thing he said was, 'I understand. We'll make it happen.' That's my husband. Catering for such a crowd, and our future mayor."

"The man has still got to get elected."

"Well, Mr. Glover, on that note, we're done. I've come to realize you've just been stringing me along for the money. I won't be recommending your services. Goodbye."

I noticed another squad car passing slowly by the entryway, or maybe it was the same one, trying for a closer look. I had to get out of there, but more importantly, I couldn't let Mrs. Noble go quite yet.

"Wait, Mrs. Noble! This is important. Did he say where this event was going to be? Your husband's life may depend on it!" I quickly pulled off my coat as I spoke to her and hung it over the payphone next to me.

"Come off it, Mr. Glover. I wasn't born yesterday. There's nothing dangerous about catering for a political dinner."

I considered my life at that moment. If she wasn't paying me, did I really need to pursue this any further? It was only a moment, though, because seeing this to the end was the only way to clear my name. There was no sitting this one out anymore.

"Mrs. Noble, Claire, you may not

have heard the news, but there was an attempt on Mayor Dore's life today at a political rally, and Lonnie Seger is involved. I have reason to believe that other highly positioned officials are being targeted, and I'd hate to see your husband get caught in the cross-fire." A bald-faced lie. Dore may still be in danger, but I had no reason to suspect anyone else was.

There was silence on the other end of the line for a long time. I began to think maybe she had hung up while I was talking, and I just didn't hear it. "Mrs. Noble?" I asked.

"If this turns out to be some sort of desperate attempt to get more money out of me--"

"Forget the money! You don't owe me one more cent. Just tell me where your husband is!"

"The Ullensvang Hunting Lodge," she said.

I'd never heard of it, but I wrote down what it sounded like she said and slammed the receiver onto the cradle.

I headed for the side entrance and pulled it open just far enough to

look both ways but saw no cops. I
looked back to see two uniforms
heading for the phone booths where my
coat still hung, so I darted out the
door and across the street to the
relative darkness of the alley on the
other side.

I needed a place to hide, to
regroup and get some information.
This wasn't it. The only person I
knew who might have the answers I was
looking for was Brian. Newspapers
never rest, so there was a chance he'd
be working on a Saturday.

I made my way north, mainly by
alleyway whenever I could manage it,
and arrived at the Post-Intelligencer
building without incident.

If Brian didn't know where this
hunting lodge was, they would at least
have some reference material where we
could look it up, and maybe even where
Seger lived. That probably wasn't the
sort of information they generally
shared, but as a candidate for public
office, he probably had to register,
and I'm willing to bet the newspapers

had access to that. If I promised
Brian a big story, he'd probably be
forthcoming with a little information.

I got to the building and chatted
with the receptionist for a while
before asking her to fetch Brian. A
few minutes later, he was down in the
lobby, but this time around, he wanted
me to come upstairs with him. He had
something he wanted to show me.

"Where are we going?" I asked as
we climbed the stairs.

"Well, first of all, I wanted to
get you out of the lobby. You know
they're circulating your picture? Not
a flattering one either. The evening
edition is heading to print right now
with that picture. You want to know
what the headline will read? No, you
don't. But I'm going to tell you
anyway. 'Local Investigator wanted
for questioning.' The byline reads,
'Fled scene of failed assassination
attempt.'"

I was suddenly aware of a burning
knot in my gut. It was probably there
for a while, but it flared up with
that news.

"As of this moment, consider

yourself my 'protected source.' I
don't want anyone to know you're here
who doesn't need to know. I'll be
calling you Simon."

He opened the door to the third
floor and let me through. Only a
couple lights were on, and the floor
was a vast array of cabinets and
stacks of cardboard filing boxes.
"This way, down at the end," he said.

"Not to derail the topic from my
imminent incarceration and public
shaming, but you said you wanted to
show me something."

"I do. Notice I didn't say I
want to tell you something. I want to
see your reaction unfiltered. It's
already set up, just right down here."
There was a series of small rooms
against the far wall, and he opened up
the door to one toward the middle. It
was dark inside. At first, all I saw
was a wooden table and chair. It
looked like an interrogation room, but
what one would be doing in a newspaper
office, I hadn't a clue. Then he
moved aside, and I saw on the table,
there was a metal box with a small
screen and some knobs on it.

"Come on, sit down. I'll turn it on. It takes a moment or two to warm up."

I sat down on the chair, with the screen of this thing a foot or so away from my face. "What is this?"

"It's a microfilm reader. We get all sorts of newspapers from all over the world printed out on a small spool of film. Once a week, I go through as many as I can, looking for stories that will appeal to local readers. Four or five of them make their way into our paper weekly. Last night, it occurred to me that this is where I probably saw..." The screen was starting to glow, and an image was slowly coming into focus. It was a newspaper with a large picture front and center.

It was a grainy photo of a man in shackles standing in a courtroom giving testimony. A judge was scowling toward him. In front of the judge's high seat was a five-pointed star with sheaves of wheat curving around it. The letters under the symbol looked Cyrillic. In the center of the room, like a lawyer in cross-examination, was a little man in military dress. "That's him!" I said, pointing at the little man. "That's Kowalczyk!"

Brian nodded. "Yes. That's what I thought. Meet Kasper Kowalczyk. Member of the Polish Military Organization, or PMO. Only thing is, that's him there," he said, pointing to the man on trial. "And this was shortly before his execution."

"Then who's this guy?" I studied the face as best I could. It was a side-on shot, and he was looking slightly away from the camera, but I was sure it was the same man I had seen twice in Hooverville and again at the club.

"This, according to the article, is one Sergey Sudoplatov. He is reportedly a member of Stalin's Politburo, working to root out anti-communist dissidents in Poland. This guy Kowalczyk isn't the only one he got killed either."

"Then what's he doing here, and why take that guy's name?"

"Apparently, he's joining clubs and promoting mayoral candidate,

Lonnie Seger. Let's assume for the moment that it is the same guy. Let's further assume that he hasn't changed loyalties. He couldn't come across under his own name. The sort of people who pay attention to who comes to the US of A are the same sort who would recognize that name. Now, tell me, what sort of club would have him as a member?"

"You're suggesting that the Brothers of Unity is a communist organization. Yeah, between the Hooverville speech, the bear on the pins, and the subversive nature of their activities, I've been thinking along the same lines myself. The question I've got at this point is, do the members generally know that? Bowerman didn't seem to have a clue. And if so, what about Seger?"

"Who knows about Seger. I've done as much research as I can into him. He showed up out of nowhere, moved to the city only two years ago, and started campaigning ten months ago. I can't find any record of him before that, and residency is the only paperwork that proves he was here for

even that long. Ten will get you one
that someone who knows his stuff could
tell you that deed's a forgery. You
need two years in the city to run for
mayor, and he has exactly that. He
has no work record, before or after,
never filed an income tax return so
far as I can tell, and he never
advertised a speaking engagement with
this paper, but we've got an op-ed
column praising his skill as an
orator. I've never heard of the
fellow who penned it. I'm starting to
doubt Seger even exists."

I sat back in the chair, stunned
by all the revelations. "No, he's
gotta exist. Otherwise, the joke
would be on them when he wins."

I started thinking out loud. In
my mind, I had my Dictaphone out,
ready for Katie to type up a few
pages. "Alright. So, he's behind in
the polls, possibly because he never
actually makes any speeches. They try
to make up for this by registering the
men of Hooverville, padding his
numbers by some small margin. Next,
they assassinate the incumbent, who's
leading by a huge margin. Now he can

come out saying whatever he wants
without contradicting himself because
no one's heard him speak yet. He
rouses the crowd and takes the
majority of Dore's votes, leaving
Langlie in a distant second."

I stood up, face to face with
Brian, who was nodding as if he was
thinking pretty much the same thing.
"Only, what do they do now? The mayor
is still alive and still has a big
lead. Are they going to try again?
What's their plan B?"

"If we're right, you threw a
major wrench in their works. I think
a second assassination attempt would
be too suspicious, but they still need
him out of the way. They'd need to
make it look like an accident."

"An accident would be difficult
to arrange, and there's only three
days until the election," I said.

"Alright, then. You know them as
well as anybody. How smart are they?
Do you think they had all their eggs
in this one basket, or are they the
sort to have a backup plan?"

"This Oberman guy running the
club? Smart. Maybe more than one

backup plan. They may have a way of
pressuring Dore to step down, but they
went with the assassination because
they wanted the voters outraged.
Angry people will do stupid things if
it looks like the ethical choice."

"So, what do we do now?"

"That depends on you. If I can
get proof of any of this, it would
make a hell of a story, right?"

"If you had proof," he agreed.
"Maybe, Mike can help with--"

"No, I'm not bringing Mike in on
this." I could see by the look Brian
gave me that I wasn't going to get
away without an explanation. But I
needed to move fast, so I cut it as
short as I could.

"You remember this X guy I
mentioned, right? I don't know much
about him, but he's watching me, and
one of his guys shows up just when my
bacon needed saving. At Dore's rally,
when the cops started beating on me,
Mike came outta nowhere and pulled me
out of there. And he was in uniform.
Now, maybe his story is true, and the
captain asked for a big blue show, but
I'm thinking, maybe he wore it as

camouflage. He didn't want to be recognized because he wasn't supposed to be there. I'm thinking he's X."

Brian considered my words, then shrugged his shoulders. "Well, at least that means I'm no longer under suspicion."

"Never mind that now. If I get you the proof, do you think you could get it printed?"

"Assuming we're not in the ledger somewhere..."

"You're thinking about it wrong," I said with a smile. "Especially if you're in the ledger. When this comes out, the people in that book are going to want to distance themselves from it quicker than a cat in a bathtub. And the Post-Intelligencer won't be able to run the risk that the Times will print it even if you don't."

A smile spread across Brian's face as he shook a finger at me. "Like rats fleeing a sinking ship. So, how are you going to get proof?"

"This Noble character, the chef. He's supposed to be catering an event for Seger tonight at the..." I pulled out my notebook to check the name

again. "Ullensvang Hunting Lodge. If
there's going to be a chance to get
Seger alone, it's going to be there.
You wouldn't know where that is, by
any chance?"

"I've heard of it. Never been.
It's across the lake, somewhere
outside Kirkland. I can get you a
map."

"That would be swell. Say, can
you also get me a camera?"

"I don't know, Drake..."

"Come on, Brian. I'm offering
you exclusive photos..." I said,
taunting him.

"Alright, alright. I'll see what
I can scrounge up. You wait here and
stay out of sight."

Chapter Twelve

Brian came through with both map and camera, a bulkier model than I was used to, but then, reporters didn't often have to hide their cameras. He also managed to smuggle me out a side door unseen with a borrowed coat. Now all I needed was a car to get me to the lodge.

Joe Freeman would be at home right now, which was a long way from here, and I would never manage to make off with it without his wife getting wise. I could argue that this was

something of an emergency, but I would
be burning an awfully convenient
bridge. Better to find a car
elsewhere.

I also needed to collect my gun.
They don't have a citizen's arrest law
on the books in Washington state. In
fact, they tend to look at it as armed
kidnapping. What I was proposing to
do was the moral equivalent, though,
and I didn't want to be left standing
there like a schlub the next time the
bad guys decided to pull iron on me.

Since I had to go by Delaney's
anyway, I figured I might as well see
if Mike was there. Now, maybe he was
X, and maybe he wasn't, but either
way, he wanted to be helpful. I
thought I could convince him the best
way to help right now was to let me
borrow his car, and anyway, it was a
better shot than anything else I could
come up with.

As I came up on the bar, I felt
the hairs on the back of my neck go
up. That instinct again. I stopped
about a block away and looked around
the corner of a nearby brick building.
There was a car, again, parked with

occupants. It was a beige cruiser
this time. It looked like someone
finally got wise that I spent a lot of
time at this joint.

I turned around and crossed the
street a block up and approached
Delaney's from the delivery entrance.
No one was watching that side of the
building. Apparently, they hadn't yet
gotten wise that I could spot a
stakeout.

I quickly crossed and stepped in
the back, scanning the room, looking
for cops. The evening crowd was just
starting to trickle in. No Mike yet.
No badges either. I took out my dad's
pocket watch. There was a good chance
Mike would be there tonight, and there
was plenty of time before the last
ferry left Madison for Kirkland.

I ducked into the booth at the
back, watching the front entrance for
cops and communists, and ready to bolt
for the back door at the first sight
of an unfriendly face.

Peggy came by the table with a
dishrag over one shoulder. "The
usual, or are you just here to get
your ventilator back?"

"The usual," I confirmed. "You seen Mike yet?"

"Not today. I take it you haven't managed to clear up your issues from last night, then?"

That actually made me chuckle. "No, if anything, I've made them much worse. Now the good guys are after me too."

Peggy nodded, a concerned expression on her face, then went back behind the bar and poured two glasses of scotch. She dropped them both on the table and sat down next to me. I didn't like that she was blocking my easy escape, but I decided it was better not to complain just now.

"Talk to me," she said.

I nursed my drink as I told her about what happened at the mayor's speech earlier that day, ending with the cops that beat the shooter to death, and how I was being sought as an accomplice.

"That's crazy, Drake! Surely, somebody saw you wrestling the gun away from the guy," she said.

"According to Mike, they just think I got cold feet at the last minute. Otherwise, why was I the only one to know what he was going to do?"

"How did you know?"

"He looked suspicious. I do this for a living, you know."

"And what about Mike? He's helping you, right?"

"Well, he didn't arrest me if that's what you mean. But no, I'm on my own on this one."

"That son of a bitch. You know, I've got half a mind to ban him from the place."

"No, Peggy, it's not his fault. Just being around me has always put him in a difficult spot going all the way back to my time on the academy and my dad's murder. Besides, he pulled me out of there when the clubs started flying. He gave me a chance to explain myself, and he let me go when the easy thing was to take me in. He's probably in a heap of trouble as it is. No, if he comes through that door in the next hour or so and agrees to let me use his car, we are more than square."

She looked down at her drink, noticing it was still full while mine

was empty. She downed it in one go
and picked up the two empties, but she
didn't get up from the table. She sat
there looking me in the eye for quite
a while instead.

Finally, she sat back in the
booth. "I don't know why I'm doing
this, Drake, I really don't. I have a
set of rules that get me through the
days as well as through the years here
at the bar. I broke one of them
already with you, and here's another
one: I don't get involved in people's
personal lives. I stand behind the
bar, and I ask men about their day,
and I keep the drinks flowing while I
nod quietly or laugh politely. At the
end of the day, I collect their money,
and I go home and wash everything
off." She stood up from the table,
the two empty glasses clinking
together in her slender fingers.

"I guess I must really like you.
But I've got a friend who's a sucker
for an underdog story, and he's got a
car that goes unused much of the day.
I'll see if I can get him down here so
he can listen to you. You tell him
your story, and you might just get

yourself a car for the night."

Peggy retreated behind the bar, setting our glasses in the sink, and picking up the phone.

I sat watching the door and thinking to myself, without even a drink to nurse. Now I had another favor to add to the list. All these favors were really starting to pile up. I owed Mike, I don't know what, but a lot. If my suspicions turned out to be true, and he was X, then I'd forgive myself a lot of that. I still had to get Peggy a replacement bottle, I owed Betty a dinner, I owed Brian a story and a camera, I owed my landlord rent, and I owed Megan a divorce.

Yeah, I do a lot of favor trade, but then that's how my people have always done things, and I was usually so good at managing it all. The favor I borrowed from one of them would help me pay off the favor I owed another. I took one out here to pay for one there, and somehow, I always seem to end up on top. Not doing well by any stretch, mind you, but managing day to day.

Peggy came back over to the table
with a second round of drinks. I did
the only polite thing and started in
on mine. Then she set a bottle of
wine on the table. I looked at her
questioningly, but she didn't mention
it.

"Okay, looks like you've got
yourself a car for the night. It's
gonna cost you a story, though, so
take your time with it and make it a
good one. Frank's about half an hour
out. You tell him your story, then
you can have the car. I'll entertain
him until you get back, and the two of
you are even."

"Even," I repeated. That was a
word that didn't come up often in my
dealings. When our deal was
concluded, I usually liked to leave
people feeling they owed me, just a
little. "So, when you say you're
going to entertain him?"

"Only the usual. I'll get him
drunk, and I'll talk to him. I'll put
way more in his glass than I do in
mine. We'll be here the entire time.
If I didn't know better, Drake, I'd

say you were turning into the jealous sort."

That wasn't it at all. I was just trying to figure out how much I'd end up owing her for keeping me and Frank 'even.' But no one gained anything by me saying that, so I kept my mouth shut.

She pulled out a corkscrew and started in on the bottle. "None for me, thank you," I said, putting a hand over my glass.

She laughed as she popped the cork out. "This is for Frank. He prefers red wine to spirits, and he'll fuss if I don't let it breathe before he gets here. He might also whine about getting an open bottle. He's fickle in that way, but you're my witness. You saw me open it."

"I'll vouch for you."

She left the bottle standing open and sat down next to me again.

"This thing you're going to do. The thing you need a gun and a car for. It's going to be dangerous."

It wasn't a question, so I didn't bother responding. Instead, I let a bit of scotch pool on my tongue and

put my attention on the feel of it
burning.

"Tell me you have a plan. Tell
me you're going to make it out okay."

I couldn't tell her that. Not
while she was looking at me with that
vulnerable sincerity. I couldn't lie
to her either, as much as I wanted to
tell her what she wanted to hear. I
let that bit of scotch roll down the
back of my tongue to sit on the cusp
of my throat while I thought of a way
to reassure her without lying to her.
Finally, I swallowed.

"Let's put it this way: I don't
like going into a situation
unprepared. My instincts have served
me well over the years, and I can
handle myself in a fight. You don't
need to worry about me. I've been in
tough situations before."

That seemed to do the trick. Her
mouth relaxed a little, and those
little wrinkles that creased the spot
between her eyebrows smoothed out.
She started working on her drink.

I was starting to worry about
her. I had worried earlier that she
might think that nothing meant

something to me, but now it looked like maybe it was the other way around. This morning she didn't say boop about it, but this evening, she seemed somewhat attached. It felt like the wrong time to talk about it, though. There was no sense in starting an argument I couldn't hang around to finish. I also didn't want to lose a good bar or a friendly bartender.

It's not like I thought she was sweet on me. Peggy was no Betty. Whatever this attachment was, it wasn't romantic.

I was still studying her face when I saw someone from the corner of my eye, entering the bar. He wore a trench coat with the collar pulled up, but the coat wasn't wet. That's what drew my attention.

He slid into the first booth, trying to look inconspicuous. He probably didn't think I'd recognize him, and I didn't know him by name, but I'd seen him around the precinct. He was a cop.

I once again wished Peggy hadn't chosen to sit next to me. My muscles were coiled like a spring, and I had nowhere to go. "Peggy, how about you sit across from me," I said, not looking her way.

"What?" she asked as if she didn't understand the request.

The cop's eyes roamed across the bar until they landed on me. We made eye contact, then he looked around the bar again in the opposite direction. He gave it less than ten seconds before he got slowly back up and walked out the way he'd come.

I downed the rest of the scotch. "Looks like I'm not waiting around for Frank's ride," I said. I started scooting out of the booth. Peggy got the hint and stood up. "They've found me. I've got to split, out the back, and quick. Get my gun, will you?"

I ran to the delivery door and pulled it open far enough to get an eyeball out. There were two more uniforms at the end of the alley, holding shotguns. I quickly shut the door and threw the bolt. I was surrounded.

I caught up with Peggy as she was stepping back behind the bar and

stopped her with a hand on her elbow.
"No dice out back either. Now listen,
Peggy. They're not going to want to
take me alive, I figure, so lead's
going to be flying, see? I plan on
making life hard for them by giving up
easy, but you've got to look after
your customers and stay low, just in
case. This is where I either get
captured or get killed."

She shook loose of my grip on her
elbow. "Yeah. I suppose it could be
like that," she said. Then before I
knew it, she slapped me in the back of
the head. "<u>Or</u>, you could do the smart
thing and vanish into thin air. Come
on."

She grabbed me by the tie and
pulled me behind the bar.

Outside, a man with a megaphone
shouted into the bar. "Drake Glover,
you are surrounded. Come out with
your hands up."

"Everybody out!" Peggy said.
"The bar's closed for the night. Make
sure you leave with your hands up, or
you might get mistaken for Drake

here."

She moved quickly to the
register, letting go of my tie along
the way. The rest of the patrons
grabbed what belonged to them and
hurried toward the front door. Peggy
hit the 'No Sale' button, and the cash
drawer popped out to the sound of a
bell.

"Never send to know for whom it
tolls," I thought, as the man outside
continued to persuade me to exit
peaceably. On the bright side, there
hadn't been any sound of gunfire as
the last of the patrons left the bar.

The drawer had a tray inside,
containing all the bills and change,
which Peggy pulled out and set aside.
Then she reached inside the empty
drawer, and retrieved my brother's
revolver, still wrapped in the
chamois. She turned and tried to hand
it to me, but I was reluctant to take
it, with the cops about to burst in.

"Pay them no mind. They can come
in if they want," she said, as if
reading my mind. She proffered the
gun again, and I took it this time,
pulling it out of the chamois and

slipping it underneath my coat and into my jacket pocket.

Peggy reached inside the register one more time, and something buzzed electrically. A square in the floorboards popped up an inch or so, with the sound of a solenoid going off. When it was flush with the floor, there was absolutely no sign that it had been there.

"Don't just stand there," she said, "get inside!" She grabbed a book of matches off the bar, and pulled a couple bills out of the tray, then put the tray back inside the register drawer and closed it up.

I pried the trapdoor up the rest of the way and looked down into the darkness below. I could make out the first few slats of a rotting wooden staircase, then nothing else.

"If you don't come out, Glover, we're coming in!" the voice over the megaphone said.

"Hoof it!" Peggy prodded with a firm hand on my back. "Otherwise, it really will be a shootout. I don't want to be here when they burst in!"

That was all the encouragement I

needed. I sat down and lowered myself onto the stairs. They looked pretty flimsy, but they took my weight without complaint. I started down into the darkness below.

Peggy followed behind me and pulled the trapdoor shut. It clicked into place, and we were in absolute darkness.

I could hear my own heartbeat pulsing in my ears, and just above that, the sound of her feet coming down the stairs toward me. I felt like I was going to fall. There were no handrails, and I had no idea how far away the bottom was. All I could do was plow ahead. I held my arms out, reaching for anything to hold onto.

My eyes were stretched open, as if doing so would collect more light. It smelled of rot and damp earth.

I reached the bottom and nearly fell trying to take another step down. With my arms stretched out in front to keep from breaking my nose, I stepped to the side and waited for Peggy to follow. I slid my feet across the floor toes-first to be sure there wasn't another drop-off.

"Eleven, twelve, thirteen. There we are," Peggy was saying under her breath. I realized she had been counting the steps. "Okay, Drake?" she whispered.

"Yeah, I'm okay," I said. "I'm over here."

"Put out your hand," she said. I slowly extended one arm toward the sound of her voice until I felt her fingers tap the back of my hand. She then grabbed my wrist. "This way," she said.

How she managed to navigate in the darkness, I didn't know. I kept getting the feeling that she was going to pass under a brick archway or something, and I was going to catch it full in the teeth. I held my other arm in front of my face, just in case.

"This is your last warning!" It somehow sounded louder from down here. "Surrender, or we're coming in!"

Peggy came to a stop, and I stood looking up. I heard the loud bang of someone kicking the door open. then running feet as cops flooded the bar. Dust trickled down into my wide-open eyes. Instinctively, I breathed in as I shut my eyes tight and felt the need to sneeze. I grabbed the bridge of my nose and squeezed hard while burying it in the crook of my elbow. Slowly the urge passed.

I still felt as if I had a pound of sand stuck under each eyelid, though, and rubbed at them as they teared up.

"You okay if I leave you here for a second?" Peggy's voice was right at my left ear.

I put out a hand and found her shoulder. "Do what you gotta do," I said. I squeezed, then let go, even though it was the last thing I wanted to do just then. I heard her footsteps moving away.

I felt like I was in a vast empty space one moment, with nothing around for maybe miles. The next moment, there could have been cold brick walls surrounding me and closing in.

There were feet running back and forth above me, and voices, but I couldn't make out what they were saying.

"Okay," Peggy said, right in

front of me, making me jump. She
reached out and took my arm again.
"Right over here," she whispered.

       She led me for a few more feet as
we took a winding path to get where we
were going. I could only imagine the
obstacles we were avoiding. Then she
stopped and let go of my arm once
more.

       I heard the sound of keys on a
ring, then one of them was slid into a
lock. It clicked, and a door opened
on well-oiled hinges.

       "Okay," Peggy said, feeling
around for my arm again. We can
chance a little light out here, but
keep it quiet. They're right above
us."

       "What do you mean, 'out here?'" I
heard her close the door behind us.

       Peggy lit a match. For a moment,
it was so bright I couldn't see
anything else, but as my eyes
adjusted, I realized we weren't just
in the basement. We were standing on
the porch of the first floor of the
building, with steps leading down to

what was once the sidewalk below,
while overhead were the Roman arches
supporting the new sidewalk above.
Shopfront windows flanked the old
brick façade on either side of the
entrance we'd just passed through.

Here's another thing few people
know about Seattle. Back in 1889, a
careless woodworker let a vat of glue
boil over, starting a fire that ended
up burning down twenty-five city
blocks in the downtown area. They
wanted to rebuild, but the flammable
wooden buildings weren't the only
problem.

High tide in Seattle brought sea
level above downtown. Yes, there was
a sea wall, but there was also an
aging sewer system, and twice a day,
things got real messy.

So, the council decided to raise
downtown by washing the dirt down from
nearby hills, but the process would
take twelve years. Long story short,
people built their new stone and brick
buildings, the city put up retaining
walls and raised the level of the
streets up to the second story. Then
they just built sidewalks at street

level, turned some of the second-story windows into front doors, and left the old first floor underground.

We were standing on the old sidewalk in between the retaining wall and the shop fronts of old-Seattle.

"The Underground!" I said in an excited whisper. "Delaney's is on the Underground!"

"Damn straight it is. How do you think I got through prohibition?" She shook out the match, plunging us into darkness once again. I heard the sounds of her locking the door behind us. "Come on, this way."

I found the railing and used it to guide my steps down to the pavement below.

"Hold up," Peggy said. "It's not exactly well maintained down here, and any potholes you'd find annoying up there are potentially fatal down here."

She struck another match, and I could see that she was kneeling by the side of the stairs. She came up holding an old hurricane lantern; the type my mother used to have in the house before they ran electricity to

Ballard. "This way, hurry."

She led the way down the old city sidewalk, with eerie, deserted shopfronts on one side, and the retaining wall that held in the street on the other. Our footfalls echoed off the walls and ceiling, driving off the rats at the edge of the lamplight.

We turned the corner to find a couple men sleeping outside the stoop to another building entrance. These were not the jobless, penniless residents of Hooverville, but the mind-numbed slaves of poppy tar, exiled from their opium den, but with nowhere to go. Nor any willpower to move them from the spot.

Now that was more what I expected to see on the Underground. The illicit trade of contraband that couldn't be seen on the streets of Seattle above, and purveyors of said contraband. Stories were told of deals made down here in secret languages, where anything was for sale. If a deal went badly, you could wind up as food for the rats, or even shanghaied off to parts unknown, never to be seen again.

We passed several more opium addicts before turning another corner. The sidewalk above had little purple panes of glass embedded in it, about the size of a checker square. They let in a little bit of light from the streetlamps outside.

A few feet down from the corner, there was another door, this one made of iron. Peggy handed me the lantern while she located another key on her ring.

"My truck is upstairs," she said. "I park back here sometimes, to leave room for the customers in front. Today, it's damned lucky I did."

"Thanks, Doll. I'll get it back to you as soon as this is over."

"Like hell, you will, Drake. Thanks to you, I'm now a fugitive too. Aiding and abetting, and all that. Besides, you don't know old Bessie. The clutch sticks in second, and you have to know just how to kick it tenderly, or else you'll flood it, and then where would you be?"

"I think I can figure it out," I said.

"Pride goeth before destruction,

Mr. Glover. No, I'm afraid you are
stuck with me now, like it or not."
She put the key in the lock and turned
it, pulling the door just slightly
ajar. This one wasn't so well oiled
and screeched like a cat in heat.

She put the keyring in a pocket
of her dress and took the lantern
back. "You ready?" she asked.

I nodded, still unhappy with the
situation, but unable to do much about
it. Peggy lifted the glass of the
lantern and blew out the wick. I
heard her set the lantern down, then
she swung the iron door wide, letting
in faint light from the street above.
At the top of the concrete stairs, a
railing at street level kept anyone
from falling in.

Peggy climbed the stairs, just
enough to look both ways, then dashed
the rest of the way to the top. I
just about shut the door behind myself
by reflex, but the last thing I needed
was that noise calling attention to my
location. I let it be and started up
the stairs.

When I got to street level, I
could see her squatting next to her

beat-up old truck across the street.
A trio of squad cars sat near the
alley on this side, with the
silhouettes of a couple men inside the
closest, shotguns at the ready. I
ducked low and ran across the street
to join Peggy.

"Get in the back," she whispered.
"You're too exposed on the other
side."

I vaulted the side and lay down
in the damp bed of the pickup, while
Peggy got in the cab and started the
ancient beast.

Chapter Thirteen

Laying in the bed of the truck, and not daring to look over the side, I could only guess what was going on out there. We stopped at the end of the street, where men were shouting, mostly about me. "Well, he didn't come out this way!" someone said.

I heard a couple other cars speed past before Peggy put on the turn signal and went right. More cops arriving on the scene, I guessed. While we were moving, all I could hear was the wind that chilled me, howling through the bed of the truck.

We drove straight for several minutes, mostly uphill, then I heard the turn signal again, and after a group of cars passed, Peggy turned left. She glided to the side of the road and stopped. I felt sure she'd been forced to stop, but then she rapped her knuckles on the rear window. I brought my head up far enough to see. She motioned with her head for me to join her, and I quickly got out of the bed and into the cab. She immediately started back up again.

"Thanks for stopping. It's cold out there."

"No problem. I could use the company. I may not look like it, but I'm shaking on the inside. I've obviously had to hide things from the police before, back in the prohibition days. The difference was, back then, they weren't carrying guns. Sure, I was risking jail time, and even that wasn't too likely. They'd probably have tried to get me to turn on a distributor in exchange for leniency. But the point is, death was never on the line. I don't know how you do it,

Drake, playing it cool while you're stuck between the good guys and the bad guys, with both sides trying to kill you."

"Well, put it in gear, and they're a lot less likely to."

"Right, yes. Of course." She pulled out into traffic, nervously forgetting to signal until after she'd merged.

"It's alright. Just take it easy. No need to call attention to ourselves. Now, turn right up here."

"Got it." She got over to the right and waited her chance to pull into traffic.

I started thinking again about the events to come. Having Peggy along was going to put a crimp in my ability to work. I had to come up with some way to convince her to stay in the car.

"It just seems so wrong!" she said, interrupting my thoughts.

"What does?"

"Just look at them all, going about their lives. While we're being hunted. I don't understand how they can just go on like everything is

normal. It's not! How can they not
feel that?"

"Yesterday, a private dick's body
got pulled out of the water near
Alkai. You didn't feel that, did
you?"

She got her chance and made her
turn. "Exactly! And why not?
Someone's life ended, and the world
just turns below him. We've got cops
looking for us, and Martha over here
has shopping to do," she said,
pointing out the window at a passerby.
"It doesn't seem right."

"You'll need to be in the left
lane. Madison is just up ahead."

"And you being so cool about it
doesn't help. It's like their
ignorance is infecting you somehow."

"I'll tell you one thing. There
are a lot of people in this world who
aren't going to have your best
interests at heart. Only a small
percentage are ever going to threaten
you, and smaller still is the number
of people who will ever draw a gun on
you. You've probably worked that out
on your own. What you may not realize
is that there are a lot more people

willing to point a gun at you than are
ever willing to pull that trigger.
Yeah, I've looked down the barrel of a
gun more than once, but I've only been
shot at a handful of times, and no
one's ever gotten me. Maybe that
makes a man cool under pressure. But
I've learned that it's not the barrel
of a gun you should be scared of, it's
the look in the eye of the man holding
it."

Peggy made the turn, and we drove
up Madison in silence. When we got to
the docks, there was a group of cars
waiting there already. We could see
the ferry coming toward the terminal
with passengers to unload from the
westward trip. We couldn't have cut
it too much closer.

Peggy paid the toll attendant
with the money she had grabbed out of
the till and put the truck into park
while we waited.

I saw a phone booth, and suddenly
decided I had a call to make. "I'll
be back before you have to get on the
ferry. I'm going to call Mike."

"Are you sure you ought to? Is
it safe?"

I stepped out of the truck but held the door while I responded. "No one here is looking for me, and nobody would think to look for me here. Don't worry. I'll be both quick and careful."

I jogged the short distance to the terminal building, where a payphone sat outside under a bare bulb. A short while later, the phone was ringing at Mike's house. His wife picked up the phone.

"Hello, Janet, it's Drake," I said. "Is your husband around?"

"Oh, hi Drake," she said pleasantly. She liked me better than Mike seemed to lately. Then again, she didn't have to put up with me nearly so often. "No, I think he went over to Delaney's after work. I'm surprised you aren't there with him."

"Right now, there's a lot of people surprised I'm not there. Listen, do you have anything handy you can write on? I've got a message for Mike."

"Sure, hang on." I heard her rummaging around through a drawer. I watched the progress of the cars being

unloaded from the ferry while I waited
for her. "Okay, go ahead," she said.

"Tell him this Polish guy
Kowalczyk--" I spelled it out for her,
"--his real name is Sergey Sudoplatov.
And he's not really Polish, he's
Russian. He's one of Stalin's
killers. Tell him the chief might
rethink that list he's on if he knows
who's on it with him. You got all
that?"

"Yeah, I got it. I don't know
what it means, but I got it."

"Thanks, doll. I owe you. It's
important that he gets that as soon as
you hear from him, okay? I'll be at
the Ullensvang Hunting Lodge. If he
wants a bigger part in this, I'm
likely to need backup. Since the boys
will want to find me anyway, it should
be easy to bring them in on this,
regardless of jurisdiction. Tell him
if he manages all that, he'll
definitely be a hero."

"Okay, Drake. You're gonna be by
on Sunday, right?"

"Wouldn't miss it. You're gonna
make some of that coffee cake, right?"

She laughed, and we said our

goodbyes. By the time I'd made it
back to the truck, there were more
cars waiting behind us.

Peggy parked the truck on the
lower deck of the ferry. I reached
for the door handle, but I felt
Peggy's hand on my arm. "Wait. I
want to know what's going to happen
next."

"Next? Next, I'm going to get
something to eat, because I don't know
what comes after that, or how long it
will take."

"But you must have some sort of
plan!"

I took my hand off the door
handle and turned to her with a sigh.
"Look, I've never been to this place,
and I don't know the layout. I also
don't know much about tonight's event,
only what a housewife overheard of
half a conversation. It sounds like
they're expecting a hell of a turnout.
The only thing I'm counting on is, if
there's a fundraising dinner with
Lonnie Seger, then at least he has to
show up.

"I'm hoping that I get a chance
to look around while no one's
watching. I hope I can get Evan Noble
alone for a minute and finally do
right by my client. I also hope I can
find something incriminating while I'm
in there. They are bound to have
cleaned out the club, and this is the
only other place I know that they
operate out of."

"And what do you do if you're
caught? You came into my bar pretty
beat up last night. I know you aren't
recovered from that, are you really up
for more of the same?"

I gave her a smile that I hoped
was reassuring, though it really
didn't feel that way. "Don't worry,
doll. I can handle myself. A lot of
this looks worse than it is. And if I
run into anything I can't handle,
that's what this is for." I patted my
coat pocket.

"Now, can we go up and get
something to eat? Whatever I have to
face, I would rather not face it
hungry."

"Ugh. I don't think I can eat.
I feel like I'm going to throw up."

"Well, then come up and keep me company. I'll eat. You might feel different once you've got a bowl of delicious clam chowder in front of you."

I don't know whether it was the soup or the guilt over company that convinced her, but she agreed to join me. We walked up the nearby staircase to the passenger section, then aft to the cafeteria. A lot of people were sitting at the tables there, but few were actually eating. Most were just enjoying the view of Lake Washington with Mount Baker glowing pink and gold in the sunset.

We grabbed a table, and I got in line for two bowls of clam chowder. While I was walking back to our table with the two bowls of soup, some oyster crackers, and other accoutrement, I got that hair-raising sensation on the back of my neck again.

I stopped, holding the tray with our lunch on it, and looked around. There weren't any cops in sight, and no muscle either. Just ordinary people, couples, for the most part,

just going about their business. No
one was paying me any particular
attention either, though of course,
they would be soon if I continued to
stand there like an idiot.

I decided it wasn't anything
after all and returned to our table.
Just as I was setting the tray down,
though, I noticed the couple at the
table behind us. He had a small brass
pin on his lapel.

I looked around the room again,
this time paying close attention to
people's lapels, and I saw them
everywhere.

"What's the matter?" Peggy asked,
a bit too loudly.

I sat down quickly. "Keep your
voice down," I said, a bit too
harshly. "We're not alone."

Peggy looked over my shoulder, a
puzzled expression on her face. "What
do you mean? Did you recognize
somebody?"

"No, not yet, and that's lucky.
Almost everybody here is from the
Brothers of Unity."

Peggy's eyes widened when I told
her about the pins. "Oh, my," she

said.

"Don't worry about it. I should have expected it. If there's a big gathering across the lake, we were bound to see a few of them on the ferry over. No, this might turn out to be a good thing. Eat your soup."

I set a bowl down in front of her and slid a spoon across the table, but she ignored them.

"What do you mean, 'a good thing?'"

"It means we won't have any trouble finding the lodge, we just have to follow one of them. Now eat your soup before it gets cold. I need some time to think."

I started in on my soup, staring fixedly at a spot on the table just past my bowl. It would be a lot easier for the two of us to walk into the place if we had our own set of pins. Would the same trick work on them twice? Maybe, if we got lucky and Henry or Ryder weren't working the door. But how was I going to get them?

I could take them by force and throw some people overboard. Only, I wasn't going to hit a lady, so that meant two men, then I would run the risk that their wives would miss them. Even if they came alone, their cars wouldn't be leaving the ferry, which someone would notice, and if they were parked in front of us, that would be another sort of problem.

"What do you need to think about, Drake?" Peggy asked.

I looked up and saw she hadn't touched her soup. "Would you just eat your damned soup, Peggy?"

She gave me a hurt expression, but she picked up her spoon and dipped it in the chowder.

"I'm sorry, doll, it's just that we're trying to look normal here." I looked around to make sure I hadn't drawn any attention with my outburst. A couple conversations had stopped abruptly, but they were pointedly not looking our way. "I was thinking, if I could get a hold of a couple of those pins, the two of us could pass for club members and maybe just waltz through the front door.

"Oh," she said, stirring around inside her bowl until she cornered a

potato. She scooped it up and ate it.
"You should have just said so. I
could help."

It hadn't occurred to me that
this life-long bartender and one-time
smuggler might have other skills as
well. "Yeah? What can you do that's
helpful?"

"Well, maybe my charms are lost
on you, Mr. Glover, but I can still be
a distraction when I try."

"Peggy... I said I was sorry."
I wasn't going to get out of this one
easily unless I played hardball.
"You... had me pretty distracted last
night." I set down my spoon and
reached across the table to touch her
hand.

She blushed despite herself but
pulled her hand away. "Really?"

There was something in her eyes a
bit like hope. It suddenly dawned on
me that maybe last night had meant
something to her after all. Maybe the
reason she didn't want to talk about
it was the age difference between us.
She was scared. Christ, my dad used
to take me to Delaney's when I was a
kid. Part of her probably still saw

me that way. She was embarrassed about robbing the cradle and scared of what I would think of her at the same time.

That was one more thing than I was prepared to deal with at the moment, though. I had to diffuse it; put it off until later.

"Hey. It's alright. This thing we've got between us, we can work it out later. Right now, if you've got a suggestion that'll get us those pins, I'm all ears."

"Easy peasy, lemon squeezy. I wait at the top of the stairs. When two of them start heading up the stairs, I go down. Then I just take a little tumble, and while they're offering to help me up, you come from behind and slide their pins off. Do you think you can do that without their noticing?"

"I've spent a lifetime practicing gaining access to a man's wallet without him noticing. This should be a piece of cake after that."

It was a good enough plan, so I went downstairs and had a smoke on the automobile deck, waiting to hear her

cry out. In the middle of my second
cigarette, I heard her. I stubbed out
the butt and started for the stairs.

Sure enough, two men were
standing over her, asking if she were
alright. "Oh, it's my ankle!" she was
saying.

I came up behind the two as
silently as possible on a metal
staircase. I got right behind the
two, and I reached over the shoulder
of the guy on the left.

Just then, the ferry's horn went
off, a loud, long burst of steam. The
two men turned toward the sound, and I
pulled my arm back just in time.

"We must be pulling into the
dock," one of the men said.

"Do you know this woman?" asked
the other.

"Yes," I said. "She's with me."
I wasn't going to be able to get at
their lapels now.

"I think I'm okay to walk," Peggy
said, rubbing her ankle. She seemed
to sense our con had failed as well.

We watched who got into which

cars, making sure we followed someone with the lapel pin. As our truck was let off the ferry, we pulled in behind a couple driving a black Chrysler. I had Brian's map unfolded on my lap to verify that they were heading in vaguely the right direction.

I almost never got over to this side of the lake, and it always seemed that going to Kirkland was like going back in time, never more so than at night. Seattle was a metropolis, a minor one, granted, but a metropolis nonetheless, and here, just fourteen miles away, it was a frontier town. The main city streets had electrical lighting, but just off the main drag, you were plunged into darkness.

Sure, the houses were a far cry better than you'd see in Hooverville, and the downtown area was probably a mark of civic pride, but there were farm plots, and you could still feel here the omnipresent encroachment of wilderness. Of nature attempting to reassert itself. If people abandoned Seattle entirely, it would still be decades before you would see deer grazing in the city streets. In

Kirkland, I'd give it fifteen minutes.

We were off the main road almost as soon as we left the ferry terminal, and the road devolved further from asphalt to packed gravel to straight-up dirt before very long. There was a neighborhood labeled on the map as 'Bridle Trails' that we would be going through, but after that, there weren't even labels. Here there be monsters.

"Give them a bit of room. We don't want them to know they're being followed. If we can see their taillights, that's good enough."

Peggy nodded.

"You nervous?" I asked.

"Well, yeah," she said. "If we had just a few more seconds, we would have had those lapel pins, then we'd be golden."

"Not golden, not by a long shot. There were people at that club, people that would recognize me, and not just the bruisers who did this to my face. The club owner, this guy Sudoplatov, but also just regular people. They weren't on the ferry, not that I saw anyway, but they could still be at the lodge. If we ran into any of them,

we'd be awfully far from golden. But
we'd have gotten in anyway, and now,
I've got to figure something else out.
But never mind that now, what did you
mean by it?"

It was a while before she
answered. "You're going to make me
stay in the truck, aren't you?"

I sighed. Before I saw the lapel
pins, I'd been thinking exactly how to
broach this subject. "The best thing
for you would be to let me out and
then just drive away."

"And go where? The last ferry
for Seattle is gone already, and it's
a long drive around the lake.
Besides, it would be just eating me
up, leaving you there, with who knows
what going on. There's no way I could
keep driving, thinking about that. I
would turn right back around, Drake.
I swear to you, I would."

I nodded, frowning. I had pretty
much come to the same conclusion.
"Same thing applies to staying in the
car, doesn't it? I wouldn't be in
there two minutes before you'd come
after me."

"So, what are we going to do?"

"The idea of handcuffing you to the truck occurred to me. There's only one problem."

"You wouldn't dare," she said.

"I don't have any handcuffs."

"I'd scream."

"And draw the wrong kind of attention to yourself? I don't think so. Why couldn't you have driven a car instead?"

"Why a car?"

"Because then I could lock you in the trunk."

"You wouldn't dare."

"I think we've established I would."

"Well then, I'm glad I don't drive a car."

"Back to your point, though. I have to take you with me. There's going to be rules or I will find a closet to lock you in."

She was silent again for a while. "What kind of rules?"

"First off, don't ask questions. If we aren't there with some legitimacy, I don't want people knowing we're there at all, and the less talking we do, the better off we are. I can't be answering your questions all night and still hope to survive in there."

"Alright. What else?"

I felt like pointing out that this was a question, but I let it go. "Second, you follow my lead. I may be able to talk my way out of any chance encounters, but not if you start doing your own thing. I've been in situations like this before, and you're going to have to trust me, and maybe do a bit of acting."

"Understood. Is that it?"

"One more thing. You stay behind me. If talking doesn't work, I may have to fight my way out of there. I can't do that with you in the way. And if they get a chance, they'll use you against me. Once they've got a hold of you, I either have to do what they say or risk that they'll hurt you. Or worse."

Her voice was shaky when she finally said, "Okay." Good. I think I got the point across to her.

The rest of the rough and bumpy drive passed in silence.

Chapter Fourteen

The entrance to the Ullensvang Hunting Lodge had a large wooden gate, featuring a carving of a Viking warrior on skis and holding a bow. There was a long driveway, but from the road, we could see the lights of the lodge.

I had Peggy drive past the gate and on down the road. A hundred yards or so further down, we pulled off to the side and got out. I checked my camera for about the fourth time to be sure everything was set up properly.

It was a lot fancier than the one I was used to. There was a dial marked 'f stop.' As long as that 'f' stood for focal length, I decided I was good. As far as the actual function of the camera, snapping a shot and advancing the film, it was pretty much the same.

We crossed the road and stepped over a short log fence onto the grounds of the hunting lodge. "I'm glad I wore flats at least, but these shoes are going to be ruined," Peggy said.

The forest floor was damp, but not soaking, and it was mostly pine needles and maple leaves. Mud would have been something to complain about, and heels would certainly have been a pain, but this wasn't so bad.

"Keep it down. They may have some toughs running security out here."

When we got close enough to see the lodge, I motioned for her to hold up, then I pointed toward a tree she could stand behind. I crouched low behind a bush and watched the folks entering the club. The lodge was made

of wooden beams, far longer than it
was wide. One massive beam rode the
roof of the lodge, and both ends of it
were carved with dragon heads, giving
the impression of a Viking longboat
run aground. Lights blazed in front
of the building. They had a large
area cleared for parking, filled up
with cars, and a stream of headlights
still arriving.

I couldn't see the entrance from
where I was, but the guests were
speaking to someone just before
disappearing inside. The windows
along this side of the lodge were
dark, except for the last one. The
window was slid open, and I could hear
a ventilation fan. That one must be
the kitchen.

I waited a few minutes to see if
I could make out any patrols. I
didn't see anyone, so I got Peggy's
attention and pointed toward the
window with the light on. She nodded,
so I got up and crept toward the back
of the lodge. As we got closer, I
could hear music coming from inside.
Benny Goodman, if I wasn't mistaken.
Must have been a Victrola this time

instead of live music.

The window was too high up for me to see inside, but I smelled fry oil, confirming my suspicions. I peeked around the back. The lodge was just as wide as it was long, and there were two doors, one on each end, with a light over each. The kitchen door was closed, but someone had propped the far one open with a rock.

I motioned for Peggy to follow, and I crept toward the open door. A puff of smoke forewarned me that there was somebody right around the corner taking a break. That's why the rock was there, to let him back in when his break was over.

When I got to the door, I motioned for Peggy to stand there and hold it. I picked up the rock and snuck up on the corner.

I poked my head around to see where the guy was. If he was facing this direction, things might get complicated. To my surprise, I recognized the little guy. It was Sudoplatov, formerly known as Kowalczyk, and his back was to me. I wasn't going to feel the least bit bad about this.

I lifted his hat and brought the rock down hard on the back of his head.

The Russian spy, or assassin, or sapper, whatever he was, collapsed. I tossed the rock to the side and caught him on his way down. Gently, I laid him face down on the sphagnum carpet and took off his shoes and socks. He had a tattoo of a five-pointed bezeled star on his right ankle. Using his shoelaces, I trussed him like a pig, then gagged him with his socks, tossed his shoes in random directions, and dragged him into the woods.

I'd come back for him later. I'm sure someone in the Secret Service would want to know what he was up to here in the States.

When I got back to Peggy, she was pacing back and forth, biting the back of her finger. She stopped when she saw me. "You were gone so long! I could hear noises, but I didn't know what to think."

"Everything worked out nicely, and I managed to get one loose end tied up already. The important part is that you held the door. Now let's get inside before anyone else comes around."

As good as it felt to get Sudoplatov out of the way, the fact was that he was a big part of this group, and his absence would probably be noticed before long.

I pulled the door open and looked inside. There weren't any lights on in the room, but the far door was ajar, and enough light streamed in to give me an impression of the room. The heads of several deer, a mountain lion, and a goat were hanging on the wall. In between were photographs of men standing, guns in hand, with their kills. In the center of the room was a glass case filled with hunting rifles on display stands and smaller acts of taxidermy.

We passed through the room, and I checked the hallway outside. On the left-hand side, there was a door in the middle, and at the far end was the one that led to the kitchen. Two more doors across the hall, and one on each end. I had a pretty good feeling the two doors on the right led to the main

area of the lodge, where the dinner
would be held. There were too many
people in that direction, and I was
looking to avoid exposure.

No, I needed to talk to the guy
in the kitchen, but only if he was
alone. I motioned for Peggy to follow
and stepped out into the hallway. Out
here, the sound of the Victrola was
unmistakable, but I could hear the
sounds of conversation over it, all
coming from the doors to my right.

Around the time I was halfway
down the hall, the door to the kitchen
burst open, bringing us the sounds of
several voices from inside. I quickly
stepped back to the middle door and
ushered Peggy inside. Ducking into
the darkness after her, I pushed the
door nearly closed. I put my eye to
the crack, watching for the hallway to
become clear again.

"Aprons off! Look presentable!
Remember who you are serving. They
paid a lot of money to be here!
Jackson, take off your toque and mop
your brow, you've soaked it with
sweat. There, good enough, let's go!"

A stream of cooks came out of the

room carrying silver trays. They
formed into two lines and exited the
hall through the two doors across the
hall. Moments after they entered, the
Victrola stopped, and a round of
applause came up. The smells wafting
past as they went through the hallway
were incredible. Whatever they were
eating tonight, it was better than
Seattle's famous clam chowder.

The last two waiters to go
through closed the doors after
themselves. I poked my head back out
into the hallway. It was hard to tell
for sure, with all the sounds coming
from the main hall, but the door to
the kitchen was still open, and it
didn't sound like more than one person
in there.

"Okay, the coast is clear. Let's
--" as I turned toward Peggy, I saw
the room we were in. For the most
part, it was storage. Shelves of
supplies stood against three walls.
But behind Peggy, against the back
wall, was that press I had seen back
at the Brother of Unity Club. It was
sitting on a table with cardboard
boxes on one side, and stacks and

stacks of paper on the other.

I closed the door quietly and crossed the room to look at the press. Brian had said it was a coin press, and he usually knew his stuff, but then what was with all the paper? I picked up the top sheet. It was damp and had the smell of a mimeograph to it. It wasn't like book paper either. More like card stock. "Hey, Peggy, got another match?" I wanted to see what was on it, but I didn't want to risk hitting the overhead lights.

"Sure," she said. I could hear her digging around a bit, and moments later, the rough striking of a paper match.

Across the top of the paper, it read "Official Ballot" and underneath that "Precinct of Green Lake." The stack I took it from had well over a thousand ballots, and there were fifteen stacks.

"Bring it closer," I said.

As she came over to join me, I could read all of the ballots. Another stack read, "Precinct of West Seattle," and others, "Precinct of Ballard," or "Precinct of Queen Anne."

They were all filled out already, with a tick mark next to Lonnie Seger, of course, but also votes for circuit court judges, police commissioner, and a number of referendums.

Peggy shook out the match as it burned down to her fingertips. "Need another?"

"No, I think I saw enough. I'm going to take a couple pictures though. You might want to shut your eyes, there's going to be a flash."

I took one straight down onto the stacks of ballots, then another one close enough to see the detail, then I stood back and got one that included the printing press and all the stacks of ballots.

The door behind us opened up, and I pulled my coat over the camera. I did the move instinctually, but it was a worthless gesture. This camera was too bulky to go unnoticed.

"What are you doing in here?" A voice said, and the light came on.

I turned around. The man was dressed as a chef in immaculate white with the tall hat. His dark hair poked out at the sideburns.

I flashed him my friendliest smile. "Just trying to get some alone time with my girl, you know what I'm saying. Didn't mean anything by it. Hey, are you Evan Noble?"

"Yes, how did you know?"

I pushed past him and closed the door. "Then the real question is, what are you doing in here?" I asked, dropping all pretense of friendliness.

"Steel wool," he said, pointing to one of the shelves. "We've got pans to clean, and the one in the kitchen is falling apart. What's going on?"

"Look, we've got to get you out of here. This club is into some truly terrible things. I haven't decided whether I believe you know about them or not, but my client is concerned for you, so I'm giving you the benefit of the doubt."

He smiled, as if this was some sort of joke. "What do you mean? We're just supporting a local candidate for mayor."

"Through intimidation, bribery, vote tampering, and assassination attempts." I watched his face fall,

but was it because the joke just got
serious, or was it because of how much
I knew about the plot? I still
couldn't tell. "The police are on
their way right now. I've found
enough evidence here to put some
people away for life, but I imagine
things are going to get rather
uncomfortable for anyone who's still
here when they arrive.

"If you're part of all this, and
you're here on principle, then you can
hang with the rest of them. But if
you're here just trying to do a job
and get paid, then I can sympathize
with that. This is your chance to cut
and run. No one will be the wiser, or
at least, no one will be able to prove
it."

"You're serious about all this."

"I'm told I'm a funny guy. You
would know it if I were joking."

"Okay," he said. "I'll go with
you. But I've got to grab my things.
As far as proof goes that I was here,
they'll be enough to identify me."

It could be a trick. If I let
him out of my sight, he could warn
Seger and Oberman, and they would get

away before Mike could get here with a few Untouchables. "Alright. But we all go."

He nodded, and I opened the door back up. He headed right, back toward the trophy room. "Stay close," I told Peggy, and left the room after him. He passed the trophy room and went to the door at the end of the hall. He looked back at us and waited until we were close before opening it.

Beyond lay another hallway that ran to the left for what looked like the length of the building. Doors to the left of the hall would once again open into the main hall, but to the right, there were several more that could only open into much smaller rooms.

Evan motioned to us and silently headed up the hallway. He stopped in front of one of the right-hand doors, then looked down both directions of the hallway. "Quickly. In here," he said.

I guided Peggy in as he opened the door, but then we stopped short.

There was Kenneth Oberman, along with a man I had never met before.

They had a map of Seattle laying out
on a desk, and what looked like chess
pieces standing at various points on
the map. They looked up as we
entered.

"Look what I managed to capture,"
Evan Noble said from behind us as he
pulled the door closed.

So, his name may be Noble, but
the man is anything but.

"Who's the girl?" Oberman asked.
He instantly had his gun out and
pointed at me, but he was talking to
Noble.

The man with Oberman looked
uncomfortably at the hand cannon. He
was a well-dressed man in his mid-
forties. His hair was salt and
pepper, cut close on the sides and
waving across the top. He had
piercing gray eyes and wore a walrus
mustache. His overall appearance was
strikingly presidential.

"I don't know. She was just here
with the dick."

"She's just my ride. She has
nothing to do with this."

"All the same, I think she should put her hands up too."

Peggy and I put our hands up.

"Much appreciated. Now, what are we to do with you, Mr. Glover? You have a habit of showing up at the most inappropriate times. And, for the record, Mr. Jackson will not be saving you this evening. I'm afraid we've severed ties."

"He said the cops are on their way," Noble told him.

"Is that so? We've gone to some expense to ensure that we own the cops. No, they won't be coming, particularly without warning me first."

"Do all the cooks know so much about your plans, Oberman, or is this mug special?"

"Mr. Noble is very special indeed. He's a very talented forger. He's the one who inscribed the plates from which we have punched our ballets. A perfect replica of the original, I am assured."

"So that's what you meant by bringing the plates. You know, your wife really bought into the whole

executive chef thing. I suppose the
gazpacho soup incident was all a
sham?"

Noble laughed. "Yeah, my wife
sees things the way she wants to see
them, and it ain't in my interest to
disillusion her. But it's true. I am
an excellent chef, it's just that
there's more to me than that. Oh, and
'gazpacho soup' is a code phrase.
It's how my contact in the governor's
office let me know that the Feds were
onto our counterfeiting scheme. So,
yeah. It kind of happened."

"So you were in Denver, forging
currency plates, probably just down
the block from the U.S. Mint, but you
had to high-tail it to the coast. Why
didn't you end up in Frisco?"

"San Francisco would have been
too hot with a Mint there as well. If
they were onto me, that would've been
the next place they looked when I
skipped town. No, we needed somewhere
smaller, but up and coming, where my
talents would be appreciated."

"So for six months, you went
shopping your currency plates around
to every lowlife in Seattle, and you

ended up with the Commies. Only they
had other ideas in mind."

"Mr. Glover," Oberman
interjected. "I don't appreciate the
implication that communists are
lowlifes. We are trying to raise the
common man to the stature of true
brotherhood with the elites."

"By sneaking around, bribing
officials, and murdering those
currently in the position you care
about," I said.

"There is a significant amount of
propaganda against the word Communism
right now. Of course, we need to work
in secret until we have enough popular
support of our candidates to show the
people what Communism really means."

"Well, your buddy Sudoplatov
could certainly tell you what it means
in Poland."

"Who?" Oberman asked. He seemed
genuinely confused.

"You really don't know then? The
little guy, Kowalczyk. He's not
Polish at all, he's a Soviet agent who
worked in Poland to root out
opposition, convict, and execute
them."

"I don't believe you. He would have nothing to gain by lying to me. While I may not approve of all of Stalin's methods, I am certainly sympathetic to his cause."

"You don't have to believe me. You can read it in the Post-Intelligencer tomorrow."

"I've had enough of this. Noble, go get my men. They can collect Mr. Glover and his driver and take them outside. Far enough away that no one will hear the shots."

Noble nodded and left the room, closing the door behind himself.

"You haven't bought everybody, you know! Plenty of people know where we are!" Peggy was equal parts scared and angry.

"Really, dear. I'm sorry you've been roped into this thing, I really am. But I'm afraid you've picked the wrong side on this one, and I can't allow any witnesses. By now, Mr. Glover is a hunted man. Everyone knows it was his plan to kill Mayor Dore. There's enough evidence in his office to send him to the chair. Anyone who knows you two are here is likely to shut up about it so as not to be labeled an accomplice."

"You act like you are so righteous, but you're killing innocent people!" she spat.

"Would it make you feel any better to know that it will trouble me? Or perhaps that you will live on in history as casualties of the revolution!"

"A revolution that begins in Seattle of all places," I said.

"You still don't understand, Mr. Glover. Well, you will at least go to your grave a bit better informed. Seattle is only part of step one in the plan, and it began years ago. The labor strikes, the sawmill closing." He put a hand on the shoulder of the man standing next to him. "Once Mr. Seger here is in the mayor's office, all that will go away. We are prepared to put new money into Seattle, and yes, some of it will be printed by Mr. Noble. Unemployment will plummet to wartime lows. There will be construction! Expansion! Road building! Mining. Every sector will be hiring, and people will flock here. The quality of life will be through the roof, and people everywhere will know it. It will be a relatively small investment with a truly big payoff. In two years, there will be a gubernatorial election, wherein Mr. Seger here will run, and as votes Seattle, so goes the state. He will be a shoo-in. But even that is just phase two.

"In phase three, the real change begins. When something unfortunate happens to one of Washington's senators, the governor will have the sad duty to appoint his replacement. And I will be ever-so-humbly willing to accept."

He smiled his cherubic little smile. "The Brothers of Unity club has chapters in cities all around America. We now control ports and shipping hubs. Products are either delayed or expedited as we see fit. And most importantly, a version of this same plan is being executed in other key cities around the nation. In just a few short years, we'll have enough votes to bring in some much-needed legislation. Maybe even an

amendment or two. You two are
intelligent people. I think you can
see where this is going."

"A lovely little bit of
daydreaming, I'm sure, but you'll
never get away with it in the real
world. One small accident with a
senator? Sure. People will buy that.
But how many small accidents would you
need to get any sort of majority? The
American people are going to be
suspicious."

"Oh, we won't need a majority.
We don't need to take the senate, just
help it lean a little in the proper
direction. It's always been so evenly
balanced in the past, but just now,
popular momentum is tilting in our
favor. It's the way of the world,
Glover. You can't fight progress. We
figure five percent is all we need.
Even if something happened, and we
lost several of our 'seed cities,' our
plan will work. Anyway, I didn't say
this unfortunate accident our senator
will have is going to be a little one.
There will be a period of mourning,
and the American people will demand
action. And they will look to us,

their new leaders, to provide this action. Trust me, Mr. Glover. We've had our very best minds on this problem for some time."

The door opened behind us, and in walked Henry and Ryder.

"Ah, gentlemen. Come on in. You remember Mr. Glover here. As I recall, the three of you have unfinished business. Fortunately for you, Mr. Glover has seen fit to give you another opportunity to make good on your duties."

Oberman returned to the desk and his business with Seger. He put his gun back in the drawer. "As for you, dear lady, I'm truly sorry. You really shouldn't sneak onto the grounds of a hunting club at night. You're likely to be mistaken for game."

Ryder took hold of Peggy's arm, and Henry reached for my shoulder. I shot my hand out and grabbed his thumb instead, then ducked under his arm and pulled it straight. From behind him, I got one good shot in at his ribs, then another at his elbow. If it had been my left, I might have repaid him for breaking my ribs, but I had to satisfy myself with the celery-like crunching sound his elbow made. My satisfaction ended there, though, because the big guy only grunted at the pain.

I placed a foot in the small of his back and pushed him at the desk. The trouble with being as big as Henry is that you take up a lot of room that other people were going to want access to. My only hope was to keep him between Oberman's gun and me while I dealt with Ryder. The big guy's right arm was going to be useless, so for the next few seconds only, I had an advantage.

I turned on Ryder, who seemed in a bit of shock. He was still holding onto Peggy's arm, and he'd turned toward me, but he hadn't acted yet. I took a swing at him, and he leaned back, dodging it easily. That was exactly what I wanted, though. I would have missed him anyway; I was only getting him off balance.

I followed up with a kick to his

knee, pushing it sideways and back.
That one was definite payback for the
lead pipe he'd used on me last night.
I spun as he fell to his left knee and
came around with an upper cut below
his chin.

I figured he'd be pretty much out
of the fight, and I had a second or
two before Henry was back in it, or
Oberman could get a shot around him.
I dug into my pocket for my brother's
service revolver and turned to aim
behind me.

Henry didn't need a second after
all and brought his left fist down
hard on the gun, sending it to the
floor. He was ready with another
punch, and I had to back up to avoid a
hell of a shot that might have broken
more ribs. It turns out Henry could
use his left as well as his right.
And without the gun, I was back in
trouble again.

Oberman had the drawer open, and
the gun was in his hand again.
"Glover," he started to say, but I was
in no position to pay attention to
him. I had to duck under another blow
from Henry.

There wasn't very much further I
could back up, so I had to go back on
the attack. The next time Henry
punched at me, I leaned back and
caught his arm on the back of my
right, pushing it further past me,
then I jabbed with my left at the
clump of muscles between his shoulder
and underarm.

He backhanded me a solid shot
across the face and pressed forward.
My back was against the door, and he
was pulling back for another haymaker.

Henry might not have been the
biggest guy I ever faced, but he could
have been the strongest, and he also
knew what he was doing. I did not
want to get hit with the punch that
was coming.

But come it did, and he knew I
had nowhere to go, so he was putting
everything into it. So, I opened up
the door and stepped back into the
hallway. He went badly off balance,
and I pulled on his shoulder with both
hands, sidestepping him and sending
him sprawling.

I took up position just inside
the room as he turned back toward me.

The narrow doorframe was going to keep him from taking any more big swings with those albatross arms of his.

"Mr. Glover," Oberman said again, with more insistence this time.

Oh yeah.

I had lost track of the gun in all this. Slowly raising my hands, I turned, but only part way. I didn't want my back to Henry. He was bound to take a bit of revenge. I backed away from the open door as he came in, so everyone was where I could see them.

"I can't be here while this is going on!" Seger said, going all red.

Oberman didn't want the sound of a gunshot, with his party just outside, but he'd do it anyway if I pushed him. Ryder was standing up too, though he was leaning against the wall and holding his left leg off the ground, the way a wounded dog would.

All eyes were on me, except for Peggy's. She dove for my gun and came back up onto one knee, shooting.

Blam! Oberman took it right in the center of his chest and stumbled back before falling to the ground.

Blam! She shot again, this time she got Seger, and a third shot brought him down, leaking heart's blood.

She spun around, and I could tell she wasn't going to stop. I hauled back and hit Henry in the jaw as hard as I could. He crumpled to the ground, and I got between Peggy and Ryder.

"It's over, Peggy. You can stop now," I said. I tried to keep my voice calm, but it betrayed me. I was halfway convinced that she was going to go on shooting, even with me in the way. Ryder, for his part, looked terrified. He had his hands up in front of his face, his eyes wide.

Peggy was breathing hard, her face had a look of madness about it. She continued to point my gun straight at me, holding it in both white-knuckled hands, but so far, she hadn't fired.

Slowly, her trembling thumb came up and settled on the hammer. She slowly eased it forward, which was good, but I would have been a lot

happier if she were pointing it
someplace else. "I did it," she said,
almost in astonishment.

"You did. But it's over now...
Just hand me the gun." I walked
slowly toward her.

Ryder bolted for the door, and
Peggy's tracked him with my gun. I
jumped back in the way, cursing myself
as I did it. "Let him go!" I said,
then softer, "He's not important."

She got shakily to her feet and
finally started to lower the gun. Her
eyes were still wide with surprise,
and she was just about
hyperventilating. "I did it!" she
said again.

"It's okay," I said, reaching for
the gun. "You did what you had to do.
When the cops get here, I'll vouch for
you. It was self-defense."

I got one hand on the still hot
barrel and turned it to the side. She
relaxed her grip for a moment, then
pulled the gun back out of my hand and
stepped away. "No! You don't
understand! I did it!" This time she
spoke with excitement.

She was staring at the bodies of

Oberman and Seger, and a smile spread across her face. She turned toward me. "I killed the bad guys! I'm the hero!"

It took a moment for what she was saying to register. "No, Peggy, please tell me you aren't X."

"I really didn't think I could do it! I was just a bit part! A bartender with a sad but strong backstory. Mostly just setting -- window-dressing! Just there so you would have a place to do your drinking! Easily forgotten. I figured I was good for the gal Friday role, or maybe even the love interest! That would have been fine with me! But then I thought if I was going to go for it, why not shoot for the moon? And I made it!"

"Peggy," I started, then I realized I had no idea how to end that sentence. I just wanted her to stop, it was making me sick. "Peggy, it's okay. We'll get you help..."

"I don't need any help! I won!" She started jumping up and down. "Everybody's going to remember me now!"

"Peggy," I started again. I
still had no idea what I could say.

She grabbed me by the shoulders.
"Come on, Drake! You've got to admit
how good I was!" She was searching my
face for something I didn't have. All
I felt was sorry for her. "You have
no idea how much work it was! I
didn't have all the talent it took to
do it by myself, so I had to make sure
the plot hooks were in place so you
would keep coming back! But in a way,
I was perfectly positioned. Everybody
talks to the bartender, and nobody
worries about what they say! You even
brought it up at one point. You said
to me that the only people you told
were Mike and Brian! You completely
forgot that I was there!

"So, I hired the only other dick
that was part of the narrative. I
typed out a note and had him put it in
the bad guy's office where only you
could find it."

"That was just plain dumb luck,"
I said. "There's no way you could
have known I'd be there."

"It wasn't luck; it was proof!
Hiding under desks isn't something

that happens in real life! If I was wrong, you'd never find the note, and you wouldn't make the meeting in Post Alley. But once you showed up, I knew I was right."

"Oh, Peggy," I tried again, but she wasn't done yet.

"And I bought him a new hat and coat so you wouldn't recognize him when you spoke! It was going perfectly until I found out you were looking for him for your other client."

"And so you murdered him," I said.

"You don't know that! It happened between the pages! But he was dead, and I had to hire someone else to tail you in case you got in trouble. I had to take out another loan on Delaney's, Drake! It took real money to do all this."

"And he was killed too. What was his name?"

"What did he need a name for! He was introduced and killed in the same scene!"

"Peggy, you killed two men."

"But I had to. Laslop was a

better detective than you. He was younger, better looking, smarter, and had more resources at his disposal. Once I got him involved in this case, he would have solved it days ago. I had to stop him. You see, Drake? I did it for you!"

"That doesn't make it any better, Peggy! You've got to see how this looks!"

"But it was necessary! It was part of a chain of events that brought the two of us to this point! Just like when I called the cops on you at Delaney's!"

I closed my eyes. How could I have been so dumb? The cops showed up right after she made a call, and I still brought her along with me. It all made sense now, and I should have seen it. What made me think X had to be a man?

"You aren't mad, are you, Drake?" she asked.

I was too stunned to speak. I tried to put every bit of how I was feeling into the look I gave her instead.

"Okay, maybe you are. And maybe

you have a right to be. It's your story, after all, you expect to get the bad guy. But don't worry, you'll be remembered too!"

By now, the party in the main room was over. People had been gathering in the hallway outside, and the doorway was crowded with lookie-loos. I put my hand over the gun that Peggy was still holding. It came easily from her grasp.

I put it in my pocket and turned away from her. She continued on with her self-congratulatory rant, but I was done listening.

I owed Brian a story, with pictures, so I started taking shots of the crime scene.

Chapter Fifteen

Soon after that, the badges rained down. The buttons who were first on the scene put me in irons, and Peggy too. She was still ranting like a lunatic, and I was still a wanted man. They took my brother's heater as evidence too. Another one of my most cherished possessions was gone. Of course, they took the camera Brian had lent me as well. At least they didn't smash this one.

We weren't the only ones getting arrested either. I told the cops about the counterfeit ballots, and they sent a man to check. Pretty soon, everyone was wanted for questioning. I'm pretty sure none of the partygoers knew they were supporting a communist takeover of America, but Noble had made it out of there before the cops showed, and he sure knew. He apparently ran across Sudoplatov on his way out as well, because the little guy wasn't where I told the cops to find him.

They led us out to waiting squad cars, separate ones, thankfully. The last I saw of Peggy, she was still ranting as they put her in the back of the boiler. "The readers are never going to remember any of you! You probably don't even have names! But I'm the hero! I won!"

The door closed, mercifully cutting off anything else she had to say. They opened up the door to put me in a car too, but just then, another bull wagon pulled up. The door swung open. "That's him! Hold it right there!"

Out stepped Captain Sears. My day was about to get even worse.

"Take those cuffs off, officer, this man was working for me."

Well, all parts of that sentence came as a complete surprise. If I was working for him, I certainly was unaware of it.

"Sir?" the officer asked.

"You heard me. I needed someone to infiltrate the Brothers of Unity, and I got word that the police force was compromised, so I hired outside help. Take the cuffs off. He's our inside man."

"But what about Mayor Dore?"

"Am I talking to myself here? That was all part of the plan. He's innocent. Let him go." There was a strain in his voice that told me it was killing him to have to say it, but he couldn't take it back now. He patted me on the shoulder and disappeared inside the lodge.

That's when I saw Mike. The two of them had driven to the lodge together and apparently had time to talk. The officer took my cuffs off and handed me back my camera, none too happy about it. I snapped a photo of him, just to rub it in.

Mike joined me by the back of the squad car. "Is it true what they're saying about Peggy? Did she really murder Seger?"

"Killed him anyway. I won't testify that he was unarmed at the time, and he was with Oberman, who was about to shoot us."

"Uh-huh. Still pretty hard to believe. I've known her for years."

"Not the way she tells it. According to her, we're all just characters in a book, and all that history you remember was backstory."

"Totally off her nut then?"

I nodded, not wanting to say it. "What did you say to Sears?"

"I told him you'd find that ledger before the Feds did, and when it turned up, his name wouldn't be in it."

"Oh, is that all?"

"No, not quite. I also told him it wouldn't cost him a dime."

I sighed. "Well, somebody better pay me something on this. I'm out a camera. How am I supposed to make a living now?"

The look on his face told me

pretty plainly this was going to be non-negotiable, and I should feel lucky I got even that. I sighed again. "Fine. I won't charge him for it. But from now on, when I come to visit the precinct, I'd better feel welcome."

I did get paid in the end. Not a lot, but some. Bowerman's lawyer had actually been hired by the club, and with it gone, the lawyer split as well. Megan got her divorce and her maiden name back. She was grateful to me and paid me back everything I had given her for the hotel stay and then some for expenses.

I managed to find another camera in a pawn shop that was just like my old one. It had a busted strap, but I knew a guy, and all it took him was a couple of seconds with a stitcher to fix me up. My friends thought I was nuts not to buy something more modern, but I liked the fit and style of the classics.

The Feds didn't end up paying me one red cent for services rendered,

but they did take up a lot of my time
with interviews. I gave up everything
I knew about this conspiracy in our
initial sit down, leaving out the
small detail about our police chief.

I also left out the address Brian
had given me in Greenwood that Seger
had filed residency under. I had a
hunch that might be where they moved
the ledger to. And when I did find it
a couple of days later, I handed that
over minus one page.

That didn't stop them from
inviting me to tell them the whole
thing, again and again, trying to get
details about that map that I just
couldn't conjure up. The only cities
I remembered for sure were San
Antonio, San Diego, and Santa Barbara.
My best advice to them was that any
place which had a Brothers of Unity
probably had a problem with ballot
tampering.

It looked like we were getting an
expanded presence of J Edgar's men in
Seattle now. They'd been here since
the start of the Great War, but since
Seattle was no longer a part of the
strategic war effort, they were mostly

chasing down stolen cars. The men I
met with promised to be a nuisance in
my life in the coming years, and I
believed them--mostly because I'd had
some juicy collars in my hands and
they both got away. They seemed a bit
embarrassed by the fact that other
field offices had been looking
everywhere for Evan Noble, and they
had no clue he was operating in their
fair city. But as bad as the
publicity was on that account, now
they knew Sudoplatov was loose in the
States, he was Public Enemy Number
One.

After paying for the camera, the
suit I rented, my apartment, a couple
packs of cigarettes, and my employee's
salary, I was flat broke again.
Nothing left over for my office over
the Chinese laundry, and this time,
they weren't letting the rent slide.
Since I would have to apply for my
license all over again and couldn't
work until I got it, that didn't feel
like a huge loss. The one thing I
would miss was Katie.

"Stop being so mopey about it,"
she said. "You'll land on your feet

again. You're like a cat that way, nine lives and all. I have faith that you'll be back in business before you know it, and when you are, you give me a ring, and I'll come running."

I did make a small amount selling the story to the Post-Intelligencer. I gave them details that the Times didn't have access to, and of course, they got the gruesome crime scene photos that they could never print. I did my best to leave Peggy out of my version of events--I felt sure that she would snap out of it sooner or later, and I didn't want this stigma following her forever.

She was now the newest patient at the Northern State Asylum. I haven't been to visit her yet. That last image of her is still stuck in my head, and I don't want to see her this way. Mike tells me she's happy there. She's got a private room and all the books she can read. "She's curious to see what happens when a fictional character such as her reads about themselves," Mike told me.

I've been debating whether to tell you this or not, but I got a few

letters from her. The first couple I
left unopened, but a man came to my
home to present me with the third. I
thought I was getting sued by someone,
Bowerman, maybe, but it turned out to
be the title to Delaney's. She wanted
me to run it in her absence, and since
I didn't have an office or a job, I
signed the papers.

So now I've got a bar and all the
debt Peggy racked up by following me
around. I'm keeping the name--
Delaney's is a Seattle establishment,
and the way I look at it, I'm just
keeping Peggy's seat warm.

With Seger's death and the club's
influence falling apart, the mayor's
race was down to Dore and Langlie, but
it came out that Dore had been
concealing an illness and was, in
fact, gravely sick. The electorate
voted in Langlie over concerns that
Dore couldn't do the job. Dore died
on April 18th, and Arthur Langlie,
mayor-elect, became mayor proper.

I couldn't help but think the
Brothers of Unity had acted on their
backup plan and poisoned Mayor Dore,
but the coroner put it down as

Influenza and Pneumonia.

"Could you tell me again, though," Brian said to me when I handed over the paper's camera, "what was it that Oberman said about 'seed cities?'"

"He said they could stand to lose several of them and still get the five percent they needed to sway the Senate their way."

"That's pretty scary. Too bad they burned all your negatives. I would have loved to get another look at that map with all the pins on it."

Wouldn't we all, I thought. But if Oberman was right about things, it was still a couple years before they would have any senators in place.

Thank you.

Thanks for reading my story, A Shadow Stained in Blood. I truly hope you enjoyed it. I have a list for people who like my stories, and I even have an exclusive novella for you if you join. All you have to do is follow this link:

https://bit.ly/2QWIHmP

Why would you want to? Well, if you liked this story, you'll probably like other things I write, and you'll hear about those here first. There will be discounts exclusive to list members, and I may ask your opinion about things too, such as "Which cover do you like better?" or "Which of these books should I write next?"

Whatever is happening, you'll hear about it first if you join my list. But I also won't spam you. After all, how fast can I write? We're talking maybe three books a year… Maybe.

Made in the USA
San Bernardino,
CA